Red ice

Books by Anthony Masters

Fiction

A pocketful of rye (1964)
The seahorse (1966)
A literary lion (1968)
Conquering heroes (1969)
The syndicate (1971)

Thrillers

The donor (1970)
The dead travel fast (1971)
The emperor on ice (1973)
Birds of a bloodied feather (1974)

Non-fiction

The summer that bled (1972)
Inside marbled halls (1979)
Rosa Lewis (1977)
Nancy Astor (1981)
The man who was M (1985)

For children

Badger (1986)

Nicholas Barker and
Anthony Masters

Red ice

St. Martin's Press
New York

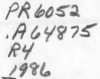
Library of Congress Cataloging-in-Publication Data

Barker, Nicholas.
    Red ice.

    "A Thomas Dunne book"
    I. Masters, Anthony, 1940-   II. Title.
PR6052.A64875R4   1987   823'.914   87-16299
ISBN 0-312-01079-6

First published in Great Britain by Constable & Company Ltd.

First U.S. Edition

10 9 8 7 6 5 4 3 2 1

To the Red Plum – NB
To Robina, who also braved the elements – NB and AM
Also to my dear friend Musa for all his wise
help and counselling – AM

Author's note

It is customary for authors to thank those who have been involved in compiling a novel of this type. So many kind people (too many to mention by name) have offered advice and encouragement, and I thank them all. I am especially grateful for the help and knowledge provided by Binnie Macellari; for the support given by the officers and ship's company of HMS *Endurance*; for the assistance of my two secretaries, Gary Lewis and David Faulks; and finally, of course, for the cooperation and expertise given by Tony and Robina Masters, without whom the whole venture would not have got off the ground.

During the course of writing this story I have been constantly reminded of the hazards that exist for those who work in the Antarctic and the South Atlantic. It is those men and women that I thank for the inspiration required to write a novel about this fascinating, at times angry, but beautiful part of the world.

N.J.B.
Cambridge
March 1986

Red ice

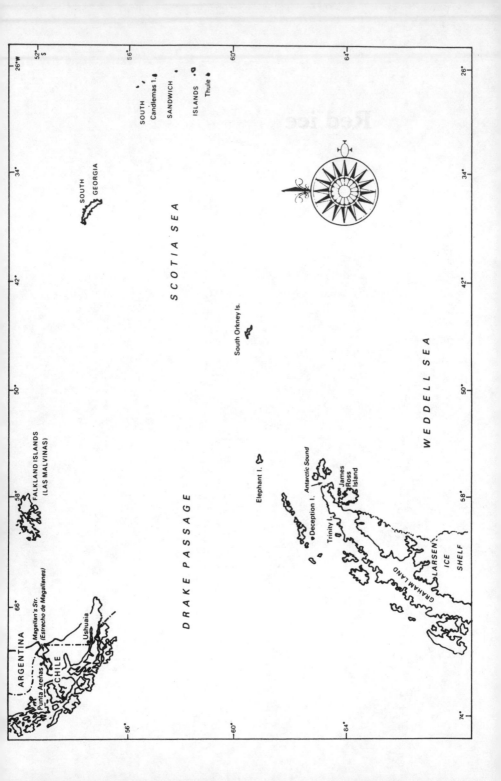

1 – Opening volley

19 November 1989
1.45 p.m.
Montevideo
The Santa Lucia faced out on to a crowded street, its cluster of
pavement chairs and tables bunched closely together. It was a
popular spot with the Embassy people as well as the Navy and
Captain Maxwell was not surprised to see Arrowsmith walk in
with a girl. He felt a sudden envy of his Lieutenant's youth and
freedom. He was only twenty-nine, bright, efficient, good-
looking, going places. His whole career in front of him.

Abruptly, Maxwell wrenched his mind back to the Attaché's
small talk, ungraciously wondering why the hell Rosemary had
married such a pompous bastard in the first place. Still – she
must see something in him, they'd been married for over
twenty years. Maxwell toyed with his *fruits de mer*, wishing
Aubrey Dunhill would go away somewhere so that he could
talk to Rosemary. But he sat immovable, pecking at a small
omelette, looking like some giant bird of ill-omen.

Lieutenant Arrowsmith had met Sally Openshaw at an
Embassy party some eighteen months ago and was now hope-
fully consolidating a somewhat interrupted friendship. He was
surprised that she was still free and did not realize that she had
been in love with him since his last visit and had been waiting
for his return in an agony of apprehension. But clearly, he had
no idea of her feelings and nor, she was sure, did he reciprocate
them.

'Is that the boss?' she asked him.

'Maxwell. He's a good bloke.'

9

'What's he like to work for?'

'A bastard.' Arrowsmith grinned. 'A nice one, though,' he added reflectively.

At twenty-two, Sally, a typist in the trade section, had come to Montevideo through her father's contacts in the diplomatic service for an 'adventure'. But her natural reserve had not made her gregarious enough to enjoy socializing in the diplomatic set. She was lonely – and had already decided to return home. The only man she had met and felt at ease with was John Arrowsmith. And he was a sailor.

'You were in the war with him, weren't you?' she asked.

'All the time. Sally – ' It seemed as if he was looking at her in a different way and she detected – or thought she detected – a sudden intensity.

'Yes?' Sally tried to keep the eagerness out of her voice as her hopes rose.

'Do you like squid?'

'Now, James.' Dunhill cleared his throat officiously. 'The arrangements for the cocktail party. I suppose you've – '

Maxwell caught Rosemary's eye and tried not to smile.

'Shall we have another bottle of wine?' she asked and Maxwell nodded.

Aubrey Dunhill frowned, not pleased at being interrupted. 'You see – the Ambassador was asking whether you were going to use the hangar.'

'We usually do.'

'We've a lot of people coming this time.'

'P'raps you need a bigger ship,' said Maxwell, 'just for entertaining.'

'You'd need an aircraft carrier.' Rosemary laughed up at Aubrey who gave her a sudden smile. It was a special smile, intimate, loving – a smile that Maxwell had never seen on his face before, despite all the years he had known him. Maxwell was shocked, unable to understand why he had been so smugly unperceptive. As the shock died, loneliness replaced it. His wife's face swam into his mind's eye. Susan and I have been

10

away from each other too long, Maxwell thought. Too long to grow together; long enough to grow apart.

'I'm going home.'

Arrowsmith looked anxious and took Sally's hand. 'Why – anything wrong?'

She smiled at him over her salad and immediately he relaxed. 'No,' she said almost sharply, 'I mean I'm going back to England at the end of the month.'

Glancing round, he caught his Captain's eye and Maxwell winked. But Arrowsmith did not smile back. Instead he jumped to his feet, knocked over a carafe of wine and began to shout.

What on earth was Arrowsmith up to, wondered Maxwell absently as he sipped at his wine. Had he lost his temper? Was he sick? Had he gone mad? As he stared at Arrowsmith in bewilderment he heard Rosemary say, slowly and very distinctly, 'Oh, dear God, no.'

Maxwell looked past Aubrey Dunhill's pinched expression to the floor of the restaurant. There was an open space around which the inside tables were grouped. It had a black pattern of flowers and was used for dancing in the evening.

'What's the matter, James?' said Aubrey peevishly. 'Have you seen someone you know?'

No one I know, Maxwell was thinking. But an old presence – a very familiar old presence. Death.

Arrowsmith could not see the grenades rolling across the floor. He and Sally were sitting at pavement level and the interior of the restaurant was slightly above them. But he had seen them pull the pins. There were three young men – almost boys – who stood watching the rolling cylinders with a kind of intense fascination that had a hypnotic quality. He was on his feet, still yelling, screaming, roaring at Maxwell who now had his back to him and was half-standing, half-sitting. Sally was on her feet too now, jabbering at him, screaming for information, while other diners were gazing at them in amazement. But not looking up, thought Arrowsmith wildly, not looking

11

up where they fucking well should be.

The grenades continued to roll across the dance floor. They were travelling in three different directions and there were almost a dozen of them. The three young men were standing in a rough semi-circle and, apart from Arrowsmith's yelling, a great silence had fallen in the Santa Lucia. It was the silence of suspended, exaggerated time. Time that did not exist.

'Oh, sod,' muttered Maxwell, 'sod it!'

Aubrey had turned round now and his shrill exclamation began the noise – the awesome noise of panic.

'They're grenades,' he screamed. 'Oh, God – they're rolling grenades at us.'

Then everyone was on their feet, sobbing, crying, pleading, screaming, shouting the fiercest epithets against the Almighty. Most of it was in Spanish. But to Maxwell it all made perfect, deadly sense. They were going to die. All of them. He felt a curious sense of relief.

The breeze took the edge off the heat and, twelve storeys up, the room was bearable – just. Below them, the town sweltered, the siesta just beginning. Somnolence gripped her but the sweltering weather seemed to have no effect on him. He was the same as he had always been since he came out of prison. Wary.

The room was bare and impersonal. It belonged to a friend who was in Europe and who had left behind only the minimum of furniture. Gabriel had been sleeping here for the last two months but he had left no personal trace.

It seemed unbelievable that the time had come for it all to begin. Julia looked at her brother, wondering what he was thinking. She never knew now. Was he wishing, like her, that they were still in those years of planning?

Gabriel opened the window and stared down at the peeling sea-front with its dingy coffee-houses. The steady breeze blew from the ocean, sending litter flying over the empty white sand of the Ramirez. Then he turned to face her, the lines on his face hard-etched in the early afternoon sunlight that filtered the room. The window banged but he didn't notice.

This morning they had walked in the park near La Carreta –
the monument to the pioneers of Uruguay. She had stared at
the bronzed oxen pulling the covered wagon with its bearded
gaucho, trying not to think, hoping, just for a little longer, that
her mind would stay blank. Now, as he stood by the idly banging window, Gabriel said: 'We must go over it again, for my
sake as much as yours.'

Her heart sank as the awesome reality of it all swept over
her. It was like the races she had swum as a young girl. Months
of training – and then the ghastly moment of looking down at
the water, waiting for the off.

'The official report says that whilst commanding the original
Falklands guardship, *Endeavour*, Captain James Maxwell was
outspoken and incurred their Lordships' displeasure.'

He spoke slowly, deliberately, making her feel childishly
nervous. When he had finished he asked her to repeat it all –
and she knew she was bound to make mistakes.

As she stumblingly began Gabriel blinked out at the hard
windy sunlight, watching a child throw stones at a boarded-up
ice-cream kiosk. There was a crunching sound and the child
fled. A dog loped into view, obviously a stray – lean, wary,
hungry. It crouched down and began to pull debris from
underneath the kiosk. Eventually, after discarding the litter, it
found something edible and began to eat ravenously. Suddenly, an image returned to Julia that she had not seen in
months, that she thought she had expelled for all time. Still
reciting mechanically she saw the women on all fours in the
barracks yard, licking plates that were set on the ground. Then
she saw herself amongst them.

' – and a detachment of twenty-two Royal Marines. Have I
got it right?'

'Yes – at last you have got it right.'

Maxwell threw himself forward as the first grenade exploded
on the far side of the room. Then another rolled on to the pavement area. Blood and brains from Sally Openshaw's head spat-

13

tered Arrowsmith as he was thrown aside by the blast. As he struggled to his feet, he saw her lying on the floor in the smoke, her body smashed into the debris of the table. One eye hung crazily down her cheek and blood steadily poured from the hole where her mouth had been. Other people were lying around her and there was a smell of shit and hot air. Looking down, Arrowsmith saw a severed hand. It was large and brown and muscular. It still held a fork.

Maxwell was lying on the floor as the blasts came. Black smoke engulfed him, the building shuddered and searing heat swept the Santa Lucia. People screamed, shouted, cried, called on God again and again. Then more blasts – and Maxwell briefly glimpsed Rosemary lying on the ground with Aubrey on top of her. Then there was a sudden stillness and Maxwell couldn't work out whether he was alive or dead. He seemed to be floating weightless in the stinking black air. Fleetingly he wondered what was going to happen next.

Julia Mendoza crossed the floor of the small apartment and sat down heavily in an armchair. Gabriel had gone out, walking the quayside, unable to bear the waiting. She felt exhausted and on the edge of hysteria. Resolutely she applied herself to her brother's motives by quietly remembering the enormity of what had happened to him. Julia always did this when she was consumed by doubt, and so far it had never failed to reassure her.

Gabriel was now a lecturer in politics at the University of Montevideo. But he had originally been editor of *La Humanidad*, a left-wing newspaper that had been banned in 1974. With his wife, and herself, he had been arrested three times between 1973 and 1976 and confined in various barracks. Twice he was sent to military hospital to recover from the tortures they had imposed on him. In April 1976 his wife, Anita Mendoza, had disappeared and no trace had ever been found of her body. Two months later, in June, both his sons, Antonio and Juan, had also disappeared. They were later discovered drowned on the shores of the River Plate. Both bodies had been partially encased in cement.

Julia rose to her feet, the grim facts in sterile order. But, for once, she did not feel they were a justification for what was now presumably happening at the Santa Lucia.

Methodically, stringing out the process, Julia began to clean the apartment. But after a few minutes it became impossible to blunt her emotions.

She went to the drinks cabinet and mixed herself a large Scotch. She felt the pliers tightening the metal wires on her wrist and tasted again the filth in the water they had plunged her head into and then the awesome shock of the electric current. Until recently the memories had not returned for years, but now they were back with persistent force. Knowing that once again she would have to deaden them still further, she poured herself another Scotch.

The suspension was over and voices returned, screaming in a relentless agony that to Maxwell was unbearable. Blood began to pour into his eyes but, as he clutched at his head, he found the wound was shallow. Apart from this he seemed unscathed, although his thoughts were in a wretched turmoil and his body still felt weightless.

But suddenly, reality returned and with it, Maxwell's initiative. A young man was jumping through the shattered window of the Santa Lucia. Unthinkingly, painfully, Maxwell followed him, cutting his hand on broken glass.

The light outside was hard, bright and almost as hot as the blasting heat of the grenades. Police sirens blared some distance away, but the traffic was jammed tight. People had taken cover, crouching down behind vehicles or seeking refuge in other cafés. From one of the larger restaurants what seemed like a vast crowd was watching them intently as if they were enraptured members of an audience.

A few feet in front of him Maxwell saw two of the men running towards a bus, but suddenly he caught sight of the young man vaulting over a car bonnet. He followed him, keeping low, his breath coming in gasps, the pain in his hand increasing.

Weaving through the traffic, the sweat pouring down his face, Maxwell began to draw closer. Once the young man glanced back and Maxwell saw the fear in his eyes. Then he heard feet pounding behind him. Arrowsmith. He drew abreast – and passed him.

A few seconds later, their quarry disappeared into a small, already crowded bar and supermarket. They plunged in after him as he literally tore his way down the central aisle, knocking aside customers and scattering goods.

'There's no way out,' shouted Arrowsmith, but he was wrong for the young man knew his territory. Raising a final desperate burst of speed, he ran towards the back of the shop, overturning a pile of cans and some supermarket trolleys as he went. Then he wrenched open the glass door, leaving his gasping pursuers to pick their way over the debris – and out on to a crowded pavement.

'Sod the bastard!' panted Arrowsmith. 'Where the hell is he?'

'There!' Maxwell saw him through a scattered trail of pedestrians.

Now Maxwell's chest was so painful that he could hardly breathe and his legs felt like weights. Arrowsmith, however, was streaking ahead towards the faded gilt of the ornamental gates and, in a few seconds, he had disappeared out of sight.

Maxwell struggled on until he reached the entrance and found himself looking down a long sloping sward of dusty grass towards a football field. He saw the young man running jerkily – as if his strength was giving out. He was followed by Arrowsmith. They were heading for a group of children, who were kicking a ball around on the bare scrubby earth. Above them, the sun was a shimmering orb, its heat searing the grass. To the left was an overgrown quayside and to the right an unmade road and a ramshackle grandstand with rows of broken seats.

Arrowsmith was gaining now, but with a last effort the young man reached the children and began to gasp out instructions. He was brandishing something that Maxwell could not make out at first, something that glinted in the hard sunlight.

A knife.

He clutched at one of the children, a girl of about eight, and hugged her close. Arrowsmith came to a stumbling halt and Maxwell walked painfully towards him. They stood looking helplessly at the scene in front of them.

'Let her go.' Maxwell repeated the statement in Spanish.

The young man shouted something they couldn't make out and Maxwell saw there was blood on his face and hands. The child was very still in his embrace.

The impasse seemed to last for hours, with time suspended under the relentless glare. Maxwell could see no shadows on the baked earth. The figures stood there, immovable, rooted to the moment, perhaps frozen for ever to that arid spot. The children, three of them, gazed at captor and captive wonderingly. But the little girl in the young man's arms seemed untroubled. She looked up at him trustingly, almost smiling. Does she think it's a game? wondered Maxwell. Is she a simpleton? Or does she know, by instinct, that he won't hurt her?

The tableau was shattered abruptly as a battered Volvo roared up the unmade road.

'Get down,' said Arrowsmith. 'For Christ's sake get down.'

For a second Maxwell could also see the snub-nosed machine gun protruding from the driver's window. Then he hit the unyielding earth, the pain in his arm biting viciously.

The bullets thudded around them, shattering the baked earth. Maxwell could hear Arrowsmith swearing. Then he sensed he was moving forward and shouted: 'Don't be a bloody fool.' He raised his head and saw him a few yards away, crawling towards the car. The children stood watching apathetically – almost as if they were watching a bad television movie.

Suddenly, the Volvo began to back away in a frenzy of screaming tyres and an over-revved engine. Arrowsmith rose to his feet and began to run towards it. As he did so, Maxwell saw the machine gun reappear, this time out of the passenger's window.

'Get down!'

Arrowsmith ran on.

'Get down, you fucking idiot!'

17

Arrowsmith threw himself to the ground just as the gun began its deadly chatter and the Volvo continued to reverse until it came to a wider part of the track. Arrowsmith got up as the driver gunned the accelerator, only diving to the ground again as bullets tore into the earth around him. The Volvo disappeared from sight in a cloud of dust and Arrowsmith lay still.

Desperately Maxwell stared around him, conscious of a surging feeling of hopelessness. Then he saw the elderly Fiat crawling through the traffic and he knew that this would be his only chance. Leaping out into the dusty road, he wrenched open the rickety door, pushed aside the driver and shouted '*Policia.*' Arrowsmith, unharmed but shaking, threw himself into the back as Maxwell forced the jolting wreck after the Volvo. As they turned the corner at the back of the grandstand, they saw it, hopelessly stuck behind a cart full of chickens that was proceeding at a funereal pace through the decrepit shanty town around them. Children swarmed on the earth pavements and there was a smell of frying. Chickens ran perilously across the road and a machine gun again emerged from the side window of the Volvo. But Maxwell drove on relentlessly, his front-seat passenger protesting vehemently beside him.

'Sod off,' Maxwell told him as he rammed the back of the Volvo in a shower of dust and grinding metal. His unwilling passenger burst into hysterical speech while Maxwell and Arrowsmith dived out on to the impacted earth. Rolling over, Maxwell found himself staring up into the eyes of a goat. It bleated wonderingly, as the machine gun chattered again and deafening pop music began to blast out of a café. Bullets thundered into the road around him as Maxwell pushed aside the goat and rolled himself into the running water of the gutter. Where the hell is Arrowsmith? he wondered. Then he saw him lying under a trestle table that was laden with fruit.

Maxwell crawled behind a small truck and waited. He could hear bullets hitting the coachwork. Suddenly they stopped. For a few seconds Maxwell did nothing. Then he cautiously poked his head round the truck and they started again. Hurriedly he withdrew and waited. He seemed to wait for an eternity. The brown legs of children occasionally flashed past, treating the situation as a game. There was a sound of a car door closing, followed by a shout. Then he heard Arrowsmith yell: 'You cunt!'

Maxwell stood up to see Arrowsmith and one of the occupants of the Volvo fighting furiously on the ground, watched by an admiring crowd. As he ran towards them, he tripped and fell heavily. Scrambling to his feet, Maxwell started to run again. Then something hit him very heavily from behind. He went down again – and this time did not rise.

The *policia* were in force outside the Santa Lucia, the entrance of which was sealed off with white tape. A large, jostling crowd watched from the other side of the street whilst the diners were being interviewed. Arrowsmith saw Aubrey Dunhill's stick-like form, white and shaking as he sat at one of the tables under the awning surrounded by broken glass. Two policemen were with him.

'Your wife – ?' asked Arrowsmith tentatively.

'They've just taken her away.' Dunhill's voice was so low that it was almost impossible to make out what he was saying. 'She can't feel anything.' He choked as the tears ran down his cheeks and his hands began to tremble violently. Then Arrowsmith went over to the blanketed heap on the floor. But before he could lift Sally's bloodied shroud, Dunhill was with him.

'I wouldn't – '

'This is my business, sir.'

'Where's Maxwell?'

'He's in hospital. We almost got the bastards, but one of them got to him first. He'll be all right.'

3.30 p.m.

The casualty department was full of children whose coach had overturned on a school outing. Most of them were only superficially hurt, with cuts and bleeding, but they all seemed in a state of shock. Quiet, staring, ten-year-old eyes were riveted on Maxwell as he was taken behind a screen on a stretcher.

Suddenly one of the children began to scream, and as if at a signal others followed. Maxwell slipped into consciousness and was back in the Santa Lucia. Soon the casualty department sounded like a slaughter-house as he rose up in bed, smelling blood and death and grenades.

The storm had intensified over the south-west Atlantic as they approached Montevideo until it reached Force 10. With the wind on the port bow, HMS *Mercator* had been rolling heavily for three days and Maxwell's nerves – and those of his officers and ship's company – had been ground fine by the heaving of the little world around them that had become a maelstrom of flying objects. Speed had been reduced to eleven knots and they had been steaming a SW course towards Isla de Lobos, the easternmost point of Uruguay. The wind had increased soon after they left the blue waters of Rio de Janeiro harbour for the muddy, shallow waters of the River Plate and Maxwell had stared down at the thrashing muddy sea with distaste.

'No sign of easing up, sir.' Dimly Forbes's voice came back to him as he struggled in mental clouds of pain and chaos.

'Optimistic as usual, Nick?'

'We're only six hours late, sir.'

'Alter course to starboard. I'm going below.'

There conditions were worse, with plates in the galley rattling out of their stowages. Sleep had been impossible, men had tumbled out of their bunks and tempers had been lost hours ago. As Maxwell had walked to the heads, he had heard someone thundering on one of the doors. It was AB Taff Evans yelling with great clarity: 'Piss off!'

'Who's that? Taff?'

'Piss off.'

'It's Dolly.'

'So?'

'I'm sick, Taff. I'm gonna throw up.'

'Do it somewhere else.'

'You've been in there bloody hours.'

'And I'll be in here for another bloody hour if I want.'

'Bastard.'

'Fuck off.'

The words began to merge into another conversation he had listened to in the ward-room. The Flight Commander, Lieutenant-Commander Sinclair, had poured coffee with the precision born of long familiarity with bad weather. Helicopter pilot, Lieutenant Ogilvy, had sipped appreciatively. Their domain was the air, not the sea, and their helicopter flying tended to set them and their breed apart from the rest of the *Mercator*'s officers. They usually hung around together, knowing each other just a shade too well.

'Sod the sea,' Ogilvy had said. An extra large lurch sent scalding coffee on to his wrist and he had sworn again.

'Blowing up a bit more, isn't it?' Lieutenant Arrowsmith had commented, coming into the ward-room like a wet wind. 'Morning, sir,' he had said, seeing Maxwell unfamiliarly taking it easy. He took off his foul weather jacket and sank down.

'Can it blow up any *more*?'

'We'll be tipping off the Beaufort scale if it does.'

Sinclair had stumbled with the coffee jug only just managing to save Ogilvy from a second scalding. He was not so lucky with himself. 'Why did I ever go to sea, sir?' he had asked Maxwell. 'You can't even bloody stand up.'

Later, there had been a briefing and Maxwell had noticed his officers were in ebullient form, knowing the much needed run ashore was about to begin. Maxwell's mood had softened as he heard his own voice saying again: 'What a bloody awful trip!'

They had laughed at the understatement, drawing him into their companionship, and he had felt some of his isolation fade away.

'Look – let's get this briefing over and then we can get down to some serious drinking.'

Some of them had been with him in the Antarctic before; others had been getting used to him for the first time. Either way, they had all known his reputation in Whitehall and how he had been sent out on a long leash to 'make good'. Making good in this case was keeping a low profile. Before they sailed from Portsmouth, Susan had told him: 'Keep down – you've got two years left as a captain. Robin and I want you early retired on a good pension – not broken!' Her voice drifted in and out of his mind until the blurred images returned him to the ward-room. He was glancing around him now and their faces sharpened. Commander Nick Forbes, his second-in-command, three times with him in the South Atlantic now, Burgess, Percy, Eccleston-Smyth, all Commanders, like directors of different departments. Cunningham, his Navigating Officer, Lieutenant Arrowsmith with whom he had gone through so much in the war, Lucas, the Commanding Officer of the *Mercator*'s detachment of Royal Marines, Lieutenant Commander Sinclair, the Flight Commander, Senior Pilot Lieutenant Ogilvy, Lieutenant Crabtree – and all the others. A good team; those who had been tried before knocking those who hadn't into shape. And, by God, they had to be good.

'The point is,' he had told them, 'this isn't just going to be a routine deployment.' He remembered they had stared back at him, the adrenalin rising. 'There's been a lot of activity at that Soviet base, toing and froing, building up supplies and equipment, nothing you could pinpoint. But it gives me the same kind of feeling I had before the Falklands invasion. Our Intelligence is not good enough.'

'You don't think they're going to have another go at the islands, sir?' Burgess had asked him.

Maxwell remembered the firmness in his own voice. 'No – I don't. And if they did, we'd be ready for them. It's something else – I'm sure of it. Something big.'

Now Maxwell felt himself sliding out of unconsciousness. Sometimes he was flooded with living memory, then he was seeing the faces of nurses, of a doctor and, once, of an anxious Arrowsmith. Then, again, he seemed to slide away and he was watching the *Mercator*, now secured alongside the jetty at Montevideo after her long passage from Portsmouth via Madeira and Rio de Janeiro. Although he had stopped clear of the harbour to hose down the salt spray, clean up the decks and even touch up some of the paintwork, the seas had still been running high and their efforts had not met with great success. Now he was looking gloomily at the great gouts of rust running down her superstructure and the peeling paint on her hull.

Irritably, Maxwell had gone below to change into his white ceremonial uniform. A few minutes later he was standing in his underpants, trying to decide whether or not he could squeeze into the trousers he had not worn for eighteen months.

'Lynch,' he had yelled.

'You'll not get into those, sir,' his steward had replied triumphantly, coming in with Maxwell's sword and medals. The telephone had rung and he had hurried outside.

With an effort Maxwell had managed to zip up his trousers. 'I'm in the bastards. Flies took a bit of – '

'Excuse me, sir,' Lynch had said primly, 'the Naval Attaché is here to take you to lunch.'

Maxwell had shaken hands with Captain Aubrey Dunhill, the British Naval Attaché in Uruguay, reminding himself gloomily that Dunhill's next job would be Secretary to the Second Sea Lord, the Chief of Naval Personnel – a chair of ultimate power and influence as far as Maxwell's career was concerned. He had known he would have to be careful – and he hated having to be careful. With any other Attaché he would have discussed his fears about the Soviet bases. He had already pounded the ears of the Ministry of Defence – to no effect whatsoever – but if he talked to Dunhill there was no doubt that he would block him. No wonder we're always so bloody unprepared, Maxwell had thought. There's something about the British love of secrecy that's wholly devious.

He had known Dunhill since they had been cadets together, but even then they had been enemies for the simple reason that Dunhill went by the book – and Maxwell did not.

Five minutes later they had been walking down the gangway whilst the pipes shrilled. The Naval car had been waiting for them on the quayside, and when they had settled into the back seat Maxwell had glanced across at him. Dunhill was very thin and his steel-framed spectacles and staccato way of speaking had not been comforting.

'Welcome to Montevideo, James.'

'Thank you, Aubrey.'

Their words crystallized in Maxwell's dull mind, as if they were on a screen. Then Maxwell saw the limousine pull slowly away, leaving the *Mercator* looking tatty and insignificant at the quayside. Forbes had been on the gangway, saluting smartly, and Maxwell had felt a sudden desire to order the driver to the nearest whore-house. That would have shaken Aubrey. Even now he could imagine his protestations and Maxwell had smiled as they drove past the bars with their bland, smiling hostesses – South American dolls propped limply against the awning supports, the disco music blaring out from behind, sharp and fiery in the white afternoon heat.

Drawing away from the docks they had passed the Palacio Teranco, built by a wealthy merchant in French style, looking cool and inviting. It was Maxwell's favourite building and he remembered how he had taken Susan in there early one morning. They had walked the high-ceilinged rooms with their imported furniture, marbled floors and statues, happy they were together in a foreign port, eluding pomp and circumstance in that rare state of being alone.

'Rosemary is going to meet us at the Santa Lucia.'

'Good,' Maxwell had replied dully. 'It'll be lovely to see her again.'

Then he remembered the car had slowed down behind a truck piled high with what looked like broken prams and the heat had closed in.

Once again, Maxwell almost surfaced and, dimly, he heard a nurse saying in a foreign accent: 'Captain Maxwell – can you hear me?' He could – but he didn't want to come to. He didn't want to think about what had happened in the Santa Lucia. Instead, he forced himself back, slipping again into welcome unconsciousness.

They had drunk dry white wine and watched an interesting argument develop between a taxi-driver and a fare who seemed to think he had been swindled. Eventually it had petered out, the contestants coming to an abusive impasse.

'Still out of favour, James?' Rosemary had asked. Aubrey

had been away from the table, telephoning someone.

'They gave me the ship.'

'Grudgingly?'

'You bet. But I'm lying doggo for a bit. Just till the smoke clears.'

'The war's in the dim and distant.'

'Not for some.'

'They haven't got anyone else with the experience.'

'Aubrey wanted me put out to grass.'

'He doesn't like trouble-shooters.'

'I wouldn't call myself that.'

'Then what do you call yourself?'

Maxwell had leant back in his chair, lazily grinning at her, sipping at his wine. 'I call myself homesick. I'm getting too old to go to sea.'

They had laughed and Maxwell realized again how much he enjoyed Rosemary Dunhill's company. But his pleasure had been abruptly terminated by the return of Aubrey. He had been dressed in plain clothes, a spotless grey suit, white shirt, old Harrovian tie and highly polished black shoes. With his emaciated form and the receding hair-line that gave his forehead a dome-like shape, Dunhill was known as the 'stick insect'. He had gazed at Maxwell through his half-moon spectacles, stuck out on the bony ridge of a beaky nose.

'And how are Susan and Robin?'

'Thriving.'

'And the stud?'

'For a new venture, it's ticking over nicely.'

'Nicely enough to retire into?'

'To start a new career in, Aubrey. It'll be a challenge.'

'I can't imagine you land-based in Norfolk,' Rosemary had said.

'Neither can I. I'll get myself a little dinghy and play at sailors.'

'Isn't that what you all do anyway?' Rosemary had asked sweetly and Aubrey had signalled the waiter. He didn't like banter.

Seconds later, they had begun to roll the grenades across the

25

floor of the Santa Lucia. Maxwell woke screaming.

Julia Mendoza sifted through the pile of ambassadorial corre-
spondence in her in-tray abstractedly, continually looking at
her watch as she did so. The internal telephone buzzed by her
side and she picked it up hurriedly, eagerly seizing the distrac-
tion. It was Kenny's PA – a young English rose called Amanda
Ashton.

'Are you busy?'

'Yes.'

'Oh dear – I just wondered – '

'Well?'

'The party in the *Mercator*. Have you got it all in hand? Mr
Kenny was a bit worried that – '

'It's in hand.'

'He wondered if you'd invited the Ramons – and the
Estrellas – you know, the people at the Maritime Museum.
And what about – Jose Sentino?'

'They've all been sent invitations.'

'Oh.' She sounded nonplussed. 'Jose Sentino said he
hadn't – '

'They were all posted in good time.'

'I see – well, I'm sorry to have bothered you.'

'Will you give Mr Kenny a message?'

'Of course – er – '

'Five years ago he offered me the job of social secretary in
this Embassy and I took it, knowing I would be competent.'

'Of course.'

'And the message is – if he would like someone to take on the
job I would be happy to tender my resignation.'

'I'm sure he had no such idea –' The English rose was completely nonplussed now and Julia smiled sweetly. God – what a
bitch I am, she thought with pleasure.

'Then tell him, with respect, that all his invitations have
been sent out.'

'Of course,' came the flustered reply. Julia slammed the receiver down.

26

'Captain Maxwell.'

'Mm.'

'You're awake at last.'

'What?'

The doctor's face floated into view, distorted by the glowing white light above him.

'You are in hospital.'

Maxwell tried to pull himself up but it cost him too much pain. He fell back, muttering: 'I know I'm in bloody hospital.'

'You have suffered some injuries.' The doctor was old and he spoke slowly in perfect English as if relishing each word. 'Two blows to the head. Inflicted at different times – times that were close together.'

'Where the hell did I get the second?' Now he was fully awake, Maxwell felt like death.

'In a side-street. I don't know the circumstances. One of your officers brought you in.'

'Lieutenant Arrowsmith?'

'I believe so.'

'And the hand?' He was looking down at the bandages.

'Minor lacerations.'

'Anything else?'

'No, Captain Maxwell. You were very lucky to have survived the blast.'

'Were there many casualties?'

'I believe so.'

'Mrs Dunhill?'

'She is in intensive care. Here at this hospital.'

'How is she?'

'Not well. But comfortable.'

Maxwell winced. 'You've picked up British hospital jargon.'

'I was trained there.'

'Mm – I'd like to go and see her.'

'You mustn't get up, Captain Maxwell. We are transferring you to a ward.'

'You're not.'

27

'Are you not aware of the dangers of concussion, Captain Maxwell?'

'Absolutely – and I'll take the risk.'

Maxwell tried to sit up – and failed again.

'Bugger it.'

'I have a feeling that you are not going to be a good patient, Captain.'

'You bet I'm not, doctor.'

Two hours later a shaky Maxwell had joined Dunhill at his wife's bedside in one of the intensive care units. She seemed lost in a jumble of equipment, much of which was embedded in her body. Her breathing was stentorian and sometimes it sounded as if it was about to shudder to a halt.

'Any change?'

'No,' Dunhill replied woodenly. 'There's no change.' He seemed almost unaware of Maxwell's presence and for a while they sat in silence, listening to the rasping of Rosemary's pressurized lungs. Then Dunhill said softly: 'Did you know responsibility has been claimed? There was a call to the television station.'

'Who was it?'

'Ola Roja.'

'Who the hell are they?' Maxwell turned away from Rosemary's waxen features.

'I don't know. It means Red Wave. Someone important was killed.'

'As opposed to those who weren't important,' said Maxwell, his head throbbing. 'Who was it?'

'A scientist – an American scientist.'

'Connected with – ?'

'I have no idea.'

But Maxwell had a pretty good idea that he did.

Aubrey pulled out a crumpled piece of paper. 'It was on the radio.' He stared down at the paper in a puzzled way, as if the words were irrelevant to his present situation. '"The execution of Dr Randolph Berens at the Santa Lucia restaurant in Montevideo was carried out by Red Wave freedom fighters and was a new strike in the liberation of the South American states from capitalist influence."' He paused. '"Unless HMS *Mercator* is withdrawn from service in these waters, more executions will follow."' He carefully folded up the paper and put it back into his pocket. Rosemary stirred faintly, letting out a low moan, and a doctor came in to check her drip feed. Dunhill looked up at him like a beseeching animal, whilst Maxwell felt the shock waves invade his already throbbing mind.

Back in the private ward he did not intend to occupy, Maxwell phoned Susan, getting her out of bed. Her reaction was predictably stoical, and he wondered how much she really cared whether he was alive or dead. On the other hand, she had been told of danger, or the risk of death, so many times in the past that she had successfully adopted the matter-of-fact façade of a sailor's wife. Unreasonably Maxwell did not want this matter-of-factness. He wanted her to scream down the phone, to fly out, to make him believe he had nearly died, but all she had said as they concluded the call was 'Keep that profile lower, Jimmy. We still want you back in one piece.'

Forbes hurried in, breaking into his ruminations. 'They've given Arrowsmith sedatives, sir, but I think I ought to get him back to the ship.'

'Yes,' said Maxwell, 'of course he must go back. I think we should all go back.' He sat down heavily on the bed. 'Oh shit!'

'You'll be under observation, I gather, sir.'

Maxwell held up a weary hand. 'I'm going to the Chief of Police.'

Forbes looked appalled. 'But the doctor – '

'To hell with the doctor,' said Maxwell.

'Captain Maxwell?' The big man had full sensuous lips and there was a gloss to him that spoke of bustling authority. He was accompanied by a short dumpy figure that forcibly reminded Maxwell of Father Brown.

'I'm Maxwell. This is Commander Forbes.'

'I am Geraldino Garcia-Lopez – Chief of Police.' They shook hands formally. 'And this is Mr Symons of your Embassy.' More hand-shaking. 'I have come from my *estancia*. I was on holiday.' He leant forwards eagerly, as if anxious to redeem himself.

Maxwell took his opportunity immediately, concisely telling him about the restaurant and its aftermath. Then he asked: 'Do you know this Ola Roja group?'

'We have never heard of them. But that is to say nothing. There are many new names – names just used for one operation. We shall be investigating. I am deeply shocked that this happened to you in our country.' He paused. 'The tragic deaths – ' He broke off. 'How is Mrs Dunhill?'

'Unconscious.'

He nodded and turned to Symons, who spoke for the first time. 'We shall be working closely with Señor Garcia-Lopez.' His voice was formal, without warmth. 'You will have police protection here until you leave. But there are questions I need to ask you now, and I shall want to come on board to talk to Lieutenant Arrowsmith when he is in a fit state to speak to me.'

Maxwell turned to Forbes. 'Get him back to the ship – I'll come on later.'

'Are you sure you're OK, sir?'

'Commander – I feel bloody awful. But at least I'm alive.' He turned back to Garcia-Lopez. 'I'm at your disposal.' Maxwell rose slowly to his feet and Garcia-Lopez looked at him in concern.

'We shall go to the registrar's office and talk where there is coffee.'

Maxwell staggered slightly. 'That,' he said, 'is a damn good idea.'

Two hours of close questioning in an unbearably hot office convinced Maxwell of one thing – that the mighty combination of the Uruguayan Police Department and British Security seemed to know next to nothing about Ola Roja and their twin objectives of killing the American scientist and attempting to frighten off the *Mercator*.

'It's just not logical,' Maxwell told them. 'Even if they had succeeded in bumping me off, there are plenty of other Naval Captains who would love to command the *Mercator*.'

'But surely,' said Garcia-Lopez, 'the original survey ship was to be withdrawn before the Falklands war?'

'As you say,' replied Maxwell, 'that was *before* the Falklands war. Now this one's more vital than ever. So you won't find the British Government quite so anxious to cut her up.'

Symons smiled – a little grimly, thought Maxwell. Did he know more than he was letting on? As if to reassure everyone, Symons said: 'I have a feeling we should view this as very much of a one-off. A group of amateurs having a go.'

But Maxwell was not so sure and once the questioning was over he returned to the intensive care unit. There he found Rosemary's condition unchanged, and Dunhill still sitting beside her. He looked up, his face grey with fatigue.

'You're still here – ' He seemed rather put out.

'Uruguayan Chief of Police and British Naval Intelligence. Had me under the bright lights.'

Dunhill nodded. 'Any further?'

'No – so I'm going to nip down to the Uruguayan Naval Headquarters before I go back to the ship.'

'Why?' His voice was sharp. 'Why should they know any more?'

'I don't say they do. But I want to check everything out.'

Dunhill got up. 'I'm coming with you.'

Maxwell was startled. 'In God's name why?'

'Because there's nothing I can do here.' He looked down at the machine that was Rosemary. 'They tell me she'll be unconscious for some hours yet.'

'But if she wakes up – you'll want to be with her.'

Dunhill, however, was already stiffly walking towards the door. 'I've said I'm coming with you and that's it.'

What the hell's going on? wondered Maxwell as he nodded puzzled acquiescence.

The dark wood panelling of the outer office was covered with oil paintings of sailing vessels and a conglomerate of ships' badges and photographs. A flag lieutenant showed Maxwell and Dunhill through this museum-like space into a modern room with a long, polished, bare desk. Behind it was a short, clean-shaven man who had an almost mechanical neatness to his spare figure. Desperately, Maxwell tried to overcome his exhaustion.

'Good evening, Juan,' said Dunhill in his Diplomatic Corps voice. 'Captain Maxwell – Rear-Admiral Ramirez.'

'I won't shake hands,' said Maxwell. 'The hand's a bit painful.'

Ramirez was clearly considerably agitated. 'I had no idea you would come to see me – after the tragic events of this afternoon.'

But Maxwell swept on aggressively. 'I thought you might know a little more about this Ola Roja group – more than your Chief of Police does, for instance.'

Ramirez turned abruptly to Dunhill. 'Aubrey – how is Rosemary? It's unbelievable – some madman – ' He broke off. 'Is there anything I can do?' he said awkwardly.

'Thank you,' replied Dunhill, his voice just controlled. 'There's nothing you can do. I shall be going back to the hospital presently.'

'You should go now,' insisted Ramirez.

'I'd rather carry out my duties for the moment.'

'I see,' said Ramirez inadequately. 'Captain Maxwell, I know nothing of this Ola Roja group. They are a completely new name to me. But what I can say is that everything that can be done is being done to bring them to justice for this outrage.'

Maxwell smiled sourly.

'Can I get you gentlemen a drink?'

'Not for me.' Dunhill sounded a hundred miles away.

'Could I have a large whisky,' said Maxwell, undeterred.

Ramirez went to a cupboard and began to rattle glasses and bottles. As he did so, he said: 'I gather you will have full police protection now.' The telephone rang on his desk and he picked it up impatiently. 'Well?' He listened, nodding. 'I shall warn them,' he said and put the phone down. 'There are a pack of journalists in the lobby downstairs. They must have followed you here.'

'Damn.'

'It would be unwise for you to speak to them here.'

'Or anywhere else.'

'That is up to you, Captain Maxwell,' he said, handing him a large Scotch.

'And so you can't enlighten me?'

'As to Ola Roja – no. But these names – '

'Could be one-offs. Yes.' Maxwell groaned inwardly, knowing he was getting nowhere. He looked at his watch. 'As you know, I was coming to brief you on my task in the South Atlantic. I'd like to do that still.'

'That's most kind. But in the circumstances – '

'I won't have any more time. I've got to get back for the cocktail party.'

'You surely aren't going ahead with that?' Ramirez looked amazed.

'Of course I am,' snapped Maxwell. 'I certainly don't want those bastards to think they've got us on the run.'

'But the security.'

'It's been redoubled,' said Dunhill, coming swiftly and succinctly to Maxwell's rescue. 'I'm sure Captain Maxwell is right. The schedule must be adhered to – everything should be as normal.'

'And the VIPs?' asked Ramirez doubtfully.

'They'll be looked after.' Dunhill's voice was crisp. 'Now – if you're going to ask Captain Maxwell questions perhaps you would be good enough to proceed. He's very tired – as I am.'

Ramirez looked considerably discomforted. 'Very well – I'm most grateful.' He cleared his throat. 'The *Mercator* – is she similar to the Argentine *Corrientes*, or the German *Meteor*?'

'No. She's an amalgam of all the Antarctic vessels and a damn good warship as well.'

'The ship's company?'

'Two hundred and six men, including twenty-six officers and a detachment of twenty-two Royal Marines.'

'Aircraft?'

'A Sea King and two Lynx helicopters.'

There was a short pause and then Ramirez said: 'I wonder

how the signatories of the Antarctic Treaty* will view the war-like potential of your *Mercator*?'

'They were all consulted during the building phase and no one raised any marked objections,' replied Maxwell flatly.

'The weaponry is very well concealed, isn't it, Captain?' put in Dunhill meaningfully.

But Maxwell was not to be drawn. 'Well, the Sea Dart launcher submerges out of sight, the Exocet is very well camouflaged and it's only the Sea Wolf that's blatantly obvious. But that, of course, is purely defensive.'

'Yes,' replied Ramirez, 'of course. Do you feel the Treaty will be renewed in 1991, Captain?'

'No, I don't,' said Maxwell and Dunhill visibly winced. 'Now that oil's been found – and there's the strong possibility of other minerals being present – I don't think there's a chance in hell. The big companies will win the day.'

Ramirez smiled, as if in appreciation of his blunt candour, but Dunhill's face was dour. 'I'm not surprised by what you say. However, our cousins across the River Plate will be a little put out, I'm sure.'

'So will British scientists. But I think you have to realize that our relations with Argentina are very much improved at the moment.'

'I'm sure they are looking to you for some kind of compromise – and for you to exert your influence amongst the large oil companies.'

'That's certainly a possibility,' replied Maxwell blandly.

The phone rang on the desk and Dunhill started, watching Ramirez intently as he answered it. After a few seconds he passed across the receiver. Dunhill listened, spoke briefly and handed it back.

* The Antarctic Treaty effectively froze all territorial disputes between the Argentine, Great Britain and Chile over their individual claims to the Antarctic Peninsula. Signed in 1959, the Treaty reserved Antarctica and its surrounding oceans and islands south of latitude 60°S for peaceful scientific purposes by all interested countries. The USA and the USSR were among the signatories. All military and political activities were shelved until further notice and at least until the Treaty is reviewed in 1991.

34

'She's regained consciousness,' he said, staring at Maxwell blankly as if he could not believe the news.

When Maxwell eventually returned to the *Mercator*, he lowered himself cautiously into the bath, taking care to avoid jarring his hand. Once he had manoeuvred himself into the hot water he felt himself unwinding, but only slowly for there was a nagging doubt in his mind. Having just survived an assassination attempt he found it a little galling to discover how the perpetrators had been so easily dismissed by everybody – including the British. And why had Dunhill followed like a terrier at his heels? None of it made sense. As his mind went on in a circular motion and his head began to ache violently, Lynch rapped on the door.

'Yes?'

'I'm afraid you have a visitor on the way, sir.'

'Tell whoever it is to go to hell.'

'That would be difficult, sir.'

'Why?'

'It's the Ambassador. He'll be here in ten minutes.'

'But he's coming to the party, later.'

'He's early. In view of what happened.'

Maxwell began to swear slowly and with great feeling.

A brown Rolls Royce flying a Union Jack purred to a halt on the jetty, the bugler sounded the alert and the *Mercator* public address system announced: 'Attention to starboard, British Ambassador to Uruguay.'

Peter Kenny walked slowly up the gangway to inspect the guard. He was a distinguished-looking man with a shock of white hair, a small, trim moustache and his skin tanned to a leathery brown. With his beautifully tailored tropical suit Kenny looked very much the traditional career diplomat.

As Maxwell stood at the top of the gangway in the cooling early evening, he wondered why Kenny had never reached the higher diplomatic posts. Perhaps his looks belied his lack of bite for it was rumoured he lacked grip.

'Good to see you, sir.'

They shook hands as the gangway staff stood rigidly to attention.

'Why the hell aren't you in hospital?' Kenny's voice was strong and rich, its tones redolent of many years of public speaking. Maxwell knew that this was his last appointment before retirement and he had recently been awarded a CMG in the Queen's Birthday Honours. 'He's unpopular.' Maxwell remembered the Mayor of Montevideo's confiding voice when they last met. 'Always promoting British commerce, but never landing us any contracts.'

'I'm OK, sir. I'm just so sorry about the girl – and Rosemary Dunhill, not to mention that poor bastard, Berens,' said Maxwell, as they walked along the upper deck towards his cabin.

'Yes,' said Kenny. 'This is the worst episode we've had in years.'

They passed a large muster of the *Mercator*'s officers who saluted vigorously.

Kenny smiled. 'I see it's business as usual, James.'

Forbes sat on Arrowsmith's bunk and lit him a cigarette. Lying on his back, his face ashen, Arrowsmith was still drowsy from the sedation.

'We almost got the bastards,' he said. 'I had one of them on the deck but the other one nobbled the old man.' Then his face crumpled and he turned away.

'She wouldn't have known anything about it,' said Forbes firmly. 'You were having a good lunch – and then that was it.' They had been through the Falklands war together and seen a lot of death. But Forbes knew this was different.

'Sir.' Arrowsmith's voice was stronger.

'Mm?'

'What will you do when you get out of the Navy?'

'Why ask that?' Forbes was surprised.

'Because I want to talk about something. Something else.'

Forbes touched Arrowsmith on the shoulder. 'Of course,

forgive me.' He sat considering and then said: 'God knows –
I'm not fit for anything else.'

'Is the divorce through?'

'Just. It's the kids I worry about. Jake's in his last term at the
Dragon, then he goes to Marlborough. It'll be the hell of a
change and now Angela's so busy with Tom – you know
they've got this catering business off the ground.'

'Good for them. But she's always been close to Jake, hasn't
she? I mean, she won't neglect him?'

'I know she won't, but all the same – I broke up a marriage
because of the sea – I don't want to make things worse.'

'And Judy?'

'She's more self-contained. Going as an au pair to Germany
next month. Anyway – she wrote me off years ago as the
absentee father.'

Forbes continued to talk, knowing that he was softening
Arrowsmith's mental return to the enormity of what had happened. He told him of his years at Dartmouth, of his home in
the Welsh hills and his fierce Admiral of a father. 'We were all
born to go to sea,' Forbes said. 'No escape whatever.'

'But you love it.' Arrowsmith sounded as if he was a frightened child, wanting to be told a story to stave off the dark.

'Oh, yes,' replied Forbes. 'But it's a wilful life – and it's
damaged the family – irreparably. I'm a selfish bastard.' He
laughed ruefully.

'You haven't answered the question.'

'What was that?'

'What are you going to do when you get out?'

'When I *have* to get out? I'm only forty-three.'

'But when you do?'

'I had thought of running a yacht-chartering business –
maybe somewhere in the Med. But I'm not so sure now.'

'Why?'

'I'd like someone to share it with.' Forbes stood up.

'Sorry,' said Arrowsmith.

'Why sorry?'

'I pushed you into saying that.'

'No, you didn't. I freely admit it.' He looked at his watch.

'I'd better go and get organized. The old man's still going to run that damned cocktail party.'

'Good for him. Show the bastards.'

'You're to stay here. You're in no fit state to – '

Arrowsmith was levering himself up out of the bunk. 'I don't want to be alone, sir. Can you see?'

Forbes looked down at him. 'Yes, I can see,' he replied slowly.

'There's one hell of an investigation going on.' Kenny sat in Maxwell's cabin sipping dry sherry.

Maxwell frowned, a sudden anger sweeping over him. 'I rather had the opposite impression.' He turned away so that Kenny would not see his hand trembling on his glass. But Kenny was quicker than he had imagined.

'You're a fool. You should be in hospital. Not running a reception.'

'I wouldn't give them the satisfaction.'

Kenny was looking at Maxwell intently. 'You're saying no one's taking this seriously enough?'

'Something like that.'

'Then I'd better tell you everything I know. To be more accurate – I'd better tell you what my hunches are. And please bear in mind I could be wrong.'

Maxwell nodded. 'I would appreciate someone levelling with me.'

'The oil problem was very much in Mrs Thatcher's mind when she defended the Falklands in 1982. Seven years later we still feel the same way. But now we're actively negotiating sovereignty the Russians would love to see disruption – and Ola Roja could be acting as their agents.'

'And the oil?'

'In ten years' time, provided our scientists are right, the West could break the Arab monopoly. We wouldn't need to be so dependent if we had oil resources here – and the Russians know that only too damn well. So the more disruption they can create via other agencies, the more they can delay the breaking of the monopoly. And of course the arrival of the *Mercator*, with all its concealed weaponry, must be seen as a threat.'

Maxwell was impressed. Kenny had never treated him to such confidences before. 'We're purely defensive,' he said wryly.

'But you're not going to let anyone break the Antarctic Treaty, are you? Or threaten the negotiations for renewing the terms?'

'It's hard to comment on that. I just take orders.'

'Yes,' said Kenny urbanely. 'Of course you do.' He paused. 'There is another matter. After what has happened I'm sure you appreciate that your people must observe total security.'

'They do,' replied Maxwell defensively, adding drily: 'In any case, they don't have the precise details.'

'Of course,' said Kenny, 'this is MOD business, not mine.'

'Do I take it that you're warning me about a possible attack on the *Mercator*?'

'I think you have to foresee every possibility,' Kenny replied.

7.30 p.m.

Maxwell felt light-headed with exhaustion as he welcomed his guests on board. The Sea King and the two Lynx helicopters had been ousted to the after-end of the *Mercator*'s flight deck and a red-and-white striped awning had been erected inside their hangar. The stanchions were festooned with old whale-gutting and carcass-cutting knives salvaged from the South Georgia whaling station by HMS *Endeavour*, *Mercator*'s predecessor. Flowers and pot plants had been lent by the Embassy and a waterfall, devised by Forbes, gushed erratically in a corner of the flight deck.

Maxwell contemplated the rigours of the forthcoming Embassy dinner without relish. The local evening newspaper had been full of the attack, blazoning a headline that, loosely translated from the Spanish, read: '3 DEAD IN RESTAURANT SHOOTING. TOP AMERICAN SCIENTIST DIES. ATTEMPTED ASSASSINATION OF BRITISH CAPTAIN.' He had ignored the flood of

calls reaching *Mercator* from the British and American press –
and had been warmly praised by the MOD for doing so. 'WE
WILL ISSUE STATEMENT,' their telex had run. 'CONGRATU-
LATIONS ON KEEPING THE SHOW GOING.'

Maxwell had telephoned Susan again, trying – but failing –
to reassure her. She had read out the headlines from the British
evening papers to him: 'EMBASSY SECRETARY AND AMERICAN
SCIENTIST SLAIN IN MONTEVIDEO. ATTEMPTED ASSASSINATION OF
FALKLANDS GUARDSHIP CAPTAIN.'

'Why?' she had asked him again and again. 'Why do they
want to kill you?'

To his satisfaction, he now realized that her stoicism had
wavered and her fears were growing. He wondered what had
triggered it off. Press notoriety? Then he damned himself for
being cynical. He was behaving like a little boy who had been
hurt and who wanted everyone to comfort him. Especially
Susan. Immediately he had tried to allay her fears by talking of
hit and miss terrorist activities. 'Nothing significant,' he had
told her. 'Just having a go.'

But she was not to be mollified now and anger had replaced
her fear. 'Why do you take me for such a fool, James?'

As they rang off, Maxwell felt a sudden rush of satisfaction
at the emotion he was wringing out of her.

The alert was sounded and whilst the White Ensign was slowly
lowered, Maxwell breathed a sigh of relief as the belated sunset
party stood rigidly to attention and his guests began to take
their leave. The Officer of the Day ordered the carry-on to be
sounded and the sunset party marched off.

Maxwell winced as an elderly Embassy official almost lost
his footing. 'They seem to have had a good time,' he said to
Forbes, who was draining the last of his whisky. 'We did well
to keep the flag flying.'

'Risky though, sir,' replied Forbes. 'Now where are you
going?'

'To the Embassy dinner party, where else?'

'For God's sake, sir – '

'I want to keep that flag flying,' replied Maxwell firmly.

Maxwell arrived at the Embassy half an hour later than diplomatic etiquette permitted. He had changed hurriedly, and then been delayed by cocktail party stragglers. Feeling a vile temper creeping over him and with his head splitting, he had been driven in an official Embassy limousine to Pocitos, a select residential suburb of Montevideo where the Embassies had been built, screened by high fences or clipped hedges from public view.

Repeatedly looking at his watch, and inwardly cursing the driver for his slow progress, Maxwell had finally spotted the mass of blue and lilac hydrangeas that flanked the graciously porticoed doorway to the British Embassy. Emerging from the car with inelegant speed, Maxwell was received by a butler and ushered down the long corridor which reminded him of an old-fashioned English country hotel. Eventually the butler led him into a brightly lit drawing room crowded with Kenny's guests.

Forbes was already there, talking animatedly to a striking middle-aged lady, and three other *Mercator* officers – Burgess, Sinclair and Cunningham, Maxwell's navigator – mingled heartily. Maxwell switched on his automatic smile and sipped at a large whisky awkwardly held in his bandaged hand. Then Kenny came up, looking even more British Raj in his silk dinner jacket, and introduced him to a local business man. As they talked, Maxwell was discreetly able to survey the other guests who had obviously been carefully selected by Kenny and his social secretary to represent a cross-section of Uruguayan, Argentine or British diplomats, politicians and service person-nel with a leavening of business men. Escaping from a round of spiritless dialogue, Maxwell drew Forbes aside.

'How are you bearing up, sir?'

'I'm not. I feel as if I'm being eaten alive. The sooner we're down in the ice the better.'

The gong sounded for dinner and Kenny ushered his guests into the dining room. Maxwell found himself placed at the high table with a titled English lady on his right and Señora Ramirez, the wife of the Uruguayan Admiral, on his left. It was not a stimulating or a relaxing position to be in. Waiters hovered, ready to replenish their glasses with red or white Chilean wines but never seeming to replenish them enough.

The attractive middle-aged woman he had seen with Forbes sat at the end of Maxwell's table, listening to Sinclair talk about rugby. There was something about her that captivated him – a sort of false jauntiness that made him wonder if she had a dry sense of humour underneath it all. She was obviously of Spanish extraction and her dark oval face, although heavily lined, was still striking in its mobile beauty. She was taking a polite interest in Sinclair but Maxwell knew she was bored. He wondered if he might bore her as much with his passion for music or, even worse, the naval anecdotes that seemed statutory in diplomatic circles. He sighed, feeling the dull constraints of his position, and Señora Ramirez smiled at him confidentially. 'No wonder you are so tired, Captain Maxwell. I admire you and your officers for keeping going. It was a terrible incident.'

'Yes,' Maxwell replied abruptly. 'I don't really want to talk about it.'

'I gather Mrs Dunhill is making good progress,' she persisted. But Maxwell swiftly changed the subject.

Since his return to the hospital, Aubrey Dunhill had not left his wife's bedside. Outside the small, private room, two policemen stood guard, one with a revolver on his lap. Rosemary was conscious now but heavily drugged against the pain in her back. The doctor had told Dunhill that she would not be paralysed. The base of her spine had been damaged, her shoulder was broken. She had severe bruising, burns and various nasty abrasions. But that was all – and she was lucky, the doctor had said. Very lucky.

Rosemary had spoken a few words to her husband and he had hesitantly explained about the grisly events in the Santa Lucia and the fact that she was now safe, protected and recovering. She had seemed reassured and was now lightly dozing. Dunhill gently relinquished her hand which he had been holding for the last hour. He had an acute case of pins and needles and, as he flapped his hand to and fro, he wondered again why they had come for Maxwell as well as for the American scientist. Was it simply an attempt to frighten off the Royal Navy – an isolated, random, ill-conceived attack? Or was this to be the beginning of something more sustained?

Dunhill again sought Rosemary's hand whilst he thought of Maxwell and his long history of nonconformity. Although it had always irritated him that Maxwell was a rebel – that in commission after commission he had fallen foul of his superiors to such an extent that he had only been given the *Mercator* by the skin of his teeth – Dunhill had long had a sneaking admiration for Maxwell. It was an admiration that he would never have admitted to anyone – even Rosemary. It lay, surprisingly enough, in a streak of romanticism, for Dunhill, despite all his bureaucracy, was not a man without imagination and something of Maxwell's unorthodox spirit appealed to him, knowing as he did that it was only men of Maxwell's breed who would keep the dwindling Royal Navy alive. Maxwell had been born to go to sea and was such an intrinsic part of British naval tradition that its decay had made him a radical. Now he was a thorn in Whitehall's side, only retained because they knew he was good.

Dunhill looked at his watch, knowing that he must get some sleep or he'd be fit for nothing. The hospital almoner had offered him a bed next door and he must take advantage of it. Gently unclasping Rosemary's hand again, Dunhill yawned and stood up. He bent over the bed and whispered: 'Good-night, my darling. Thank God for saving you.'

As the ladies reluctantly withdrew, the men huddled round the freshly replenished port decanter. Maxwell groaned inwardly as the Head of Chancery began to question him about South American politics, but by expert manoeuvring born of long experience he managed to make his escape.

Kenny smiled cynically as Maxwell described the report he had to finish, but as the other British officers began to make their excuses, he escorted Maxwell to the door. For a few minutes they stood at the top of the Embassy steps, looking out at the velvety darkness which was unbroken by sound or movement.

'Be careful, James,' he said.

'Yes, sir,' said Maxwell softly.

'Everything OK, sir?' asked Forbes, coming up behind him.

'Yes,' replied Maxwell slowly, 'everything's fine. Want a lift?'

Forbes looked uneasy. 'We were going into town.'

Maxwell shook his head, feeling schoolmasterly. 'We can't afford to take any risks. Make it short.'

'Yes, sir.'

There was silence for a moment then Maxwell said: 'I'll be happier when we get back to sea. When we get into the ice.'

'It's a different world,' Forbes agreed.

'Certainly a safer one,' replied Maxwell.

But Nick Forbes's mind was elsewhere. The woman he had met at the Embassy had made a very particular impression on him. Years of womanizing had made Forbes employ a routine points system. Six for a near miss, ten for an average screw, twenty for memorability. And so he had continued his sexist way. This time he thought it was different, yet the cliché worried him. Why should he find Julia Mendoza so different? Was it because he'd had the fleeting impression that she despised him?

20 November 1989

2 a.m.

Dunhill woke with a headache. It was stuffy and claustrophobic in the narrow, windowless room and he had an urgent desire to rise immediately from his bed, seek fresh air and find some coffee. He was sitting on the edge of the bed, pulling on his socks and shoes, when he thought he heard a noise next door. He listened intently and caught it again – a kind of muffled sigh, just discernible through the wafer-thin wall.

Hurrying out into the corridor, he saw both guards were

awake and in position. Dunhill felt a wave of relief and tried to get a grip on himself. Then he heard the sound again, accompanied by a quiet movement.

'Who's in there?'

'The doctor, *señor*. He is on his rounds.'

'Is she all right?'

'A routine visit.'

Dunhill paused, taking all this in. It certainly sounded reasonable enough. Then, as if guided by a sudden instinct, he opened the door.

The night was hot, musky, and the taxi-driver's potent little cheroot glowed in the front seat of the battered Fiat. Next to him, Julia looked alien, part of a foreignness to which Forbes was not privy.

'When this scare's over and we're back in Montevideo, can I take you out to dinner?'

'I'd like that.'

The taxi drove away into the darkness, leaving Forbes alone on the steps of the Embassy. For the first time in years he felt elated.

Rosemary was propped up in bed, her eyes closed, and the young doctor was bending over her. He straightened up as Dunhill came in, and smiled. He was slight with dark hair tumbling over his forehead, a dazzlingly white coat and a stethoscope slung round his neck. His smile was reassuring.

'She is making good progress,' he said. 'Your wife sleeps very peacefully.' He came up and shook Dunhill's hand. 'You are a very lucky man – she's had a narrow escape.' He walked slowly towards the door while Dunhill looked down at Rosemary. It was true – she did look very peaceful.

'Will she completely recover? I mean – she won't be paralysed or anything?'

'No,' replied the doctor, 'she will make a complete recovery. Of course it will be slow and she will be with us for some weeks. But she will recover.'

'I'm very grateful for all you're doing.'

'It is a pleasure, *señor*. Your wife is a very popular lady here and she is much respected.'

'Thank you.' Dunhill was on the verge of tears.

'And now I must continue with my rounds.'

'Of course.'

The doctor walked to the door. *'Buenas noches,'* he said, hurrying out into the corridor.

'Buenas noches.'

Dunhill was alone with her at last and his joy was the greatest he had ever known. It had taken this, he thought, to bring him alive. Now they would both start afresh. Reborn.

Walking towards the bed, he saw that her mouth was slightly open – as were her eyes. Moving nearer he saw that Rosemary was very still and after a few seconds he had the curious thought that she was not breathing. Dismissing these idiotic reactions – reactions brought on by his own shock and fatigue – Dunhill reached for Rosemary's hand. Yes – it was still warm. What was the matter with him? Thank God for that good man of a doctor. He would officially thank him, they would take him out to dinner, they – But it was her eyes. They didn't blink. And her chest – there was no rise or fall. Was he going mad? He bent over her, the sweat pouring down his face, his heart thumping. There was no rise or fall. But, of course, there would be an explanation. What could it be? Dunhill stabbed at the emergency bell.

'You're going to get better, darling,' he began to repeat over and over again. 'Isn't it wonderful that you're going to get better, darling?'

4.35 a.m.

The phone rang in Maxwell's cabin and he was awake immediately. 'Yes?'

'Forbes, sir.'

'What is it?'

'It's Rosemary Dunhill. She's dead.'

46

Maxwell shook his head, trying to wake himself up. For a few seconds he merely felt puzzled. There was no sense of shock, sorrow, nothing. Only surprise. Then he began to come to as Forbes said: 'They penetrated the hospital.'

'Who?'

'Ola Roja. Some bastard posing as a doctor. He injected her with something. Don't know what it is yet – but it killed her. Dunhill found her.'

'Christ!'

'All hell's been let loose. Press everywhere.'

'Here?'

'On the quayside. British press on the phone – and the MOD want you.'

'I bet they do.' Maxwell's voice shook and Forbes didn't know whether it was sorrow or anger. Or both. 'Poor Aubrey.'

4.40 a.m.

'Why?'

'*Señor* – we don't know. He had an identity tag. Everything.'

'Your security is pathetic!'

'Yes, *señor*.'

The hospital administrator's office was crowded with officials and there was an atmosphere near to panic. Telephones shrilled, one of the guards wept in a corner and Dunhill stood, refusing to sit down, shaking from head to foot, his voice shrill with grief and shock.

'Shit!'

Peter Kenny stood beside him, his hand on his arm. 'Please, Aubrey – you must sit down. You were quite right to ring me. I shall handle the whole investigation on your behalf, personally.' Kenny gestured to one of the nurses and she came towards them.

Dunhill sat down heavily on the swivel chair behind the administrator's desk while she gave him an injection. 'You bastards!'

Kenny picked up the telephone. 'This is the British Ambassador. Put me through to HMS *Mercator*. I want to speak to Captain Maxwell.'

'James.'

'Yes.' Maxwell was sitting in his cabin, furiously angry and still deeply shocked.

'Peter Kenny. You've heard about Rosemary Dunhill.'

'Yes.'

'Is every man on board?'

'Yes. What the hell's going on?'

'It's an incredible situation down here – everything is out of control.'

'I'd like to see Aubrey.'

'No chance. I've got an army unit coming down to the quay-side to guard *Mercator*.'

'They're here already.'

'And you sail in the morning.'

'I've been trying to persuade the MOD to let us go mid-morning. I want to talk to Aubrey – '

'I want the *Mercator* at sea. It'll ease the situation here.'

'I expect it will,' said Maxwell. 'But what are they doing about catching these bastards?'

'There's a full-scale operation being mounted here and the Army's been brought in. City's swarming with police and mil-itia. Can't say any more than that. Get to sea, man.'

2 – The *Escuardo*

25 November 1989
7.26 p.m.
Montevideo
The room was thick with smoke and the scent of coffee. Gabriel sat at the H.7. radio, sweating, fingering the headphones that were clamped to his ears. Julia was beside him, wondering how much more damage they could sustain before the operation was abandoned. She had never seen him so angry, the sudden appearance of emotion transforming him, bringing him almost alive again.

'Put Morales on. Over.'

'Morales.' The static was fierce and the voice was faint, distorted.

'The *Escuardo*. What in the name of God has happened?'

'Sending out a mayday signal – ' His voice faded and returned. ' – explosion. Over.'

'What occurred? Over.'

The static increased. ' – explosion. No further information. Over.'

'We are losing control. Repeat. We are rapidly losing control. I am coming out to assume command. Over.'

Morales crackled back. 'Message understood. Over and out.'

Gabriel put down the headphones and turned to Julia. He looked finished. 'The mistakes at the Santa Lucia – ' For a moment she thought he was going to cry. 'Now the *Escuardo*.'

'What are we to do?' she asked inadequately.

'The operation will continue,' he said. 'And there will be no more mistakes.'

'What am *I* to do?'

Gabriel stood up. 'Wait for instruction,' he said.

49

'Are you sure you should join Morales?'

He nodded, walking to the window and looking down at the white heat of the streets. 'The two ships are the centre of operations. I must be on one of them.'

7.40 p.m.
South of the River Plate
Since they had left Montevideo, the sea had been relatively calm as the *Mercator* cut through the South Atlantic at sixteen knots. At first a number of small fishing vessels had been sighted close to the continental shelf east of Mar del Plata and later the occasional merchant ship was detected ploughing its way south to Patagonia or Magellan. But on leaving the coastal waters the ship's company once again began to settle into the familiar isolation of their own floating world and the feeling of purpose that went with it. Gradually the horrendous events in Montevideo began to recede into the background and it was only Forbes who was restless. Maxwell felt he needed to put space between himself and further conjecture and even Arrowsmith appeared to be calmer, although he was still under doctor's orders and confined to his cabin. So when the mayday call came through, it gave the bridge of the *Mercator* an unpleasant shock.

'They're trying to get a bearing on the signal, sir,' said the Officer of the Watch. Ten minutes later he was able to report: 'It's coming from two-seven-zero, sir.'

'We'd better alter course and investigate,' said Maxwell, ordering the ship to flying stations and scrambling the Sea King.

Almost instantly, the *Mercator* increased speed to nineteen knots and was developing full power on her Olympus gas turbine engines while the electronic warfare team were trying to confirm the bearing of the distress call. In the meantime, the communications staff attempted to raise the distressed vessel as Forbes alerted the sickbay and galley staff. By 20.00 the sun had set and the remainder of the ship's company had just finished supper.

Maxwell returned to the bridge at 20.40 and at 20.45 Forbes

contacted him from the operations room.

'The Sea King has a radar contact forty-five miles to the west, sir. We're closing to identify visually.'

Five minutes later, Forbes rang again. 'The Sea King reports a small stern trawler, sir.'

'What's her condition?'

'Sinclair says there's smoke coming from the superstructure and – ' Forbes's voice faded for a moment and then returned. 'He's just reported that he's sighted flames aft and there's no sign of any boats or life-rafts. The sea's moderate to rough and it's perfectly possible to launch boats or life-rafts.' Forbes's voice faded again and then he reported more clearly: 'Sinclair says the trawler's lying beam-on to a south-west swell and a wind of about fifteen knots. The smoke is laying a long black trail up to the north-east. He's continuing to circle.'

Later, Forbes rang again to give Sinclair's latest report. 'There's a damn great hole in the superstructure and the remnants of a boat hanging from the davits. There are two unharmed life-raft stowages but no life-rafts.'

'What about the crew?' asked Maxwell impatiently.

'No sign of them apparently, sir. Hang on – I'll put you on Sinclair's transmission.'

In a few seconds Maxwell heard Sinclair's voice. 'Ship in distress is a stern trawler, probably Argentine, having suffered a serious fire possibly caused by an explosion in the superstructure starboard side. Light is fading but am carrying out a search for survivors in the vicinity. Out.'

Maxwell got back to Forbes. 'Tell the sickbay to stand by.'

'Sickbay's already on alert, sir. I'll give them the latest details.'

'Good. Tell Sinclair not to go in too close.'

Within a few minutes Sinclair spotted a survivor on the trawl warp, which was hanging vertically over the stern. He spoke rapidly over the headphones to Leading Aircrewman Thomas: 'Stand-by to winch down for recovery of survivor.'

As Thomas was being lowered on the winch wire, strop in

51

hand, he realized that at any moment there could be another explosion. It was not a reassuring thought. When he neared the stern of the trawler it became clear that one of the trawl warps was fouling either the screw or the rudder and the survivor was holding on for grim death. His face was grey with exhaustion and he kept muttering softly in Spanish. Thomas wondered if he was praying.

'It's all right, mate, we'll soon have you in the helicopter,' said Thomas in what he hoped was a reassuring voice as he tried to get the strop over the man's head. But he soon discovered the survivor was not only numbed by his predicament but that he had no idea of what was being said to him. 'Let go of the wire, old son,' said Thomas reasonably enough as they heaved up and down in the swell. A few seconds later he cast reason to the elements as he yelled: 'Let go of that fucking wire, you stupid bastard!' But still the man did not respond. Eventually, Thomas, by much forceful persuasion, managed to make him let go of the warp. In seconds the dazed, still-muttering survivor was being hoisted into the Sea King with Thomas behind him.

'Another survivor, sir, just floating clear of the trawler,' reported Ogilvy, who on this occasion was acting as Sinclair's observer in the temporary absence of Lieutenant Norman Jarvis, who was laid up with flu. Ogilvy welcomed the opportunity to see some action after the monotonous passage to the South Atlantic.

'Thanks,' said Sinclair as he quickly manoeuvred his helicopter above the next survivor. He turned with a grin to Thomas. 'It's time to go down again, Dai.'

With a sinking heart, Thomas was lowered again towards the grey-green swell. It was almost completely dark now but the moon rode high over pale scudding clouds against a jaundiced sky. This time, the survivor was wearing an old cork life-jacket and was floating clear of the ship. As Thomas swung round, he could see the man was barely conscious and his head was rolling from side to side. There was a long, deep wound in his forehead and his clothing was splattered with blood. It was difficult to make out much more in the darkness, pierced only by the landing light of the helicopter. As gently as he could, Thomas wound the strop around the survivor, but just as he was about to give the signal to lift off, he noticed that the man's foot had been completely blown away. As they were lifted over the sea, Thomas's stomach heaved. He retched time and time again as he stared at the swirling cloud and tried not to think of the red spongy substance that was the abrupt conclusion to the survivor's leg. Ogilvy guided them carefully into the helicopter and Medical Petty Officer Barnes placed the man on a stretcher and immediately injected morphine.

'You all right, old son?' he asked.

Thomas nodded, closing his eyes against the reality of it all, opening them reluctantly to face the interior of the helicopter again.

'You sure you're all right?' asked Barnes.

The first survivor began to mutter again and Barnes scrambled over to his side.

'What's he saying?' snapped Sinclair.

'I don't know, sir,' said Thomas. 'I don't speak Spanish either.'

'We can't bugger around here with two blokes in this state,' pronounced Sinclair.

'No, sir,' replied Thomas, offering up a prayer of gratitude that he would not have to go back to the trawler – at least not just yet.

Sinclair called the *Mercator*. 'Request pigeons.'

'Zero-nine-five degrees, seventeen miles,' the helicopter controller replied.

'Am returning immediately on a course of zero-nine-five. I have two survivors: one is in a state of shock and the other bleeding profusely from multiple wounds. Both will need immediate medical assistance. Out.'

On the bridge of the *Mercator*, Maxwell turned to his secretary. 'Get down to the sickbay and find out what the hell went on.'

Fortescue raced down three ladders and along two flats to the sickbay, confident in the knowledge that his fluency in

Spanish had made him a key figure. When he arrived he discovered that the survivor who had lost a foot was unconscious and the ship's doctor was about to perform an operation on his leg. The other man, however, was fully conscious.

'What happened?' asked Fortescue in careful Spanish.

The man said nothing, staring up at him blankly with cloudy eyes.

Slowly, Fortescue repeated the question and the man whispered something he could barely hear. Then he realized he had said: 'Explosion.'

'What happened to the others?'

'I don't know.'

'How many crew?'

'Fourteen. Captain,' he said, pointing feebly at the other survivor.

'What caused the explosion?'

But the man was slipping back into unconsciousness.

'Do you think there are any other survivors?' Fortescue put an urgent, threatening note into his voice.

'Maybe.'

'Where?'

'Engine room – fish hold – in sea.' His voice was becoming weaker and tears welled from his eyes.

Fortescue hurried back to the bridge. He had not been involved with death before and he felt strangely unreal.

About forty miles to the south-east of the *Mercator*, Gabriel Mendoza sat drinking whisky with Alberto Morales on board the *Santa Fe* – the command ship of a group of oil rig support vessels off the Uruguayan coast. As Mendoza poured more whisky, Morales felt the adrenalin flow for the first time in years – so many years. Previously he had felt a child in Gabriel Mendoza's presence, but now, despite being twenty years his junior, he felt Mendoza was his guest and he was master of their battered, heaving, tawdry little world.

Morales had interrupted a merchant navy career to work on behalf of his father, Ruben Morales, stevedore, labour union leader and a political director of the 26 March Movement who had died under torture in the Punto de Rieles penitentiary where he had been sent as a 'national security measure'. Gabriel Mendoza had been his father's oldest friend and he, Alberto, had much to thank him for. Indeed, had it not been for Gabriel's money and the use of his small country hideaway he would have been arrested too.

'Is the sickness passing?' he asked.

'With the whisky,' Gabriel replied.

They were silent and Morales did not feel it was necessary to speak. He had been with Gabriel when the police found his sons, had witnessed the grief that had destroyed him. Now there was only anger, all-pervading, biding its time – and his own loyal gratitude.

'You say we have been plagued by misfortune. But it is only our inexperience that has nearly destroyed us.'

Is he thinking aloud? wondered Morales. Or does he actually want an opinion? He plumped for the latter – and then realized he was wrong. 'If they search the *Escuardo* they will find the code books and then the system will be vulnerable. Isn't our only answer to blow the *Mercator* out of the water? Now.'

Gabriel frowned and took off his glasses, polishing the lenses with his handkerchief. A lock of silver hair flopped over his forehead and he pushed it back impatiently.

'Eventually we may have to but we would be fools to rush in. If we destroy him now, we'll have half the British Navy here.'

'So what are we going to do?'

'Let Maxwell destroy himself.'

'But if he alerts the British Government – '

'As you know – that will be difficult.' Gabriel raised his glass and suddenly smiled. It gave his normally expressionless features a startling flood of warmth. Like the sun sweeping some arid back street.

Once again the Sea King swooped over the sea in the pallid moonlight, its searchlight picking up the name of the trawler.

The landing light from the helicopter was powerful enough to illuminate most of the *Escuardo*'s upper deck and Sinclair could see that the fire in the superstructure was no worse than before. Because of this he decided to lower Leading Aircrewman Thomas and Medical Petty Officer Barnes on to the deck of the trawler so that they could carry out a detailed search.

Landing on the foc's'le, Thomas and Barnes made their way aft together. Clambering up to the bridge, they discovered the starboard bridge wing had disappeared completely and Thomas shone his torch about uneasily.

'There's a bloke over there – or what's left of him, poor bastard.'

Barnes joined him to stare at the remains of a man who was draped over the engine room telegraph. Most of his stomach, legs and an arm had been blown away.

Thomas went to the side of the bridge and threw up as Barnes laid the corpse face down and searched for something to cover it. Then he turned back to Thomas.

'How you doing?'

'I'm sorry,' said Thomas, trembling violently.

'We must get down to the next deck.'

'If we can find some fire extinguishers and some breathing apparatus we might be able to get into the accommodation area,' said Thomas, trying to show initiative in case Barnes thought him incapable of doing anything other than throw up.

Barnes paused; then he said: 'Raise the Sea King and tell them to bring some fire-fighting gear from the ship.'

Thomas got out his portable radio, but just as he turned towards the bridge ladder a dark figure rose up at him and he screamed like a wounded animal.

'Looks like a boiler went up,' said Forbes.

'Mm.' Maxwell stared up at the sky. The racing clouds were now covering the face of the moon, looking like dirty linen lit by a feeble torch. 'How's the bloke in the sickbay?'

'The one without a foot? He's OK – the doc's sewn him up a bit and he's out like a light.'

'He's not said anything?'

'Not a word.'

There was an uneasy silence. Then Forbes said: 'Arrow-smith's still very dodgy.'

'Keep an eye on him,' said Maxwell, irritably. 'I don't want any weak links.'

'I know, sir, but he keeps getting the horrors.'

'To hell with it,' said Maxwell wearily. 'I can't say I blame him. But keep tabs.'

'I thought that bloke had resurrected himself,' gasped Thomas, frantically pointing towards the corpse by the tele-graph.

Ogilvy looked at the dismembered body. 'Messy,' he said.

Thomas swallowed. 'I was just going to call up the Sea King for some fire-fighting gear. Then we were going to see if there were any more survivors.'

'I've already ordered the gear, so I thought I'd drop in and give you a hand with the search.'

'Do you know your way around these ships, sir?'

'No, but Lieutenant-Commander Sinclair does. He was in command of a Fishery Protection Vessel. Always boarding trawlers.'

'Lot of bleedin' use that, sir, with him up in the air,' pro-tested Thomas.

Ogilvy treated him to a withering smile. 'He can direct the search and let us know if the fire gets any worse. The *Mercator* is only five miles away, so she'll soon be able to douse things down.' His voice held an icy edge.

'Yes, sir,' said Thomas, realizing he had gone too far.

'In the meantime, we'll start on this deck, and if we can get through the smoke, we'll search every compartment.' Ogilvy hurried over to Barnes. 'But for God's sake stick close.'

They began their search in the chart house, followed by the winch control room, and then went on to the cabins. The *Escuardo* was a mess – but it was obvious that this had hap-pened well before the explosion. Bedding, papers and personal belongings were all over the floors. Radios had been smashed and several empty bottles of whisky and vodka littered the flats.

'What do you reckon, sir?' asked Barnes.

'God knows,' said Ogilvy as they cautiously continued the search to the accompaniment of the steady crackle of flames and the smell of acrid, oily smoke which occasionally billowed in their direction, fanned by a rising wind.

They soon discovered that the fire had been contained to the starboard side of the superstructure because a Minerva fire sprinkler system had been activated. There was a considerable amount of water on deck, as if someone had been boundary cooling the fire area, and this was confirmed minutes later when they found a running hose some four feet aft above the passage. Then, at the top of a ladder, they found another body slumped over the handrail.

'Your turn, doc,' said Thomas. 'I can't take any more bits of blokes.'

Barnes went over to the body and after a few minutes examination they heard him laugh.

'What's up?' asked Ogilvy.

'He's pissed.'

As the *Mercator* began to close in on the *Escuardo*, Maxwell could see the smoke and flames for himself. 'We've only got Barnes, Thomas and Ogilvy on board, haven't we?'

'Yes, sir.' Forbes sounded anxious.

'The whole lot might go up at any moment.'

'I just wondered if it might be booby-trapped,' said Forbes.

'If it *is* booby-trapped and we bring this ship alongside, we'll be blown to hell. Better let the advance party go on checking her out.' He paused. 'I wonder what on earth caused this balls-up?'

As they dragged the man along the passage he started to come round, moaning and talking in heavily slurred Spanish.

58

Thomas swore as they heaved and pushed him up the ladder until they were on the port bridge wing.

'Leave him here,' said Ogilvy. 'We must get on with the search. They think this wreck might be booby-trapped, and if it is it might go up at any moment.'

'It's so reassuring to be the only lucky bastards on board,' commented Thomas.

Ogilvy spoke into his radio: '982, this is *Escuardo*.'

'*Escuardo*, this is 982.'

'Ogilvy here, sir. We have another survivor.'

'What kind of medical treatment does he require?'

'Only aspirin, sir, he's drunk. We're continuing our search. Out.'

Forty minutes later Ogilvy reported he could find no signs of booby-trapping and Sinclair, after radio consultation with Forbes, decided to winch the advance party back into the Sea King.

Sinclair then returned to the *Mercator*, refuelled, loaded up a fire-fighting party and flew back to the *Escuardo*. One by one they were winched down on to the trawl deck until all twenty-three members, led by Lieutenant Hughes, were on board. Hughes was a highly experienced senior engineer and Maxwell had put him in charge because of his knowledge of fire-fighting techniques. Equipped with a 'Fireball' pack, which weighed about six hundred pounds and contained extinguishers, fire-suits, breathing apparatus and lights, they mustered in their protective clothing on the trawl deck, where they split into two teams and started to move forward. Lieutenant Hughes, in command, with Eales and O'Leary, remained on deck armed with portable communications, controlling the fire-fighters' progress while at the same time remaining in contact with the ship and the helicopter.

Each team made their way into the superstructure on the end of a long coil of orange line so that the control party could make a speedy rescue if necessary. After about seven minutes the team searching the starboard side of the *Escuardo* were confronted with renewed carnage and Hughes reported their gruesome findings back to Maxwell.

'One of the mess-rooms has been virtually demolished, sir. There's bits of bodies all over the bulkheads and blood everywhere. A fire's smouldering in the galley and we're tackling what we think might have been the core of the explosion.'

'Good work – but don't damage the evidence,' was Maxwell's reaction.

Hughes then arranged for boundary cooling to be set up around the fire-stricken compartments and the fire was slowly contained. An hour later, when Hughes was sure the fire had been isolated, the starboard team entered the galley and extinguished the remains of what might have been a cooking-range fire.

'I still can't see why there was an explosion, Giles,' said Hughes to Ogilvy.

'There's obviously been a drinking session, judging by the mess.'

'Yes, but why an explosion?'

At that moment Thomas entered. 'Excuse me, sir.'

'Yes?' Hughes looked at him irritably.

'I found a heap of Russian books in one of the cabins.' Thomas sounded almost apologetic.

'Christ!' Hughes was almost dead on his feet after supervising the fire-fighting for so long. 'Now the shit'll hit the fan.'

Ten minutes later a fire-fighting officer on the port side called Ogilvy. 'I've found some textbooks, sir. They're fire damaged but I think some of them are in Russian.'

Ogilvy went straight down to the charred remains of the wireless room. On the table was a mass of burnt paper and card. Ogilvy picked up his walkie-talkie. 'This lot will give the old man a seizure,' he announced triumphantly.

'They sound like Russian cipher key cards,' Maxwell said when Ogilvy told him. 'Now what the hell is that trawler being used for? Over.' He sounded angry and frustrated.

'It looks as if they were either involved in some collaborative scientific work or the Russians had chartered the ship with a small crew from the Argentine.'

'Have you looked at the log?'

'Yes, sir. They've been operating in an area just north of the ice edge in the vicinity of Elephant Island, looking at the distribution pattern of krill and ice fish. At the time of the explosion she was making her passage north with an occasional period of trawling to establish some more information on Patagonian hake.'

'And you say the fire's under control?'

'It's been extinguished, sir.'

'How about her engines?'

'They're intact, sir, but the bridge controls to the engines are badly damaged.'

'What do you recommend?'

'That the *Mercator* should tow her into the nearest harbour, sir.'

'You're sure there aren't any explosive devices on board?'

'We've checked, sir, but we'll check again.' Ogilvy felt a rush of confidence at the old man's caution.

'Do that. How many dead?'

'About twenty-five, sir. We're going to lay them out on the trawl deck. But if we're going to tow her in, it's going to be difficult to establish a flooding boundary round the damaged area.'

'Fair enough. But before you do anything, make sure you check her out. Twice more if needs be. Out.'

Ogilvy turned to Hughes. 'I think the old man reckons we're doing a good job.'

'Glad he's satisfied.'

'But he wants us to search this wreck again before she gets towed in. Just in case we haven't found the booby-traps.'

26 November 1989

5.00 a.m.

'Funny, isn't it?' said Forbes.

'I wouldn't say so,' replied Maxwell drily. 'Unless twenty-five corpses are your idea of a joke.'

It was an early grey dawn and the *Escuardo* lay a few hundred yards away from them, smoke curling up into the washed-out sky. Men in fire-fighting gear moved about her decks and a hose gently played on the starboard superstructure. Gulls wheeled over the two ships and the wind of the previous night had dropped, leaving a sluggish, oily sea.

'An Argentine trawler carrying Russian scientists – there'll be the hell of a row.'

'I'm not sure the *Escuardo* is an Argentine boat, but I'm having it checked. The whole thing's damned odd. And there's something else that's even odder.'

'What's that, sir?'

'I've signalled Whitehall, the Embassy in Buenos Aires, the Argentine Navy and the port authorities in Bahia Blanca.'

'And what was their reaction?'

'That's it – there wasn't one. They just didn't want to know.'

By 9.15, the *Mercator* had the *Escuardo* in tow at about six knots in moderate sea conditions, headed up on a north-westerly course, putting the sea and swell just abaft the port beam. This was particularly unpleasant for the *Mercator*, let alone the *Escuardo*, which was rolling heavily at about twenty degrees either side of the vertical.

Twenty of the *Mercator*'s ship's company were now on board the *Escuardo*. Five men, headed by Hughes, were in charge of the tow, and the rest, headed by Ogilvy, had the unpleasant task of laying out the parts of the bodies that had been found scattered around the mess-room and galley. By 11.00, all the grisly human flotsam had been dumped on the trawl deck and covered with a tarpaulin.

Feeling distinctly ill, Ogilvy led a further search for evidence, but nothing out of the ordinary was found until a check through the captain's belongings revealed an interesting discovery. Ogilvy immediately radioed Maxwell.

'Amongst his belongings, sir, there's a Russian manual on mineral exploitation in Antarctica which contains specific appendices on oil and uranium.'

'We'll get Fortescue on to that – he's fluent enough in Russian to give us a rough translation.'

'There's something else he could look at, sir. There are loose plans in the manual that Hughes reckons relate to some kind of sea-bed sonar system.'

'Any idea of vicinity?'

'It seems to be between South Georgia and the South Sandwich Islands.'

'I'm coming on board. Out.' Maxwell turned to Forbes. 'I must go and see what the hell's going on,' he said.

'Yes,' replied Forbes. 'It's not exactly the everyday story of trawling life, is it, sir?'

'Anything else?' asked Maxwell after he had been winched down on to the rolling deck of the *Escuardo*. Ogilvy and Hughes had arranged the manual and its plans on the table in the cleaned-up wheelhouse which smelt of charred wood and disinfectant. They stood beside him, as if making some kind of religious offering.

'No, sir, but there's a safe in the captain's cabin.'

'Break it open.'

'Isn't that illegal, sir?' Hughes sounded deferentially hesitant and Maxwell exploded.

'For Christ's sake, man, do it! We've got enough evidence already to prove the *Escuardo* was operating outside the terms of the Treaty, packed full of Russian equipment. What else do you want? An explanatory letter from the Kremlin? Get on with it.'

The sea was mounting to an uncomfortable swell now, whilst the wind increased to Force 7. Both vessels were rolling violently and Maxwell could see a single albatross circling round the *Mercator*, whilst at her stern a school of dolphins danced exultantly in the spray.

Turning abruptly, he went below with Ogilvy to take a look at the laboratory.

'I reckon this was being used for biology *and* for geology by the look of things. Is that what you think, Giles?' said Maxwell when he had looked round thoroughly. Without waiting for an answer, he added briskly: 'Get Hughes to take some photographs, will you?'

'Yes, sir.'

'One thing before you go – '

'Yes, sir?'

'We haven't found out what caused the explosion. Any theories?'

'Well, I've been thinking and it seems possible that some kind of highly combustible material was being brought across the passage to the lab whilst a party was going on. Maybe the *Escuardo* was heading back to Monte or Mar del Plata for a crew change and to land some of the scientific data.'

Maxwell looked at him with sudden respect. 'That sounds plausible. I suppose they were having a final fling.'

'Pretty final for some of them, sir.'

As Maxwell stared thoughtfully at the wrecked equipment in the disaster area that still smelt of drink and sudden death, Hughes burst in.

'Chippy's got into the safe, sir.'

'What's in it?'

'Some manuals, key cards and a few bottles of chemicals, sir.'

'Right. Get each document photographed and put them back. Then go into the wireless office and the satellite tracking room and do the same.'

'Yes, sir.' Hughes departed briskly and Maxwell turned back to Ogilvy. 'That should make for some interesting translating.'

When Maxwell was winched back on to the *Mercator* he found an 'immediate' signal from Whitehall awaiting him. It read:

FROM MOD UK NAVY TO HMS MERCATOR INFO HMA BUENOS
AIRES. YOUR 252045Z NOV
1. PRESENCE OF RUSSIANS BEING INVESTIGATED. TOW
TRAWLER TO PUERTO BELGRANO NOT BAHIA BLANCA AS
ESSENTIAL ARGENTINE GOVERNMENT INSPECT FINDINGS.
2. REPORT ETA.

On the bridge Maxwell showed Forbes the signal.

'I suppose they want us to tow her back to the Argentine naval base to strengthen our case, sir.'

'Well,' said Maxwell confidentially, 'it was made very clear at the last Antarctic Treaty Conference that some countries were operating outside the terms of the Treaty, but there was no concrete evidence. Now we've got some.'

'It should stir things up all right.'

'That's what the Russians seem to be keen on doing.'

'Do you think the Russians want to exploit the Antarctic – outside the Treaty terms?'

'No, I don't see that. They've got plenty of oil themselves – and uranium.'

'Then – '

'I had a thought when I was on board the *Escuardo*, but maybe it's a crazy one.'

'What's that, sir?'

'Over the last few years – since the war – four drilling rigs have been set up in the Antarctic.' Maxwell paused. 'Supposing the Russians wanted to destroy them?'

'There'd be the hell of a price to pay if they did.'

'If there was evidence. But suppose they didn't leave any?'

'How?'

'By using an underwater explosive system.'

'You mean setting off the mines automatically?'

'Yes, they could deal with tankers that way too.'

'Christ! You mean those plans in the *Escuardo* – ?'

'I'm only jumping to conclusions. In fact, I'm very likely wrong.'

'But if you're not – ' Forbes stared at him and Maxwell wondered if he thought he was exaggerating.

'Then there'll be a bit of a spin on at the MOD.'

'You can say that again. But – '

'Yes?' Maxwell looked at him expectantly, as if he almost wanted his theory disproved.

'Why would the Russians want to carry out all this sabotage?'

'To disrupt the whole damned development. They may not want the oil themselves, but I'm sure they won't want anyone else to get it. And if they knock out the odd rig or tanker, leaving no evidence, they'll create enough mutual suspicion and fear to put every bloody nation out of the oil race – whatever the Treaty says.'

'Christ! We could be in the middle of World War III out here. What the hell are we meant to do?'

'Stick around,' replied Maxwell. 'And don't get frightened off.'

'So that's why they tried to kill you,' said Forbes quietly.

For the past six years Julia Mendoza had been living for Gabriel, and to that end she had been establishing credibility in diplomatic circles. Admittedly her first appointment had been arranged, but after that Diego had told her she was on her own.

Now, as she pounded the typewriter, Julia was beginning to wonder if the long slog towards acceptability had been worthwhile, for with Gabriel at sea she felt isolated, stranded, with no obvious point. All she had left was her routine, the dull round of the Embassy work, her lifeless apartment a few blocks away and the odd dinner or cocktail party that she attended because it was essential not to get out of the swim.

The loneliness was the hardest aspect of the life she had grown used to since she came out of prison. But because of what they had done to her, Julia could not bring herself to go to bed with any man. It was with this in mind that her most immediate problem began to clamour for attention. Forbes. A relationship with him was essential, but how could she keep a man like him out of her bed? Clearly he was a practised womanizer. Yet there was something else about him that she could not define. Then she realized what it was. He was afraid of her.

6.15 p.m.
Off Puerto Belgrano
At precisely 6.15 p.m., three tugs arrived from Puerto Belgrano: one for bodies and casualties, the next to take over the towing of the *Escuardo* and the third to berth *Mercator*. Max-

well, already regretting his theorizing to Forbes, was brusque and short-tempered.

'What's new on the survivors?'

'Not a lot, sir. Fortescue's done a good interrogation, though.'

'Well?'

'One bloke claims to be Argentine, and he says the skipper is Argentine too.'

'And he's still in the land of the living, is he?'

'Oh, yes – he's been patched up nicely.'

'Will he say anything?'

'Not a word and I don't think he's likely to. Not to us – or to anyone else.'

'At least we've got some concrete evidence.'

'Yes, sir.'

Maxwell looked at him warily. 'You don't think it's enough?'

'Hard to say.'

'Mm.' Maxwell's sense of disappointment was growing fast. Forbes must think him a fool for shooting his mouth off and inventing such a garish scenario – a 'cops and robbers' show for Antarctica. 'Anything more?' he asked, clutching at straws.

'I had a look through the skipper's papers, sir, and there's confirmation he was born in Mar del Plata.'

Maxwell hesitated. 'I suppose you think I should start writing thrillers.'

Forbes looked at him steadily. 'I've never really seen you as a second le Carré,' he said.

She had been visited by Diego in prison and knew that he had originally been a policeman – one of those who roamed the streets of Buenos Aires at night in his unmarked Ford Falcon, one of those who sat behind the wheel in dark gloves and half-open shirts, wearing chains round their necks with crucifixes and Virgin Marys and St Christophers. They would be on trains and buses or in bars. Waiting to pick up their quarries.

He's a completely changed man now, she thought, watching

him while he emptied part of a bottle of wine into the *tuco* pan. As he put the *tallarines* on to cook he said: 'The children will be in for supper soon. We don't have long.'

Julia never understood how he could have been a policeman – even when he was younger. He had blocked his ears with swimmer's plugs and put on the two-way radio at full volume so he did not have to hear the pleadings of the victims in the back seat. Often they were clubbed into unconsciousness and their heads were laid on rags so they would not soil the car seats. Then they were thrown out on the roadside, their bodies raked by gun-fire and destroyed by a grenade. And all the time he had blocked his ears and surrounded himself with the blast of music until in the end it had sickened him too much. Now he stood watching the *tallarines*, smiling.

'I hear your brother is taking a closer interest.'

'He is with Morales.'

'Probably a good idea. And you – you will be taking advantage of the chink in Captain Maxwell's armour?'

'I've already met Commander Forbes. I don't anticipate any difficulties.'

'I hope not. Things have not gone well.'

'That is because we are too scattered. You cannot expect him to shoulder responsibility alone.'

'Your brother is in a very senior position. He is expected to take responsibility as a unit commander. As to the scattering, that is essential. It is all part of the system. Ola Roja is like a lizard. You cut off its tail and it grows another.'

Yes, thought Julia. And we are the first tail. She heard the sound of children's voices and Diego said: 'You'll eat with us.' Even this, like everything else he said, was a command.

3 – Perspective

26 November 1989
9.00 p.m.
Off Puerto Belgrano

The atmosphere in the ward-room was tense. A few days ago Maxwell's officers had been ready for action. Now, in the wake of the events in Montevideo and the macabre findings in the *Escuardo*, they were subdued and on edge.

What are they thinking? wondered Maxwell as he looked round the table at Forbes, Burgess, Percy, Eccleston-Smyth, Cunningham, Lucas, Sinclair, Arrowsmith, Crabtree and Ogilvy. Did they imagine he was holding out on them – that he had more information than he was prepared to disclose? He knew he had to reassure them – but how? There was so little he knew himself. Maxwell plunged in uneasily.

'Look – I don't need to go into detail over what's happened. You all know the facts. At our last meeting I said this wasn't going to be a routine deployment. And by God it hasn't. I told you about the build-up of the Soviet bases. I also told you the MOD had not placed us on alert but told us to keep a look-out – whatever that means. Since then we've looked out at some pretty ghastly events. I know how shocked you are – and I know how much the situation has affected the ship's company. But we have to keep two goals in the very front of our minds. The first is to maintain morale, the second is to find out what the hell is going on. We also need to keep the situation in perspective and not to jump to any conclusions about who, or what, we're up against. I gather some pretty weird rumours are circulating throughout the ship, ranging from the start of World War III to a Russian take-over of the South Atlantic. Rumours start when there is a shortage of hard facts and I'm afraid that's what we're faced with. I honestly know nothing more. Ola Roja apparently claimed responsibility for the Santa Lucia. No one seems to know who they are and no one knows who killed Mrs Dunhill, or why. Then there's the *Escuardo* affair. There's been little official reaction to that yet, but I intend to find out a damn sight more as soon as possible. Any questions?'

'Should we be placed on a war footing, sir?' asked Lucas.

'That's an MOD decision – and they haven't made it yet.'

'Are we likely to be attacked, sir?' Arrowsmith's voice was uneven.

'I've no intelligence on that. I think we have to be ready for anything. Nick?'

'I was just wondering, sir, whether this terrorist organization that no one seems to know anything about are equipped to operate at sea.'

'That would be new,' said Crabtree. 'Terrorism at sea.'

'It's possible,' replied Maxwell.

'Sir – '

'Yes, Nick?'

'Is there any thought in your mind that the MOD just aren't giving us any proper briefings or objectives?'

'It *had* occurred to me – of course it had. But they need proof of Russian sabotage – and we can't supply it at the moment. And now, gentlemen, I need to give you details of our programme.'

Have I reassured them? wondered Maxwell. Or do they think I'm still holding out on them? He looked round the table but his officers appeared suddenly inscrutable.

10.30 p.m.

Using the scrambler, Gabriel spoke with Julia – and despite the distortions, she detected a more confident note in his voice.

'We shall write off the *Escuardo*. I should have anticipated Arturo's lack of grip. Using him was a mistake.'

'Are you all right?'

'I'm very seasick. I'm told it will pass.'

'I'm sorry. I made contact with Forbes – but the security clamp-down has made progress impossible.'

'You will have to go to Stanley. They won't consider security such a high priority there.'

'Diego says you are doing the best thing.'

'It's the only thing.'

Julia put the short-wave radio back into the panel behind her freezer, walked to the window and opened it, breathing in the warm night air of Montevideo.

Opposite her flat was the lifeless park where she had met Gabriel a few hours after he had been released. He had returned as an old man, with his ravaged body, his prematurely aged face, and the jet black hair that had turned so horrifyingly to white.

Gabriel had walked along the tile pavement, joining her by the wooden seat on the grassless earth. He had walked slowly, unhurriedly – as if he was exercising in a prison yard. But his face was devoid of expression as he kissed her on the cheek, and his kiss was dry and cold. Almost immediately he had told her about his recruitment to Ola Roja and what Diego had said.

'We are privileged to have been chosen,' he had told her.

'We?' she had repeated at the time. 'We?'

Gabriel had nodded. 'What else is left for us?' he had asked her and, of course, she had had to agree. There was nothing then, and nothing now.

After all the risks they had taken in the *Escuardo*, the next three days were a considerable anti-climax for every member of the *Mercator*'s ship's company, in particular her Captain. Amidst great bureaucratic slog the salvage papers were eventually signed up. Meanwhile the *Escuardo* was searched by a large number of plain-clothes officials, led by a dumpy and enigmatic Symons.

But the most frustrating aspect was that Symons never came near him and Maxwell was left in angry isolation. As a result he had nothing to tell his ship's company at a time when their morale desperately needed boosting. He had been back to the hospital for a check and was now, somewhat reluctantly, declared one hundred per cent fit by his English-speaking doctor. The bandages were taken from his head, and a new dressing was put on his hand.

'You're very lucky, Captain,' the old man had repeated. 'And you take risks. You might not be lucky so long.'

Then, just as Maxwell's temper was reaching its peak, Dunhill arrived on board the *Mercator*. Despite everything, Maxwell was determined to treat him gently and he did all he could to suppress his anger.

'Any further developments?' Maxwell asked hesitantly.

'It's all a matter for the security people now,' said Dunhill pompously.

'I see.' Maxwell made a further effort to control himself. 'I'm sorry I was at sea for the funeral. I would have wanted to be there.'

Dunhill gave him a strange little formal nod. 'Thank you.' He cleared his throat and Maxwell, having tried compassion, returned to the attack.

'I do feel the presence of Russians in an Argentine trawler is very disturbing.'

'That's for the security chaps to work out. I expect you'll want to get going now, won't you?' He was within an ace of being point-blank rude and Maxwell had the feeling Dunhill would like him to get going straight away.

'Yes, I would,' he replied helpfully, and Dunhill visibly brightened.

'Well, there's nothing to stop you. You've done absolutely the right thing, and we'll be looking after that little mystery of yours from now on. I'm putting everything in Tennant's hands. He's the new Counsellor and Consul General. I don't think you've met him yet, have you?'

'Not yet.'

'We must get you together some time. On your way home, perhaps.'

'I'll look forward to it.'

'Of course, Tennant is adamant that there should be no press leaks.'

'That could be tricky. It's not every day a Royal Navy ship tows a fire-damaged trawler into a South American port.'

'Oh – we've fed them the fire bit. It's being carried now.'

'But not the Russian bit?'

Dunhill gave him a chilly smile. '*Not* the Russian bit, old boy,' he said.

'He understood death, sir, and came to terms with it.'

Maxwell had invited Ogilvy to dinner and they had started talking about Shackleton.

Maxwell gazed curiously at him. 'Why do you feel that is so important for you?' he said.

'I had a fairly shitty time in the war, sir. I got shot down and almost lost my nerve. It was the devil's own job getting back into the air.' He paused and then asked abruptly: 'Do you know the poem called "Prospice"?'

'Browning.'

'Yes. It was used as a kind of talisman between Shackleton and his wife, Emily. It throws a lot of light on his state of mind – his attitude to death. I know it helped me to get back into that cockpit.'

A dim memory returned to Maxwell. 'Doesn't it begin something like "Fear death? to feel the fog in my throat – "'

'"The mist in my face," ' continued Ogilvy.

> '"When the snows begin, and the blasts denote
> I am nearing the place,
> The power of the night, the press of the storm,
> The post of the foe;
> Where he stands, the Arch Fear in a visible form,
> Yet the strong man must go;
> For the journey is done and the summit attained,
> And the barriers fall." '

'We must all fear death, in different degrees,' said Maxwell. 'Especially when it brushes us.' He got up and rang for Lynch to clear the table.

'How's the hand, sir?' asked Ogilvy, wondering if brandy was to be produced. It was.

As Maxwell poured a generous measure into his glass he said: 'Bloody sore. But I'm lucky.' There was a slightly impatient note in his voice and Ogilvy knew he would welcome a change of subject.

'I gather the Argentines are pumping more money into their navy, sir,' he said. 'Do you reckon they might have another bash at the Falklands?'

'I'll tell you what *I* think,' said Maxwell abruptly. 'There are three focal points in the Argentine maritime strategy: the Beagle Channel, the Falklands, and the Antarctic, and they have one common denominator – at least in Argentine opinion: all three belong to them.'

Ogilvy laughed. 'Fundamentally the situation still remains exactly the same as it's ever been, although Argentina and Chile have patched up their quarrel over the Beagle.'

'Yes,' said Maxwell, 'the British still have sovereignty over the Falklands but the Argentines aren't giving up their claim. However, if we take the broader case of Antarctica – Chile, the Argentine and Great Britain all claim the same area which includes the Antarctic Peninsula and most of the Weddell Sea. And the Antarctic Treaty won't be continued in its present form unless an amicable solution can be found. In the meantime, now we're friendlier with the Argentines we're not too worried about the naval build-up.'

Ogilvy nodded, hoping that Maxwell would take him further into his confidence. 'The Argentines are potentially strong economically, aren't they, sir? Surely it's to the West's advantage for them to strengthen their forces. It could lead to a South Atlantic Treaty Organization which would include the USA and Great Britain and contribute a hell of a lot to the defence of the Atlantic.'

'We can see the sense of that, but the Russians won't. They'd do a lot to bust up any improvements in the Argentine/British relationship with the Treaty review date so near.'

'So the *Escuardo* could just be a catalyst, sir – a deliberate attempt to make us distrust the Argentines?'

'It's possible. Since the 1982 war we've all woken up to the fact that there's going to be an oil rush in South Georgia. Once the airstrip and deep-water facilities are finished, then it's all go. So if someone wants to bugger it up, now's the time.'

'And you think they've started, sir?'

'It's possible,' Maxwell replied cautiously.

30 November 1989
11.30 a.m.
Port Stanley
As the launch approached the jetty at Port Stanley, a maroon London taxi displaying the Royal Cipher on its doors backed towards the steps and the Governor's chauffeur got out. Maxwell shook his hand warmly – he was an old friend.

'Been in the wars, sir?'

'Something like that.' The easy clichés, their lack of formality – it was a homecoming for him and for the first time in days Maxwell felt relaxed as he sat in the back of the taxi for the short drive along the road by the foreshore. As they drove past the steamer ducks stomping about in the shallow water on the foreshore, heading towards the brightly coloured houses with their red galvanized tin roofs, Maxwell talked idly to the driver, trying to banish the events of the last few days from his mind. He knew he would talk them over again with the Governor, but just for a few minutes he wanted peace.

'Glad to be back, sir?'

'I love it here – it's a wilderness, that's why.'

The driver laughed.

'I know what you're going to say,' said Maxwell. 'Try living here – that would change your mind.'

'No, sir, I wasn't going to say that. I reckon I love it too. You know I went back to London last month?'

'I didn't. What did you make of it?'

'I spent every hour of every day wanting to come back. It was crazy – but you're right. It *is* a wilderness and I was yearning for it. All the time. And now I'm back – I shan't be leaving again.'

Maxwell wound down the window and breathed in the salt-laden wind. Suddenly he wished he could live this moment for ever.

The Governor of the Falklands, Sir Bernard Gillett, met Maxwell at the front door of Government House. He was an impressive figure, tall with a mass of curly black hair. Popular with the islanders, he had a keen intellect and Maxwell had always enjoyed his company. Gillett had volunteered for the post because his cousins had farmed in the Falklands and had told him of their unique atmosphere. He had not been disappointed and had come to love the mood of these damp, windy islands and their wildlife.

'It's good to see you, James. You had a very lucky escape.'

'Others didn't,' replied Maxwell, returning to reality with a bitter jolt.

'How's Aubrey?'

'Putting up a good front.'

'Yes – he'd do that,' said Gillett. He led Maxwell into the office and poured out whisky. 'You'd better tell me about that damned trawler.'

When Gillett had listened to all Maxwell had to report on the subject of the *Escuardo*, he said: 'I've got a bit of information for you. She wasn't a registered Argentine ship.'

'Then where the hell *was* she registered?'

'Cuba,' said Gillett with a wry smile. 'Now come along and see Diana.'

With his mind hammering away at Gillett's revelation, Maxwell followed him through a green baize door into a drawing room which was furnished like an English country house.

Lady Gillett was some years younger than her husband, with fair hair and a slim figure. She was a General's daughter and her father had been in Cyprus when Bernard was working for the High Commissioner. They're an elegant pair, thought Maxwell. They should be in some senior ambassadorial post rather than here in this wilderness.

'It's good to see you, James. Thank God you're in one piece.'

He kissed her. 'I'm damn lucky,' he said.

76

That afternoon they drove out to Mount Pleasant in the Gilletts' Land Rover. Once, a couple of years ago, he had brought Susan to this wild landscape but he suspected – he knew – that it was not her kind of beauty. The sombreness of the Falklands had depressed her and she was relieved when they flew back to Buenos Aires.

As the vehicle bumped along the track, geese rose from the marshes below and a flock of sheep, disturbed by the noise of their engine, ran down the gaunt slope. They had occasional glimpses of an entirely empty coastline, its features named hauntingly, evocatively – Horse Paddocks, Halfway Cove, Rincon de los Indios, Letterbox Hill. After a while, they left the Land Rover and walked down to Sparrow Cove. The sky was grey, the sea was grey and the spitting, driving rain looked grey too.

Sea-lions drowsed hugely on the flat pebbles of the beach, emitting the occasional deep bellow, like a massive belch, while their young ambled clumsily around them. There were clusters of penguins on rocks in the boiling surf and others strutted the water-lines.

'Which one is Aubrey?' asked Bernard.

Maxwell laughed, watching the fine mist coming in off the sea.

A little further up the beach there were great swards of fine white sand where the seals lay like hulks of timber, twitching their noses, opening their large black eyes and scratching themselves before returning to the sea.

'If you had more time, James, we'd take you out to Kidney Island – it's a bird-watcher's paradise,' said Diana.

'Or we could rent a cottage and get the hell out of it for a few days.' Bernard sounded wistful.

'I'd give a lot for that,' said Maxwell, his gaze returning to the penguins. 'What's that type called?'

'Jackass penguins. They can attack, you know. Very ferocious, beating their tiny wings.'

'Their eggs make super omelettes,' Diana added.

'Don't let the conservationists hear you say that,' said Maxwell.

'Well – of course I'd only make the omelettes in a survival situation.' Diana gave him an appraising glance. 'Are you feeling a bit more relaxed?'

'Out here – yes.'

Reluctantly, they tore themselves away from Sparrow Cove, walked slowly back to the Land Rover and drove on to Port San Carlos where the British troops had landed in May 1982. The vehicle flashed past the familiar scattered wooden-framed buildings and the long, low schoolhouse as they headed towards the white gate that led up the long drive to the weather-boarded home of George Davison, a farm manager who was an old friend of Maxwell's. But, welcoming them in, Davison said: 'I hear you've been in stormy waters, Captain.' The cliché and its instant reminders abruptly terminated Maxwell's temporary relaxation.

'Back to earth, James?' whispered Diana as they trooped through the hall.

Yes, thought Maxwell. Back to bloody earth. But it was the sea he wanted.

4 – The *Santa Fe*

4 December 1989
11.00 a.m.
Montevideo
'Bernard.' Her voice was slightly hesitant. 'It's Julia – Julia Mendoza.'

But she need not have worried, for Gillett was instantly welcoming. 'How are you?'

'Very well.'

'What can I do for you?'

Julia looked out on the park again, saw the tiled pathway and shuddered. It would be good to get away. 'I was wondering if you'd do me a favour.'

'Of course – if I can.'

'Can I rent one of the cottages?'

'We'd love you to – on condition that we see something of you.'

'You'll definitely be doing that. I'm really looking forward to seeing you again.'

'Then come and stay with us.'

'No, I need the break on my own. I feel exhausted. Peter seems to have been particularly social recently.'

'That's the way it's been here. The *Mercator*'s just put in.'

'Is she going to stay long?'

'No – she's off out again. But she ought to be back in a few days. Have you met Maxwell? He's a fascinating character – bit of a tearaway.'

'I've only met Commander Forbes. Briefly.'

'Nick? Very good chap. Bit set in his ways though. Anyway – when can we look forward to seeing you?'

'At the weekend.'

'Marvellous. You'll take Stornoway?'

'Yes, please. I love that big hearth.'

'OK. I'll have it aired and stocked up.'

'There's no need to go to so much trouble.'

'Oh, yes there is. Diana would slaughter me if I didn't. You don't realize how fond we are of you.'

When Sir Bernard Gillett had put down the phone, he walked back into the sitting room where he found his wife listening to Britten's War Requiem.

'Heady stuff,' she said as she turned it down. 'James gave it to me two Christmases ago. Do you remember?'

'Yes – can't stand his musical tastes, as you know.'

'Who was that?'

'Julia Mendoza. She wants to rent Stornoway.'

Diana's eyes lit up. 'Julia – it'll be lovely. She hasn't been for months.'

'I think she's up against it.'

'The usual?'

'She just hasn't got the stamina for that job.'

2.30 p.m.

Off Port Stanley

The phone buzzed on the bridge.

'Captain.'

'Communications Officer here, sir. The Royal Marines at Stanley have received a report from one of the West Falkland farms that six vessels have anchored in the lee of Weddell Island, sir. There's no reason for them to be there and we've been asked to investigate.'

'Right – launch the Sea King and bung it full of marines.'

'Yes, sir.'

'Sounds a bit dodgy, sir,' said Forbes.

'They're probably support ships to the oil rig,' replied Maxwell. 'Just taking shelter. But we can't be too careful. We need to send someone out on the Sea King who speaks good Spanish.'

'Arrowsmith fits the bill there, sir.'

'Yes – but is he well enough?'

'As you say, it's probably a routine check-out.'

'OK, Nick. Tell him to get ready.'

Twenty minutes later the Sea King was airborne with a hurriedly equipped section of Royal Marines and a load of arms, food and survival equipment. It was a fine afternoon but the wind was blowing Force 7 to 8 from the south-west and there was a large sea running in the vicinity of West Falkland. In fact it was a typical Falkland day – one which could change from bright sunshine to driving rain in a very few minutes with consequent highly dangerous variations in visibility.

Maxwell was all too well aware of these problems as he stood on the bridge with Forbes, watching the Sea King hover above them.

'Ogilvy enjoyed his dinner with you very much,' said Forbes. 'He needed the boost.'

Maxwell stared at the foam-flecked grey-green waters. 'He had a rougher time in the war than I thought,' he said.

'What do you think those chaps out there are doing then?' asked Forbes, abruptly changing the subject and, for a moment, Maxwell wondered if he had objected to his dinner with Ogilvy – that in some way he felt Ogilvy was horning in.

'Prospecting illegally.' Maxwell shrugged.

'The Sea King will see them off, sir.'

Maxwell picked up a pair of binoculars and began to scan the helicopter's progress. 'Weather's worsening,' he said.

As the Sea King headed west over Fox Bay towards Beaver Island, flying at a height of four hundred feet, visibility became reduced to about half a mile. The green undulating slopes of the Falkland hills were replaced by a swirling impenetrable blanket of white cloud, but the Sea King's radar had no difficulty in locating the area where the intruders were reported to have anchored. Slowly the helicopter began its search and it was not long before the observer, Lieutenant David Crabtree, reported a number of stationary radar contacts to the east of Weddell Island, tucked under the lee of the land in

Queen Charlotte's Sound.

'I've got them,' said Crabtree. 'Bearing three-one-zero, seven decimal two miles, about five contacts in one group and another two contacts to the north.'

'Well done, David,' said Ogilvy, back to his usual job of Senior Pilot. 'Let's take a look.'

A few minutes later half a dozen scattered vessels appeared out of the murk. 'What are they?' asked Ogilvy.

Crabtree stared down intently at the blobs on the ocean and then said: 'They look like a small fleet of oil – or gas – rig support vessels. They're sheltering from the south-westerly gale – and they're flying the Argentine flag.'

'Which one seems the most important, David?' asked Ogilvy.

'It looks as though the *Sante Fe* has a helicopter deck, but it won't be strong enough for us.'

'OK,' replied Ogilvy. 'We'll drop Arrowsmith – he speaks Spanish – and he can take Lucas with him.'

As the Sea King hovered over the *Santa Fe* a crewman came out on deck. He grabbed a pair of bats and started to wave the Sea King in and slowly Arrowsmith and Lucas were winched down. As this happened, the mist came in, thicker and closer, until the figures on the *Santa Fe* were completely lost to sight.

'It's like winching them down a well,' said Crabtree as the Sea King rose higher.

'They are Diego's instructions,' said Gabriel, 'not mine.'

The grubby ward-room contained the six operatives who made up the Ola Roja cell on the *Sante Fe* and the atmosphere was charged with hostile anxiety. Morales alone seemed unconcerned.

'This is not how we should be operating,' said First Officer Caterino. 'Two mistakes should not be compounded by a third.'

'A third would finish us.' Luis Sabini, Chief Engineer, was furiously angry.

'I'm afraid I disagree with you, gentlemen.' Gabriel was impatient. 'We may need this little initiative. You must appreciate the submarine is approaching and it is essential her activities remain undisturbed.'

'The *Mercator* will monitor her movements directly she's in radar range,' said Caterino smugly.

'I'm sure they will. But this little diversion can do no harm. We are bound to come under suspicion soon. Let that suspicion be cleared now and then we can be sure of being left alone. We have no equipment on board, so a search will be welcome – at this stage. You must appreciate that our rendezvous with the system ship is only a week away. After that, a search would be most unwelcome – and would definitely finish us.'

'I still don't like it,' said Caterino. Gabriel knew Caterino had Sabini's support and that the unease of the others was growing.

'I'm afraid you will have to learn to like it,' said Gabriel. 'After so many errors, we need an insurance policy for the future. It is all most providential.'

The telephone rang and was answered by Morales. He listened, nodded and gave some muttered instructions. Replacing the receiver he turned back to the assembled company with a smile. 'We can proceed,' he said. 'At the moment there are only two of them. It's our chance and we must take it.'

Ogilvy and Crabtree waited for Arrowsmith and Lucas to make radio contact for over seven minutes whilst Ogilvy tried to contact them again and again as the Sea King hovered over the ship. 'Boarding party – this is 982. Boarding party – this is 982. Nothing heard.'

Eventually Crabtree said: 'I don't like it.'

'Neither do I.'

The mist was dense now and, although they were not far above the *Santa Fe*, they could see nothing. It was like flying in cotton wool and both Ogilvy and Crabtree began to lose their sense of time and place.

'Boarding party – this is 982. Boarding party – this is 982. Are you receiving me?'

Silence. The Sea King continued to hover. And a surge of fear rose in both of them.

'What the hell is going on?' asked Crabtree.

'God knows.'

'Keep trying.'

'Boarding party – this is 982. Boarding party – this is – '

'Hang on!'

For a few seconds, like the parting of strands of fibre, the mist lifted. Crabtree craned forward and muttered something Ogilvy couldn't hear.

'What is it?' Ogilvy's voice was sharp with anxiety.

'There's a launch leaving the ship – it's going up the convoy on the starboard side.'

'I'll call the old man. Foxtrot Hotel. This is 982. Request Captain to Senior Pilot.'

Maxwell came on the line. 'Captain speaking.'

'Sir, they've been gone for twenty minutes now and we've lost radio contact. We've also seen a launch leave the *Santa Fe*, heading up the convoy on the starboard side.'

'Keep trying for another five minutes. If you still can't raise them, get Browning to take in the marines. Out.' Maxwell's voice was sharp.

Ogilvy continued trying to contact Arrowsmith and Lucas, willing one of them to reply, but the radio was completely dead. Then, reluctantly, he told Browning, Lucas's number two, to prepare to board the *Santa Fe* with the detachment of marines.

In a few minutes the Sea King was hovering low over the deck whilst the marines abseiled down the winch wire.

Julia Mendoza packed slowly and methodically. When she had finished, she lay down on the bed, gazing round her impersonal room. Six years had passed since she had left prison. They had been curiously insubstantial years. From the start she had at least partly succeeded in keeping the agony at bay during the long office hours. But when she was back in her apartment it began all over again, and she would spend sleepless nights reliving the hell of Punta Carreta prison. Now it was easier but her life had become a narrow cage, whose bars she welcomed. There was plenty of social life in the diplomatic service and, to all intents and purposes, she lived it to the full. But she lived it for occupation, and when men wanted to have a relationship with her, to sleep with her, she disappeared. But she only vanished into her cage again.

So her existence had narrowed down to the only person she loved and needed: Gabriel, the brilliant wild boy brother of her adolescence. Now, of course, like her, he was a shadow. But she still sought comfort in two things: the dangerous present he had created for her and which bound them together in inextricable purpose and the childhood she now regarded as a glorious escape route.

The Mendozas' cattle hacienda and salted meat factory had been built from small beginnings by her great grandfather, and by the time she was a child it was thriving. She remembered her father as a remote man of affairs, her mother a concert pianist, often away on tour. Her childhood had been one of servants, of nannies – and of Gabriel. Their parents' absorption with their own lives had thrown the children together and their relationship was dependently close. Weeks, months would pass and they would see no one else. At first they yearned for other children. Later they became so used to their own company that outsiders were unwelcome. Then they were separated – by expensive private schools – yet still they lived for each other in the holidays when they rode out into the vast plains of pampas with only the horses and the herds of beef cattle for company.

Gradually their separation became unbearable and although Julia was not as openly rebellious as Gabriel, she did badly enough at school to incur the wrath of both their parents. Gabriel, however, made them apoplectic. Not only was he expelled from one school for organizing a strike against the staff, but he also began to take an increasing interest in the workers on his father's estates who worked long hours for low pay. At first, Julia was sure that he did this simply to annoy his unloving father, but later she knew that he saw the workers very much as he saw himself – isolated, taken for granted and ill-used. At university Gabriel turned to politics and was sent down for running a subversive magazine. Then he began to read law but by this time both parents had virtually disowned him, and he was banished from the family estates to live in a squalid apartment in Montevideo on a very low and grudging allowance. She, on the other hand, had trained as a conventional enough secretary, for her own bitterness was different and she was simply determined to be independent and to turn her back on her unselfcritical parents. She, too, moved to Montevideo and began to work with Gabriel. It was not long before they were as close as they had been before, both deeply involved in the work that would lead to their arrests.

But now, thought Julia as she restlessly rose from her bed, they've made him an automaton – a man without a soul bent only on revenge. And was she much better?

'Yes?'

The seaman stood at the entrance to the deckhouse, looking impassively at Browning.

'I'm looking for Captain Lucas and Lieutenant Arrowsmith.'

'Why are you looking for them here?'

'What?' Browning was flabbergasted. 'What the hell are you talking about?' His marines stood behind him, poised to take any action he ordered. At that moment, however, he could not think of any action to order. There was a tense silence.

'Look, two of our men boarded this ship. Where are they?'

'I don't know.'

'Damn it, man, they were winched down from our helicopter on to your deck.'

'They're not here.'

'I want to see your Captain.'

The seaman shrugged. 'Very well.'

Leaving half the detachment of marines on deck, Browning took the remainder and followed. Eventually they found Captain Morales in his cabin, writing at a small table. He was in his early thirties with a small beard. He looked intelligent but barely welcoming.

'Yes?' he rapped out abruptly.

'These men have boarded, sir, looking for two others.'

'Two others?'

'They say they were on board.'

'I have no one on board, gentlemen. Except for my own crew. No strangers.'

'This is absurd,' said Browning. 'I'm Lieutenant Browning from HMS *Mercator*. Two of our men, Lieutenant Arrowsmith and Captain Lucas, boarded your ship.'

There was a pause whilst Morales stared back at him questioningly.

'I've told you – no one has boarded us, gentlemen.' His voice held a final note.

'Captain Morales – these men were winched down from our helicopter on to your deck,' said Browning aggressively. 'They were met by a member of your crew. They've got to be here.'

Morales smiled patiently. 'If anyone had come on board I would have known. There must be some mistake.'

Browning was completely nonplussed. As he was about to burst into speech again, Morales said, more sharply: 'And why should they come here anyway? I don't understand.'

Browning ignored him. 'The launch,' he said. 'We saw a launch leave this ship – about fifteen minutes ago.'

'Yes – that's true.'

'Where was it going?'

'To the *Rio Grande*.'

'Could the launch have had our men on board?'

'Definitely not. Strangers do not board my ship and go out in the launch without my knowledge. However, you are welcome to search the whole group if you wish.'

'We'll make a start here,' said Browning unhappily, 'and work our way on. I hope you appreciate how serious this situation is.'

'The situation – as you call it – is quite inexplicable to me. You say that two of your fellow officers were winched down on to this ship – for reasons you have yet to explain to me – and

87

refuse to accept my assurance that we have not seen them. I repeat: I am master of this ship and if anyone had boarded it they would have been brought to me immediately.'

Back on deck, Browning called Ogilvy and told him the inexplicable news.

'Bloody ridiculous!' was his reaction. 'We landed 'em. They must be on the ship somewhere. You can't *lose* people. I'll report back to the old man. Out.'

Whilst Browning and his marines searched the *Santa Fe* Ogilvy spoke to Maxwell. His reaction was as amazed as everyone else's.

'They can't just disappear. They're bound to be on board. Out.'

An hour later, Ogilvy reported that the *Santa Fe* had been thoroughly searched and there was still no sign of Lucas or Arrowsmith.

'It's absurd,' said Maxwell. 'We're wasting our time.' He turned to Forbes. 'I'm going on board to take charge of this game of hide and seek.'

'Where the hell can they be?' demanded Forbes.

'God knows – unless they were in that bloody launch. Either way, I'll sling a charge of kidnapping against this lot. Can you get through to the MOD and send them a sitrep*? We seem to have come across a bunch of pirates here.'

Maxwell then spoke to Ogilvy: '982 – this is Foxtrot Hotel. Come and pick me up. It's time I had a word with this Morales. Out.'

'You don't think they've done anything to them, do you, sir?'

'Done anything to Royal Naval officers? Can you imagine the stink it would cause if they had?'

'Where the hell are my men?'

'My dear Captain Maxwell – I haven't the slightest idea.'

'They were landed on this ship.'

'I'm sure there must be a mistake. If they were landed here I

* Situation report.

would have known. I promise you that.'

'You do appreciate the kind of problem that would arise if you were foolish enough to keep them against their will?'

'I resent that comment.'

Maxwell registered the change from passive condescension to sudden anger – and was pleased. He continued to push him.

'You also appreciate that you are in breach of the Anglo-Argentine bi-lateral agreement by being here at all?'

'We are moving back to Argentine waters tomorrow.'

'That's not good enough. You're in breach,' snapped Maxwell, taking out his walkie-talkie in response to an urgent signal from one of the marines. It was Forbes.

'I have the MOD signal, sir. It reads:

"1. Search all ships in vicinity for missing officers.
2. Use force in case of necessity but avoid casualties if possible.
3. Search oil rig and instruct drilling operation to cease immediately.
4. Argentine Government in full agreement."'

'Thank you,' said Maxwell, one eye on Captain Morales.

'What action, sir?' asked Forbes.

'The marines will re-search this ship and then move up to the rest of the group by Sea King. They will then search the rig. Both the group and the rig are to be covered with a one-missile-armed Lynx. Also, bring the *Mercator* to within range of close armament.'

'Yes, sir. Out.'

Maxwell turned to Captain Morales, who had raised his eyebrows but recovered his control.

'Strong words, Captain.'

'There'll be hell to pay if they've come to any harm,' said Maxwell.

By 7 p.m. the Sea King was hovering above the next ship in the group and the Lynx was in her covering role. Meanwhile, Maxwell, whose angry frustration was turning into foreboding, remained with Captain Morales.

'Bugger it, man,' he said to Morales. 'They can't disappear into thin air.'

'There is one possibility.'

'Well?' asked Maxwell suspiciously.

'It was rough at the time you said they boarded. Could they not have gone overboard?'

'Ballocks! Two experienced officers?'

'It has been known to happen,' said Morales defensively.

'Not in my book. Besides, before the mist came down, my helicopter observer saw them quite clearly talking to one of your men.'

'Talking to one of my men?' said Morales sharply. 'Why has no one mentioned that before?' He picked up the phone. 'I'll check immediately to see if anyone is missing.'

'Your men just drop overboard, do they? And no one reports it!' said Maxwell sarcastically.

Morales frowned. 'There has been no reason to check.' He snapped some sharp orders into the phone, a new immediacy in his voice. They sat in silence until the phone rang. Morales picked it up immediately and Maxwell watched the frown deepen on his face as he listened. Slowly he put the receiver down.

'Well?'

'I regret to have to tell you – one of my men *is* missing.'

'Are you absolutely sure?'

'I'm having it re-checked. His name is De Kroop – a South African. Apparently he is nowhere to be found at present.'

Maxwell stared at him. 'If he *is* missing, what conclusion would you draw from that?'

Morales's voice was grave. 'That there has been a terrible accident, Captain Maxwell.'

The search for Arrowsmith and Lucas continued for another twelve hours in filthy weather. All three helicopters and both launches were used and the six oil rig ships and the rig itself were thoroughly inspected – but with no success. It was as if the three men – if there *were* three men involved – had disappeared into a void.

Maxwell was completely baffled. Back on the bridge of the *Mercator* he raged to Forbes: 'Those bastards have done something to them!'

'We've got no proof, sir, none at all.'

'Then where the hell are they?'

'God knows.'

'Give the order to check those ships – and the rig – all over again.'

'Yes, sir.'

As Forbes departed, Cunningham asked: 'What the hell is all this about, sir?'

Maxwell spoke hesitantly. 'I'm just wondering if they found something in the *Santa Fe* that they shouldn't.'

Cunningham gazed at him with sudden interest. 'I just don't see how three blokes could fall overboard. Do you, sir?'

'They couldn't have seen that clearly from the helicopter in the mist, but even so – ' Now Maxwell was hesitant. What could they have seen? he wondered. It was all pure conjecture.

The internal ship's telephone rang and Maxwell picked it up quickly, praying for news.

'Sinclair here, sir.'

'Yes?' There was hope in Maxwell's voice.

'We've come across some wreckage.'

'What kind of wreckage?'

'It's not a boat, sir. It seems to be bits of packing cases.'

'Can you take a closer look?'

'We have, sir. There's some kind of marking on them but we can't make it out. It looks as if they've been paint-sprayed over.'

'Can you winch someone down?'

'Will do, sir. Out.'

The disappearance of Arrowsmith and Lucas had horrified the ship's company.

'I'd like to know what the bloody hell's going on,' said Taff to Dolly, who was washing up coffee cups with unusual vigour. 'First the *Escuardo* – now the *Santa Fe*. It's all too much of a bloody coincidence.'

Grey detected that beneath the bluster in Evans's voice there was rising alarm. 'I don't know what to think, Taff,' he replied calmly.

'I do – someone's out to get us.'

'Go on.'

'I reckon that *Escuardo* wreck was a booby-trap that didn't go off. Now this *Santa Fe* lot have got two of our blokes. What next? I ask myself.'

'You serious?'

Taff grinned unhappily. 'I don't know, mate. What do you think?'

'I think they'll turn up.'

'Where – in the bastard oggin'?'

Four hours later Maxwell decided to return to the *Santa Fe* himself. The bits of packing cases had turned out to be a red herring for once the paint had been delicately scratched off the lettering, the name of a well-known Argentine frozen fish company appeared.

Sitting with Sinclair and Jarvis in the Sea King, Maxwell felt defeated as he gloomily watched the moonlight wanly lighting the still turbulent sea and the six vessels that were continuously being scanned by the helicopter's spotlights. He saw marines and ratings on deck, busily moving about, and on the horizon he could make out the gaunt shape of the rig. Once you knew there was a problem, he reflected, modern technology made it possible for every detail to be clearly monitored. But in all naval operations there was the combination of the weather and human error which could never be entirely eradicated. On this occasion, poor visibility and lack of detailed observation had resulted in the complete disappearance of two British officers despite all the facilities the *Mercator* could provide.

Once winched down, he went straight to Morales's cabin, where he found him guarded by a burly marine.

'Captain Morales, for the last time – where the hell are my

men?'

'And for the last time, I simply don't know.' Morales was under considerable strain now – and it showed.

'You will be taken back to Rio Gallegos where there's going to be an inquiry. Have you got anything you want to say?'

There was a pause, then Morales said slowly, as if choosing his words very carefully: 'Do I take it you have the co-operation of the Argentine Government?'

'I have their total co-operation.'

'I see.'

'And I'm holding you personally responsible for the disappearance of my men.'

'You seem to have forgotten that I, too, have lost a valuable man.'

'You make my heart bleed,' said Maxwell derisively.

5 December 1989
10.00 a.m.
Off Port Stanley
When the Argentine destroyer arrived to escort the group back to Rio Gallegos, Maxwell set course for Port Stanley. An RAF Nimrod from the Falklands base continued the search for Arrowsmith and Lucas but Maxwell's gloomy mood hardened as he spoke on the radio link to Simon Tennant, the new Counsellor and Consul General to the British Ambassador in Buenos Aires. He had not met or spoken to him before and after the conversation was finished Maxwell felt he had made an enemy.

Having described in detail the incidents with the *Escuardo* and particularly the *Santa Fe*, Maxwell expected a horrified reaction at the apparent loss of two British naval officers. Instead he received what seemed to be token regret.

'I'm very sorry, old boy, but I'm sure the whole tragic business must have been some kind of very unfortunate accident. And this theory of yours. I can't think why your chaps should be bumped off just because they saw something they shouldn't – whatever that might be. It's all a bit war-comic, isn't it?'

'So you're not concerned about Argentine ships carrying

Soviet equipment on board?'

Tennant's voice became crisper. 'Of course I'm concerned. The UK have already issued a formal protest about Russian scientists operating a trawler with an Argentine crew under a Cuban flag. But in this case you have no proof that the *Santa Fe* was carrying anything she shouldn't.' He coughed impatiently as if to say – now are you satisfied? But Maxwell was not.

'I'm sorry – I'm deeply concerned about the loss of my men.'

'I'm sure you are and so am I.'

'I believe that they may well have been murdered.'

'That's a very serious allegation, and according to all reports has no substance whatsoever.'

'I know – and I also realize it could cause a major diplomatic incident between us and the Argentine.'

'There are already enough problems.' Tennant sounded dismissive and Maxwell tried to control the emotion in his voice.

'So you're not prepared to take this any further?'

'I haven't seen a full report yet.'

'I'll be sending one in right away.' Maxwell paused, knowing that Tennant didn't want to prolong the conversation. 'My view is that the Russians are spoiling for trouble in the South Atlantic and these incidents prove it. They want to disrupt our oil exploration and they're already working at it.'

'I shall be looking at your report carefully.'

There was a long pause then Maxwell said curtly: 'I'm most dissatisfied with this conversation, Mr Tennant.'

Silence.

'And I shall be taking the whole matter further.'

'That is entirely up to you, Captain Maxwell.'

They concluded the conversation with icy farewells and Maxwell turned to Forbes.

'You got the gist of that?'

'Yes, sir.'

'Well?'

'They're soft-pedalling, sir. They don't want to rock the boat.'

'But the boat *is* going to be rocked, and bloody quickly. By *me.*' Maxwell picked up a biro, and broke it in half.

'Those poor bastards,' he said. 'They're only paperwork now.'

The ship entered harbour at noon. Maxwell went ashore and was taken straight to Government House where he reported his conversation with Tennant in full.

'What kind of man is this bastard Tennant?' he concluded vehemently.

Gillett gave a rather jaded smile. 'Not your kind of man, James.'

'Meaning?'

'He boxes clever. Of course he's new and finding his way round Argentina.'

'Where did he come from?'

'He was one of Kenny's team in Montevideo.' There was a pause then Gillett added: 'Look, James, Tennant is going low-key on this. He doesn't want trouble. He needs more information to act on.'

'Or just more trouble.'

This time the silence was electric as both men realized a considerable gulf was widening between them. Gillett broke it hurriedly.

'You know I'll do what I can for you, James, but you've got to realize that all this could be just a disastrous accident quite unconnected with anything that's gone before.' He shook his head. 'John Arrowsmith – how ironic.'

'Isn't it?'

'Will you stay for lunch?'

'I'm waiting for news of my men.'

'It'll be relayed here just as quickly. Anyway, there's some people I should like you to meet. The Kingsleys. Miles Kingsley is an island doctor – but he also works for Naval Intelligence. I think he'd be interested in what you have to say.' Gillett went to the drinks table and returned with two large whiskies whilst Maxwell waited thoughtfully, wondering how useful Kingsley might be. I've been thinking a great deal about the oil potential of this part of the world recently, and putting myself in the place of the Soviets who would, I'm sure, enjoy stopping the West reaping a substantial harvest. With the recent oil strikes here – and the potential they indicate – it could be enough to completely change our policy in the Middle East. We wouldn't need to buy nearly as much oil from OPEC.'

'That's true,' replied Maxwell cautiously. 'But their usual methods of subversion wouldn't work in this part of the world. I mean, there's no indigenous population except here in the Falklands. Also, as signatories of the Antarctic Treaty, they have as much right to share the oil as we have.' He paused and then continued quickly: 'I'm sure the most serious problem they could cause is to place explosive equipment on the sea-bed. Witness the plans we found in the *Escuardo*.'

'To snarl up the Argentine/British relationship?' asked Gillett.

'As a beginning. They could use submarines, of course.'

'But to use submarines would simply cause another war.'

'So could the underwater devices – if it was discovered who was really doing it. But if Ola Roja claimed responsibility – '

'You mean you think these underwater devices could be for blowing up ships?'

'Well, if it worked it could be a much more subtle method than using submarines.'

Gillett leant forward in his chair, rolling the whisky round in his glass.

'Or do you think I'm an alarmist?' asked Maxwell.

'I don't know,' said Gillett slowly. 'Let's see how Kingsley reacts.'

But Kingsley didn't react, as Maxwell was soon to discover when his wife arrived alone, saying that he had had to go out on a medical call.

In her late thirties, Lucinda Kingsley had a directness and personal warmth that Maxwell found very striking. But all he could think of were Arrowsmith and Lucas and twice he disappeared to phone Forbes for news – of which there was none.

'How long will you be here?' Lucinda asked suddenly over

coffee.

'I'm not quite sure. I'm awaiting instructions.'

'Will you come to dinner this evening?'

'I don't think – '

'I'd like you to meet my husband. It was a pity he was called out this morning.'

Maxwell rose to his feet, looking at his watch. 'Very well.'

The telephone rang and Gillett rose to answer it. 'It's for you,' he said.

Maxwell picked up the receiver apprehensively, listened, made a few comments and then slowly replaced it. 'They're calling off the search,' he said.

'That bastard Morales is going to get away with this scot-free.' Maxwell's officers had never seen him so bitterly, helplessly angry before as he discussed the situation with them on the bridge.

'There's going to be an inquiry here in Port Stanley,' said Forbes.

'I can tell you the outcome now – death by misadventure.'

'And there'll be the official naval inquiry, sir.' Burgess knew how platitudinous this sounded.

'Yes, I'm sure. What has been done about next of kin?'

'They've been informed, sir,' replied Forbes miserably.

'I'm not sure we shouldn't go on searching, using our own helicopter.'

'We've already done three sweeps, sir,' said Crabtree.

Maxwell shrugged. 'I know it's hopeless now. But I'm just so angry that this kind of thing can happen – and there's so little we can do because we are not getting sufficient support from the Foreign Office.'

'Are you going over Tennant's head, sir?'

'I've already signalled Whitehall again, but they merely sent their regrets over an unfortunate incident that could have been an accident. They also pointed out that the date of the civilian inquiry would be brought forward. God knows what that means – probably next year instead of the year after next.'

97

Maxwell hit his palm with his fist. 'For Christ's sake – Ogilvy was hovering overhead. He'd have seen them fall over the side.'

'It was very misty, sir.'

Maxwell eyed Forbes angrily. 'Are you ratting out of this, Nick?'

'No, sir,' Forbes retorted firmly. 'I think the whole thing stinks. I'm just trying to eliminate any prejudice.'

'Yes,' said Maxwell. 'It did cross my mind.'

'What do you mean, sir?'

'That I might just be wrong.'

The Kingsleys' house in Port Stanley was a long, low, weatherboarded building with a veranda that gave the impression of belonging to the American West. It was even called 'The Ranch'. Inside, any similarities ceased. The walls of the living room were covered with large, startling photographs of the islands and their wildlife, while the furniture was modern, comfortable and anonymous.

When Maxwell arrived he found they had another visitor – a tall man with long hair flowing over the collar of his dark jacket and a leonine beard that made his gaunt, weatherbeaten face benign.

'This is our friend, Jan Petrowski – Captain James Maxwell,' said Lucinda Kingsley. 'Jan is skipper of the *San Juan*.'

'The mighty British Navy,' said Jan as they shook hands.

Maxwell smiled warily. 'And you?'

'The *San Juan* is a trawler, not to be compared with your fine ship.' There was an awkward silence then Petrowski abruptly changed the subject. 'I hear you've been up against some problems, Captain,' he said, raising a hand as Maxwell began to speak. 'But there's no need to tell me – I understand about security. The only thing is – ' he laughed ' – it's all over the island. The two ships and the Russians.'

'I should have known that.'

'And this is my husband,' said Lucinda quickly.

Miles Kingsley shook hands with Maxwell. He had the

somewhat distracted air of a permanently busy man yet his deep-set eyes were inquisitive, discriminating.

For a while they sipped drinks and made small talk, but soon the conversation centred on Kingsley's hobby – photographing wildlife. 'The best are in my study – like to have a look?' He glanced tentatively at the others. 'Jan has seen them many times before and Lucinda – she knows every last detail.'

'Go ahead,' said Petrowski. 'It'll give me a chance to seduce your wife.'

'You will be going back on board the *Santa Fe*?' she asked.

'Directly the inquiry is over.'

'It was a good piece of work.'

'Our first.'

Gabriel and Julia Mendoza were reunited in a safe house in Rio Gallegos. They were dining with Morales who was equally ebullient.

'They took the ship apart – and found nothing.'

Gabriel carved up his enormous steak with relish. 'She is clean – and will be returned to us within a day or so. After that, the *Santa Fe* will no longer be an object of interest.'

They ate for a few minutes in silence. Then Gabriel said: 'Did you contact Gillett?'

'I've got the cottage – ' Julia poured out some more wine and sipped at it reflectively. Then she turned to her brother. 'Gabriel – am I going to the Falklands just for the sake of having something to do?'

He met her eyes but she saw that he was looking through her. Suddenly they seemed to have so little contact.

'No, Julia. Befriending Forbes is useful work.'

'He's hardly likely to tell me anything of importance.'

Gabriel shook his head. 'I disagree. He is a potential weak link. A heavy drinker, a broken marriage, too long Maxwell's subordinate. You must be persistent.'

She shook her head. 'Since you've been on the ship – I just feel very isolated. Out of touch.'

'That's the way this organization should be,' said Morales

99

sanctimoniously. 'Lots of little cells.'

'Why don't you fuck off somewhere?' she told him quietly and, for the first time in months, Julia saw her brother give a genuine smile.

Miles Kingsley put the photographs back in a folder and told Maxwell: 'There's not a lot I can do for you.'

'Now where have I heard that before?'

'It's evidence we need. The *Santa Fe* was clean.'

'The *Escuardo* wasn't.'

'It didn't add up to much – that's the problem. You must appreciate that if any accusations are made without foundation there could be an appalling incident with the Soviets.'

'I understand that. But why am I being deliberately blocked?'

'You're not. They're scared shitless of what you might do.'

'Then recall me.'

'On what grounds?'

Maxwell exploded. 'I'll give them bloody grounds. And I honestly don't see the point of this conversation.'

'Listen, Captain Maxwell, let me try and explain my own position. Just after the war I was asked to keep an eye on the islands and I'm ideally placed as a doctor to do so. I'm following up a lead now that I don't want to talk to you about. Not now, anyway. But I must tell you, unofficially, that I think you're on to something. You must, however, keep a lower profile or you'll play right into their hands.'

'Whose? That's the point.'

'Ola Roja – the Soviets – both, I don't know. But what I do know is that you should continue your investigations. And a damn sight more discreetly. I think we have to leave it at that.'

As he spoke the telephone rang. Saved by the bell, thought Maxwell as Kingsley went to answer it. A few seconds later he impatiently put the receiver down and swore. 'I'm off again. Sometimes I miss social occasions entirely, usually I miss at least half of them – and very rarely I actually manage to see people home at the end of an evening. I'm not going to do that tonight.'

They returned to the dining room and he explained himself all over again. Lucinda smiled back at her husband, their eyes met and Maxwell could feel the bond of intimacy between them. For a moment he yearned for Susan, and then realized it was the first time he had done so in weeks.

Amidst renewed apologies Kingsley departed and Lucinda served dinner. The meal, composed of stuffed aubergines and a delicate lamb casserole, was a success. Maxwell and Petrowski got on well and, to their own surprise, did not regale each other or Lucinda with the standard seafaring anecdotes. They talked instead of the Falklands and their beauty, photography and the future of the islands. So it was to everyone's real regret that, some time after midnight, Petrowski heaved himself to his feet and said that he had to go back to his trawler.

He shook Maxwell's hand. 'I enjoyed talking with you.'

'Why don't you come on board?'

'That would be delightful. I shall bring you some fish. Patagonian hake.'

'That's a real delicacy,' said Lucinda.

Maxwell looked at his watch. 'I must be moving soon.'

'Stay with Lucinda,' said Petrowski. 'Keep her company for a little longer. She's on her own so much.'

When he had gone, Lucinda said: 'He's a good man.'

'Yes – I liked him very much.'

'And you've managed to relax. I know that's what Bernard had in mind for you.'

'So, it's all a plot?'

'Absolutely.'

She rose and lit a cigarette. 'I love the Falklands but sometimes – increasingly – I yearn for England. For us all to be together – all the time. Of course, Miles is invaluable here. He's very busy, very dedicated.' For a moment Maxwell thought she was going to say something else. There was an awkward pause, which she broke abruptly: 'I make myself busy too – but for less good reason.' She laughed. 'I'm busy being busy.' Then she said abruptly: 'Why don't you pour us some brandy?'

101

Maxwell walked across to the drinks cupboard and found the brandy bottle. He filled their glasses and sat down heavily on the sofa, suddenly feeling drunk.

'You're all in.' She stood up restlessly and began to move about the room. He watched her slight, graceful body and the physical desire rose in him until it was unbearable. Hurriedly, Maxwell stuttered into speech: 'I'm not being very good company.'

She came across to the sofa and sat down next to him. 'I don't give a damn,' she said. The ensuing silence was very tense and the desire surged in Maxwell again until he knew he must touch her. But in the end it was she who made the first move by leaning forward and gently kissing him on the bridge of his nose. It was an affectionate gesture and for a moment he thought he had miscalculated everything. Then she began to unbutton her dress.

It had been good – and as Maxwell left the house an hour later he felt relaxed for the first time in weeks. They had made love with a quick ferocity. Both had needed it so much and both had lain back afterwards, exhausted, satisfied and content. He had thanked her and she had laughed, saying he sounded as if he was giving an official speech. Maxwell had laughed too and then she asked him if he wanted to make love to her again. He did.

Now, at the water's edge, the *Mercator*'s boat was waiting for him and they cast off into a languid black swell.

There was no moon and Maxwell had the impression of being on a sea that had no distance, no horizon. Hunched against the biting air, he fell asleep for a few moments. Briefly, he dreamt and the dark sea turned to a dark lake across which he was rowed by a skeletal boatman. On the shore he had left, Maxwell saw Susan and Robin waving to him from a half-lit summer beach. Guilt, like an old friend who knew how to wound, began to overcome him.

5 – Escalation

6 December 1989
9.30 a.m.
Off the Falklands
The next morning was cold and grey with winds gusting up to thirty-five knots. The cable party were closing up to shorten in to three shackles with a view to getting under way at 10.00. Dressed in foul weather clothing and heavy jumpers, they went about their work in the hope that there would be no delay on the upper deck and they could soon return to the fug below.

Once under way, Commander Forbes and the Master at Arms, Bill Brand, did a full round of the accommodation to see that everything was properly stowed, for heavy seas were expected. Although the ship was making an easterly course and the prevailing wind was from the south-west, Forbes knew she would roll heavily if she had to turn to the south for a helicopter flying into the wind.

At 11.00 Maxwell broadcast to the ship's company. He was listened to with considerable attention.

'The loss of Lieutenant Arrowsmith and the OCRM, Captain Lucas, in circumstances which are far from clear, will be the subject of a full naval inquiry. However, although I would like to be able to tell you that all that can be done *is* being done, unfortunately, this is not the case. The fact is that I am far from happy at the official low-key response to this tragedy. All I can say is that I shall be unsparing in my efforts to put pressure on the authorities to discover exactly how these men were lost.

'Since our arrival in the South Atlantic we have been involved in two major incidents, and I would like to thank all the ship's company for their hard work and initiative and for the many risks they have taken. I greatly appreciate each indi-

103

vidual contribution.

'We are now back on our operating schedule and are currently heading for South Georgia, the largest of the Falkland Island Dependencies – an area which is important as the forward operating base for large tankers as well as support ships to the oil companies operating in Antarctica.'

Maxwell paused. 'Whaling and sealing were a thriving concern in South Georgia until the early sixties, when the industry was closed, leaving behind rusting machinery, stores and accommodation. Slowly but surely the stores were then pilfered by passing ships and the buildings fell into dereliction.' As he spoke, Maxwell saw the haunted buildings of the old whaling factory, with bars of Sunlight soap in the sinks and plates and cutlery still scattered around the kitchens. Elephant seals had invaded some of the buildings at Grytviken and lay inside, great mounds of dank flesh in the darkness. Maxwell almost lost his words as the memories flooded back and he hurriedly continued: 'But the jetties, the flensing pens and the foundations of the major buildings remained intact.

'But in 1982, the Argentines flexed their political muscles when scrap dealer Constantin Davidoff, backed by the Argentine Navy, tested British resolve over the sovereignty of South Georgia. Davidoff and his men were illegally landed at Leith by the Argentine Navy in March 1982, and the situation escalated into a political confrontation culminating in the Falklands War. After British forces recaptured South Georgia, the port facilities were improved considerably, mooring buoys were laid, jetties and buildings renovated. The base at Grytviken was enlarged and when the oil industry arrived in mid-1987, two American-based multinationals set up camp in Grytviken and Husvik, and a European-based company took over the old Salvesson whaling station at Leith. All these installations are within a few miles of each other, lying on the northern coast of South Georgia.

'So that, gentlemen, is your detailed briefing on where we are heading. Once again, thank you for your support.'

The briefing was heard with mixed feelings for it came as a tremendous anticlimax to the clearly unsatisfactory state of affairs surrounding the disappearance of Arrowsmith and Lucas. The general opinion was best expressed by Taff Evans when he said: 'The old man may have done his best but it's not good enough, is it? We've been told to stuff it – and I'd like to know why.'

Alone in his cabin, Maxwell lay on his bunk, remembering how Miles Kingsley had told him to keep a low profile. He was aware that he could be seriously reprimanded for telling the ship's company that he was dissatisfied with Whitehall's response to his reports, but he knew that it was essential to keep the men behind him – although he was sure they must still feel he was withholding information from them.

His thoughts soon switched from these immediate problems to Lucinda. Ever since they had made love, Maxwell had been consumed with a painful mixture of guilt and elation. Nothing like Lucinda had ever happened to him before and he felt partly obsessed by his physical desire for her, partly by his need for her companionship. She had very suddenly become an all-consuming passion for him and he wasn't sure he could cope with it. The hardest part was that this sudden, maybe never-to-be-repeated love-making had made him realize just how far he and Susan had drifted apart. What were his leaves now but a pastoral sojourn of marital responsibility? Yes, they made love – there was no problem there. He mowed the lawn, played tennis with Robin, went on family outings, visits to friends and relatives, cocktail parties, planned for retirement. It was a full life. Yet half way through his leaves he knew he was yearning for the sea again, and however much he loved Robin, however much he tried to involve himself with Susan's life, Maxwell knew that he had no real place there.

But now Lucinda had touched some deep-seated feeling in him that had not surfaced for years, letting loose an insatiable, guilty obsession with a future that could never be allowed to happen.

Hurriedly Maxwell got up and sat at his desk. This was the most traumatic period of his naval career where every decision counted. Yet he was now putting it all at risk with a longing that was as absurd as it was dangerous.

105

Mercator was ploughing her way East at a speed of sixteen knots towards the bleak coastline of South Georgia when Robertson, the Officer of the Watch, heard a shout of 'Man overboard. Port side!' He took action quickly: the seaboat was manned and the way taken off the ship.

Maxwell, hurrying up from his cabin, ordered the position of the man to be watched carefully as the safety drills they had originally practised at Portland came smoothly into operation.

'Who is it, sir?' asked the Chief Bosun's Mate.

'Able Seaman Butterfield,' replied Robertson.

'Naturally he's got a life-jacket on?' asked Maxwell, still trying to think himself away from Lucinda Kingsley. 'Officer of the Watch, use more wheel, and come astern on your port engine.'

Soon the *Mercator* was alongside Butterfield, who was bobbing up and down in the cold, grey water. He won't last long, thought Maxwell, we've got to be quick.

'Carry on with the seaboat, Commander, but put the Swimmer of the Watch in the boat this time,' he said sharply. Usually his system was to have a swimmer dressed in a slightly inflated rubber suit so that he could dive over the side on the end of a lifeline, but today the South Atlantic was so rough that the swimmer went down with the seaboat. The *Mercator* provided a good lee and very soon the crew, together with a medically trained rating, were lifting Butterfield into the inflatable. The operation had taken less than four minutes and Maxwell said approvingly to Forbes: 'That was damn good.'

'It also proves something, sir.'

'What?'

'How easy it is to go overboard.'

'Are *you* trying to say I was over-reacting?' Maxwell felt his anger rising childishly.

Forbes shrugged hopelessly. 'I'm sorry, sir. I just don't know.'

Maxwell recovered his temper with difficulty, trying to remember that one of Nick's values was to be a damn good sounding board, even a devil's advocate. So why was he abusing the very qualities he needed in the man? Did it have to do with the fact that he, James Maxwell, was no longer fully concentrating on the job? I've *got* to pull myself together, he thought, before I do real damage.

Once back on board the *Mercator*, the unconscious Butterfield was lifted on to a stretcher and taken below. Ten minutes later he came to and started swearing. McBride, the ship's doctor, rang Maxwell.

'He tells me I'm a cunt – so my prognosis is that he's improving.'

Maxwell smiled and put the phone down, but within seconds it rang again.

'Ops room, sir.'

'Yes?'

'We've detected a possible submarine.'

'Give me the details.'

'We'd completed a passive all-round sweep with the Type 184 Sonar when we detected what we thought was positive submarine contact on a bearing ahead. I've just re-checked – and it's a submarine all right, sir.'

'Right – we shall remain passive and follow the submarine's movements.' Maxwell turned to Forbes. 'This could be interesting.'

They hurried down to the ops room together with Carrington, the Operations Officer, and listened to the cavitation caused by the submarine's propeller.

'It's a nuclear submarine without doubt, sir,' said Nielson, the Sonar Director.

'Officer of the Watch, come left to zero-four-five,' rapped out Maxwell.

'Nick – '

'Sir?'

'Order the EW team to close up, will you? I know they can't achieve very much, but at least they can listen out for any radio or radar transmissions that can confirm the bearing of that submarine.'

'Yes, sir. Once we can detect the kind of transmission, we

107

can sort out the classification.'

'And the nationality,' added Maxwell. His spirits were rising. Could they be making some progress at last – something to jerk the MOD out of their complacency? And there was something different about Nick too. Something more decisive, more alive. Maxwell suddenly realized that he had grown used to the person Nick had become – and was now seeing him afresh as he really had been a few years ago. It was a strange feeling.

Twenty minutes later, Carrington was able to confirm: 'An SSN or SSBN* heading for South Georgia. But why?'

'Hardly likely to be an SSBN, Robin,' said Maxwell. 'At what target would he be launching his missiles – Buenos Aires or Cape Town?'

'Well, that's a relief, sir,' said Forbes. 'At least we're not about to engage in full-scale nuclear war!'

'It must be an SSN on a surveillance mission, sir, but whose?'

Unfortunately, *Mercator*'s equipment could only provide a bearing, for if the sonar were to be switched on in the active mode the submarine would be able to hear the sonar transmissions and take evasive action. So Maxwell ordered the Olympus engines to be started in case they needed more speed and the *Mercator* continued to follow the submarine down the bearing.

'It's got to be American, Russian or French, and if it were American we should know about it. I wonder what the hell she's up to?' said Forbes.

'Excuse me, sir.' The operator's voice was urgent. 'The EW team report they've detected submarine search radar on bearing zero-four-five.'

'And what does the frequency indicate?' asked Maxwell. He was hoping against hope that he was going to hear what he wanted to hear. And he did.

'It's Russian,' said the operator calmly.

'Interesting,' remarked Forbes.

'What now, sir?' asked Carrington.

* Ballistic Missile Submarine.

108

'We can't do more than follow her and see what she's up to,' said Maxwell. 'Let's hope they'll think we're some kind of oil rig support vessel from Punta Arenas. If not, she could prove elusive.' He turned to Forbes. 'We'll follow her at a passage speed of sixteen knots.'

Gradually the weather grew worse until the wind from astern was gusting up to sixty knots – a storm that Maxwell knew was following a well-worn route from Drake's Passage off Cape Horn, which was a notorious area for turbulence. Forbes stared through the bridge window at the darkening sky.

'The sea looks angry.'

'We're going to be in for a blow,' said Maxwell, with sudden satisfaction. This is what he enjoyed – a hunt in a vengeful sea. It was so much less complicated than what happened ashore. And he knew Forbes felt the same way. They looked at each other, experiencing the thrill of silent companionship.

When it came the storm was vicious, the sea running high, flinging vast sheets of spray over the *Mercator*'s bows. A stinging rattle of rain dashed in knife-points at the wave crests and above them ragged clouds seared a pallid night sky. The moon was no more than a pale orb and the wind picked at the rain-lashed crests which broke and were swallowed in their churning foam. The height of the waves seemed enormous – and their self-destructive speed incredible – terrifying to watch even for those who had been through worse storms. And there were worse storms.

The windows of the *Mercator*'s bridge, despite the driving force of the wipers, were almost entirely obscured by spray and all Maxwell could occasionally see was the hurtling mass of parchment-coloured waves, like a landscape washed of colour, a field furrowed crazily by some demented ploughman. But despite all this, the *Mercator* forged determinedly ahead and passive sonar contact was maintained.

Thirty-six exhausting, mostly sleepless hours later, the storm had driven itself out. Leading Seaman Cooper, who was in charge of the sonar watch, reported a bearing alteration and it soon became clear that the submarine was altering to starboard.

'The point is,' said Maxwell, 'is she going to head round the south-east corner of South Georgia, or is she just trying to shake off her "tail"?'

'If we alter to starboard to follow, sir, she'll guess we're not just an ordinary merchant ship,' said Carrington.

'And if we don't,' replied Maxwell, 'we shall probably lose her.'

'Yes, sir, but if we maintain our course and speed we should be able to follow her movements for some time without arousing any suspicion. Anyway, we'll probably be able to detect her when we get round the other side of the island.'

'Good thinking,' said Maxwell. 'She may be trying us out. Let's see if she resumes her old course when she's made certain we're not following her.'

The *Mercator* maintained her course and returned to diesel engine drive so she would sound more like a merchant ship to the submarine. Then, a further six hours later, the Soviet abruptly altered course to port to cross *Mercator*'s path, while increasing speed to about twenty knots. Maxwell soon found it was possible to determine her range by bearing movement, and it slowly became clear she would pass about three miles ahead. Back on the bridge he gave instructions to watch for any periscope sighting, but he knew it would be difficult for the submarine to look up sea against the rough conditions to determine exactly what kind of ship *Mercator* was. Fortunately, very few of *Mercator*'s weapons were visible and most of her electronic equipment was concealed.

Eventually the submarine passed ahead at a broad inclination and then resumed course. Either they had come in close to inspect the *Mercator* or they had altered course due to the contours of the sea bed.

Maxwell turned to Forbes. 'I'm sure they're playing a little waiting game – just carrying out a series of surveillance operations and collecting information on the volume and type of shipping operating in and out of South Georgia. I know the Russian fishermen were brassed off when they lost their sheltered anchorages, because they had used them to transfer their catches to factory ships.'

'What were they catching?'

'Ice fish and Antarctic cod mainly, but sometimes they'd have a blitz on krill. But it wasn't the anchorage that upset the British scientists at Grytviken – it was the debris that floated inshore as well as those streams they dammed for fresh water.'

'So the Russians were actually changing the ecology?'

'That's right – it was a bloody shame. The elephant seals have been driven further out west and the king penguin colony in St Andrew's Bay has vanished. I also have a strong suspicion they were killing seals.'

'I don't suppose much action was taken against them.'

'You bet it wasn't. Good old British phlegm – the usual pragmatic approach. A note was sent from London to Moscow, asking them to bugger off and at the same time offering them an anchorage facility at Candlemas.'*

'Of course,' said Forbes, 'there were several advantages in offering them that facility.'

'Oh, yes,' replied Maxwell. 'It was likely to be a deterrent against the Argies re-establishing their presence in the islands. Also the islands of the South Sandwich group are normally icebound for about four to five months of the year which should put the clappers on the Russian fishing effort. So I suppose the FCO considered that of all evils, giving the Russians an anchorage there was the best possible backhanded compliment.' Maxwell laughed. 'Only the penguins would object.'

9 December 1989

2.00 a.m.

Off South Georgia

The *Mercator* continued to track the Russian submarine, using passive sonar. At 02.30, Maxwell was called to the operations room. There, fifteen sailors were clamped in head-sets, intently watching the video display units and intermittently tapping out coded questions to the computers. Red and green lights flashed from the various electronic units and a sense of

* Candlemas in the South Sandwich Group.

deceptive calm pervaded the atmosphere. Directly Maxwell arrived he had a complete presentation of surface and sub-surface activity.

'The submarine's altering course again, sir,' said Lieutenant-Commander Carrington.

'Where's she heading?'

'She's altering course to starboard and heading for King Haakon Bay,' Carrington replied immediately.

Maxwell wondered if he should give orders for the *Mercator* to follow, or to continue on her course, but eventually he decided that any alterations now would be spotted. 'We'll continue along our intended track as if we're unaware of her presence,' he said. 'And to hell with it.'

For the next two hours the Russian submarine's movements were followed with meticulous care. Then Carrington broke the monastic atmosphere of calm plotting.

'They're headed for Queen Maud Bay, sir.'

'Is that anchorage charted?'

'Yes, sir. It's used occasionally.'

Thank God for Carrington's reliability, thought Maxwell. One cock-up now and we'll look such bloody fools.

'We'll be losing track of them once we get behind the island,' added Carrington and Maxwell nodded.

'We'll go slow-ahead. Once we're in the lee of the island we can monitor her progress – she's bound to use her radar and periscope when she's close in. She may even surface.'

'We've lost contact now, sir.'

'OK.' Maxwell switched his intercom to the Officer of the Watch. 'Come down to slow-ahead on both engines.'

'I wonder what she's going to do now, sir?' asked Carrington.

'I'll lay a bet that she's either going to put a party ashore, or she's going to lay something on the sea bed.'

'Do you know what they're up to, sir?'

Once again Maxwell cursed himself for failing to reassure them sufficiently. Maybe they all thought he was still holding back on them. He must check with Forbes.

'I'm just guessing at the moment,' he replied abruptly.

112

That afternoon Maxwell despatched one of the Lynx helicopters ostensibly to carry out a Life/Science survey on nearby Willis Island. He told them to take photographs of the penguin colonies from a height of two thousand feet so that estimates of breeding numbers could be sent to the British Antarctic Survey for analysis. But he also told Ogilvy to take a further set of aerial photographs of the King Haakon and Queen Maud Bay foreshore.

'What happens if we spot the submarine?' asked Ogilvy.

'Get the hell back to Life/Science work,' said Maxwell, 'or you'll blow it.'

Piloted by Ogilvy, the Lynx climbed to four thousand feet, flew over Bomford Peak, following the foreshore at an altitude of three thousand feet. Once they were over King Haakon Bay the observer, Lieutenant Crabtree, noted that there was so much kelp there was no chance of the submarine pushing through. A few minutes later they saw that Queen Maud Bay was clear of weed although the south-westerly swell dictated an impossible landing.

Suddenly, Ogilvy said: 'I'll take her down to four hundred feet, David.'

'That will really give the game away and the old man will be livid,' Crabtree retorted.

'Well, I'll make it six hundred feet then. I can't see a periscope but what I *can* see is fresh marks on the beach in that little cove to the south-west of Queen Maud anchorage.'

'Probably a reindeer went down for a swim.'

'Ha fucking ha! Let's go and see.'

As they descended it soon became clear there was a short track in the grey shingle leading about twenty feet up the beach from the sea – as if a small craft had been pulled up. But they could see nothing.

'Christ!' Ogilvy shouted.

'What's up?' Crabtree's voice was sharp with urgency.

Then Ogilvy laughed. 'I thought I saw a grey Russian uniform behind that rock, but it's only an elephant seal.'

113

'You're making me nervous,' replied Crabtree. 'There's nothing much here except that mark on the beach, and that could have been caused by a seal – I suppose.'

'Most unlikely,' snapped Ogilvy, his sense of humour vanishing abruptly.

Crabtree sighed patiently. He knew Ogilvy and his flashes of anger. 'Let's climb again and go back to the penguins,' he suggested. But just as they were leaving the bay Crabtree caught sight of something. 'Is that a seal or a buoy over there?' He took out a pair of binoculars and gave a grunt of satisfaction. 'It seems to be a – ' His voice rose in excitement. 'Well I'm buggered! Giles – there's a small aerial on top!'

'Let's take a closer look.' Ogilvy brought the helicopter over the grey swell and now they could both clearly see the buoy and its antennae. 'Maybe the submarine's in trouble,' said Ogilvy.

'I wouldn't have thought he was likely to advertise himself. Hey – look at that!'

The buoy had now completely disappeared.

Ogilvy said: 'They must be in trouble out in deeper water and transmitting via the buoy. What a bit of luck for us.'

Crabtree and Ogilvy flew back to the *Mercator* and went straight to Maxwell who had his Ops Team with him in his cabin. Together they analysed the events of the day. Eventually Maxwell called Browning up to the bridge, briefed him and then said: 'I want you to take four marines and dig into an observation position above Queen Maud Bay tomorrow night. Carrington will go with you. I may have to leave you all there for four or five days, but I want you to lie as low as possible and watch the Russians. They will only move at night, so you'll need all your vision aids.'

Later Maxwell said to Forbes: 'We're on to something, Nick.'

'Can we handle it, sir?'

'I don't know, but I think we've got to try.'

'Nick?'

'Sir?'

'Come in and sit down.' Maxwell, slumped in an armchair in his cabin, had been thinking quietly for an hour or so on his own. It had not been pleasant. First of all he had condemned himself completely for making love to Lucinda. Years of duty, of responsibility, of 'doing the right thing' had emerged as a strong force in him. Strong enough to overcome his obsession with her, to bury it somewhere in his consciousness and weight it down with sturdy morality. Strong enough too to make him uneasy about his other actions – his other obsessions.

Forbes, sensing his mood, sat down without saying anything.

'I've been over-reacting,' Maxwell said. 'Obviously, something's going on, but I think it's a monitoring system – in fact I'm sure it is. All the evidence in the *Escuardo* points that way. Frankly, the Santa Lucia disaster shook me so much that I reckon I've had everything out of perspective – even down to Lucas and Arrowsmith.'

'I wouldn't reject any possibility, sir.'

Maxwell shrugged impatiently. 'We've been through a lot, Nick. This is our last commission together. I didn't want you to think I was getting senile.'

'No, sir.' But Forbes was determined to be objective. 'I still wouldn't rule anything out, sir.'

'Quite – and that's why I'm going myself instead of sending Carrington.'

Forbes looked at him quizzically. 'The MOD won't go for one of their Captains doing a spot of adventure training, will they?'

'I don't give a damn what they go for,' said Maxwell. 'I can't take decisions – or make judgements – sitting on my arse. Never could.'

The following day the *Mercator* anchored off Leith Harbour whilst the landing party was kitted up with enough clothing, food, equipment and tents to last them for several weeks if necessary. The island was one of the most windswept, ice-cold, inhospitable places in the world.

At 15.30 the Sea King was launched with Maxwell aboard and followed the north coast to Possession Bay, where it then altered course to the south-west across the Purvis Glacier and into King Haakon Bay.

When they had been winched down, the landing party pitched their tents over snow holes in a gully, leaving a lookout on the rocks above to cover the bay and the small beach which Ogilvy and Crabtree had pointed out to them before returning to the *Mercator*.

Maxwell and Marine Boyle took the first two-hour watch from the vantage point at the north end of the rocky ledge above their camp. It was twilight as they lay in the rough tussocky grass between the black slippery rocks. Depressingly, Maxwell realized he was not in a position which could afford any shelter from the prevailing south-south-west wind and he only had the prospect of becoming colder and stiffer as his vigil wore on.

At 21.00 they were relieved by Donaldson and Browning. So far nothing had moved, except for the occasional fluttering of a sea-bird and the short breakers from the main swell hitting the beach. Watch-keeping continued throughout the night and the following day. The conditions remained bitingly cold but of the Russians there was no sign. Then, at approximately 16.30 on the third afternoon, Maxwell spotted what looked like a box floating off the entrance to the bay.

Crouched beside him, Browning said: 'It's a fish box off a trawler, sir.'

'It's been stationary for a hell of a long time,' replied Maxwell.

Fifteen minutes later Browning reported: 'I can see another box, sir, just five degrees to the right of the first one.'

Later he saw another and the other members of the landing party scrambled slowly up the icy rocks to have a look. By now there were four boxes laid across the entrance to the bay. Maxwell and Browning debated their next move.

'The submarine must be laying something on the sea-bed, sir,' said Browning.

'Sonar or mines?'

'Heaven knows – and why here anyway, in this God-forsaken spot, sir?'

Maxwell said: 'But that's exactly why they *are* here – because no one is ever likely to venture into this cove. Even if they did, all they'd see would be a row of fish boxes.'

Then with startling rapidity three of the boxes disappeared, leaving only one bobbing about on the surface.

'Christ!' breathed Browning as a telescopic aerial began to extend upwards until the box looked like a toy boat.

They watched for another ten minutes – and nothing further happened. An uneasy tension gripped Maxwell and he was sure the others felt the same. The night was very dark and the moon only occasionally emerged from behind the scudding clouds.

Then they saw a speck on the horizon. Gradually it became a small inflatable boat, heading towards the cove. Ten minutes later it landed and they counted four men. The intruders climbed out on to the beach and pulled their craft up about twenty feet before they crossed the vision of their silent watchers and headed towards a cluster of shadowed rocks. They were carrying a long pole and a number of boxes.

The first two men climbed to about a hundred yards beyond the beach and then started hacking away at the rock. The other two continued to transport equipment up to the site and then joined in with the digging. Meanwhile, the marines lay glued to their infra-red night vision enhancers, watching every move. Maxwell shivered in the freezing darkness as he apprehensively watched the primeval landscape.

After about three hours the landing party erected the mast for a few moments. Then they brought it down again while a small saucer-shaped aerial was attached.

By this time the *Mercator*'s marines were so numb with cold that Maxwell reckoned it would be hard enough to stand, let alone take action if they were discovered. Then Browning, burning for a pee, finally lost control of his agony and felt the warm liquid seep into his trousers. It was the ultimate misery of his long, silent, freezing watch.

Eventually, the mast was erected to what looked like its full extent, about twenty feet above the rocks. It seemed to Maxwell as if it was firmly secured and he noticed that a wire led to another box which one of the men had been burying in some gravel. Various unidentifiable tests were then carried out until food was produced and a relaxed picnic held. The marines watched with growing hunger pangs. Half an hour later, the landing party dismantled the equipment and made their way back to the rubber boat. When everything had been stowed away, they started the engine and disappeared round the headland.

With relief Maxwell ended the vigil and he and his marines lurched to their feet like rusty automatons, stretching and beating their numbed limbs, attempting to restore some circulation. Then Browning told Boyle and Cockburn to share sentry duty for what remained of the night.

Before he left them Browning said: 'I'm pretty sure they won't be back, and I know it's a bloody cold night, but we've got to keep an eye on that beach. We don't want to be caught napping.'

'Are we going to have a closer look in the morning, sir?' asked Boyle.

'Yes, but we'll have to be bloody careful,' put in Maxwell. 'They could be observing that beach whether we can see them or not.' They walked away into the night, leaving the freezing sentries to the rasping cold of the new dawn.

As soon as there was enough light Maxwell decided they should continue the visual search for the fish box, but there was no sign of it.

'That aerial they erected last night could be a satellite tracker/receiver fitted in some way with a transmitter so it can signal to the fish-box aerial,' reflected Maxwell.

'And maybe that activates a set of ground mines or a sonar,' replied Browning, following his own line of thought.

'Or something much more innocent,' said Maxwell. 'I'd love to have a closer look at that aerial, but obviously they took the whole lot away with them. What worries me is that they may well be keeping a watch from some vantage point or other – even if it's only through a periscope.' He turned to Browning.

118

'When you signal the ship, say that our samples have been exceptionally good.' He looked round the barren rocks with distaste. 'Suggest recovery at 10.00 today.'

'Very good, sir,' said Marine Cockburn, who had been wondering for some hours if he had contracted frostbite.

Browning chipped in: 'If it *is* a mine system, sir – isn't it a pretty roundabout method? I mean, only a Seaman Officer could have thought of that one. A marine would just plant the bomb or mine on the tanker's arse.'

It could be a secondary method of detonation,' said Maxwell doubtfully. 'There would be a minimum explosion, but maximum hull shattering – and no ship around to give away who did it.'

'That means a three or four hundred thousand tonner could go under in seconds. That's incredible, sir.'

'But possible. After all – laser beams directed from an instrument on the sea-bed could shatter the hull of a large ship and split her in two almost immediately.'

Browning looked incredulous. 'There's no such device, is there?'

Maxwell shrugged. 'I remember reading in some classified report or other that the Americans were developing an underwater weapon using the laser principle.'

Browning was silent for a few minutes and Maxwell could see that he was becoming increasingly agitated. 'Shit!' he said eventually. 'This is like a bloody nightmare.'

'We're only guessing.'

'Yes, but suppose we're right. We could have stumbled on the beginning of World War III.' His voice was hoarse with alarm, and quite suddenly Maxwell felt the same chill of reality.

Quickly, he said: 'Now – having looked at that side of the coin, why not look at the other?'

'What's that, sir?' Browning sounded disappointed.

'It could all be part of a reporting system to keep a tally of ships using the South Georgia harbours.' There was a long silence; then Maxwell said briskly: 'Let me have all the details of this investigation on paper so I can compile a formal report to the Flag Officer Third Flotilla. That way it will go to the MOD, *not* to that fool Tennant in BA. And in the meantime, I know I don't have to remind you to keep this operation completely secret.'

'My men understand that, sir.'

'I'm glad of that,' said Maxwell. 'Tell them they've done a bloody good job.'

Once back on board, Maxwell thought the situation over again in his cabin. Either way he was determined to take positive action, but Tennant's gallingly dismissive attitude acted as a curb on his impulsiveness. This time he was determined not to make any statements without concrete evidence to back them up, so he took the decision to send both Lynx helicopters out to search the west coast of South Georgia for any further installations. They could also photograph every Russian fishing vessel in the vicinity and Forbes could check with the oil companies operating from Leith, Husvik and Grytviken that they had not recruited any Soviet labour – or had any suspicion of infiltration amongst their employees. Then, in the unlikely event that it *was* true, if the unbelievable *was* happening, he would send his report to the MOD and stuff that bastard Tennant.

For the next two days Maxwell's plan was put into operation and the *Mercator* buzzed with rumour at the helicopter activity and the massive photographic work which was being undertaken. But the marines, carefully supervised by Browning, remained silent about their mission, despite the open curiosity of their colleagues. Only Forbes and a handful of senior officers really knew what was going on – and some of them only knew what was good for them.

But much to Maxwell's frustration the results of the operation yielded nothing. The oil companies were either highly offended and denied everything, or were intrigued and denied everything, or even co-operative and denied everything. There was no trace of the submarine and despite intensive scanning it seemed to have completely disappeared. As for the few Russian fishing vessels, they appeared to be operating normally with no suspicious equipment visible on board.

Then, on the afternoon of the second day, an exhausted Ogilvy came over his radio to Maxwell.

'There's something odd about the deserted whaling station at Husvik. Fresh tracks up the beach – and some oil drums moved to gain access to one of the sheds.'

'Thank God for a lead at last,' replied Maxwell. 'Suggest you land for a discreet recce.'

'Going down now, sir. Out.'

The old whaling station at Husvik was a sombre place. There seemed to be an atmosphere of pervasive gloom amongst its half-demolished sheds, rusting giant storage drums, broken jetties, whalebones and the stench of rotting seal oil. Around this deserted ramshackle settlement, the volcanic cliffs of South Georgia closed in. Tussock grass covered the swampy ground near the sea, and beyond this were tundra-like regions leading up to the snow-covered peaks. Mosses and lichens seemed to grow everywhere, adding to the desolation with their soft, damp growth. Kelp proliferated round the shore, and as Ogilvy and Crabtree walked across the wiry grass towards the buildings, Ogilvy quoted: '"Lands doomed by nature to perpetual frigidness".'

'Who the hell said that?' asked Crabtree, trudging beside him.

'Captain James Cook, claiming South Georgia for the British Crown in 1775,' said Ogilvy. 'Not a tree to be seen, nor a shrub even high enough to make a toothpick.'

'God – this is a weird place,' said Crabtree apprehensively. A strong northerly wind set a wrecked asbestos roof clanging and the mournful clamour sounded like acid bells from the steeple of the clapboard church – also ruined – further up the valley.

'When did they pull out?' asked Crabtree as they walked over the gravelly beach with its whale vertebrae and bones littered amongst broken winches and hausers.

'The whalers? In the sixties. They left the place in moth-

121

balls, hoping to return – but they never did. Then Davidoff came in 1982 and started hacking the place about.'

'Look – here are the track marks we saw.' They led up from the beach through some thrown-aside oil drums to a ramp, at the top of which stood the dark, yawning mouth of a huge shed with a rusting winch high above it.

'The gateway to hell,' said Ogilvy.

'Where?'

'That's what they used to call it. The whales were dragged up here, trussed up to the winch – and then they started to tear them apart.'

'Were they alive?'

'Yes.'

'My God! It's an appropriate title then.'

They stood on the slippery ramp, whilst the wind made the wires in the winch sing a strange rattling, whistling song. Resolutely, Ogilvy and Crabtree walked on up, the sea a dark sheen behind them in the dull afternoon light. The great iron doors were closed and they both had a job tugging one of them open. It gave suddenly, almost sending them toppling down the slope. The interior was dark and a strong smell wafted rankly down to them.

'What the hell's that smell?'

'Whale,' said Ogilvy. 'Long dead.'

Cautiously they went inside to find themselves in a huge shed. High up in the darkness they could dimly make out a series of pulleys, steel hawsers and rotting rope; on the uneven surface of the floor there were rotting wooden tables and piles of equally rotting packing cases.

'Real little home from home, isn't it!' commented Crabtree.

'Hallo – what's over there?'

'Looks like a pile of fish boxes.'

They walked towards them. 'They look new,' said Ogilvy. He tugged at one of them and the blast threw them off their feet, its force seeming to spiral up to the blackness in the roof. As Ogilvy lay on his back, with a burning pain in his hand, he saw the tin panels above him begin to disintegrate. Then they fell toward him, like sharp slivers of dull red glass.

'That Lynx is in trouble,' yelled Carrington. 'Sound Emergency Stations!'

The alarms shrilled in the *Mercator* and as fire-fighting equipment was rushed to the helicopter deck, Maxwell stood by in the communications office while Carrington tried to raise Crabtree. But it was Ogilvy who responded, his voice on the edge of hysteria.

'Foxtrot Hotel, this is 983. Foxtrot Hotel, this is 983.'

'983, this is Foxtrot Hotel. Do you read me?'

'Foxtrot Hotel. This is Ogilvy. Crabtree's hurt.' His voice rose shrilly. 'I'm going to make a bumpy landing. Do you read me?' His voice rose again. 'I'm going to make one hell of a bumpy landing.'

'983, this is Foxtrot Hotel. Hallo, Giles. This is Robin Carrington. Take it nice and slow. We're all ready for you and emergency landing procedures are completed.'

As the Lynx came in, Maxwell waited on the for'd end of the flight deck. Ogilvy put the helicopter down without needing any of the safety measures. Once the rotor had stopped, Maxwell dashed across the deck with Forbes and Carrington, who had suddenly appeared from below. Their relief was evident as Ogilvy staggered out, one of his hands covered in blood and a long, livid graze down his cheek. Crabtree followed with a cut on his forehead and his hair matted with blood. Surgeon Lieutenant McBride arrived with a stretcher party who took them down to the sickbay. As Ogilvy was carried below he said to Maxwell: 'Sorry about the panic, sir.'

'What panic?'

'The way I brought the Lynx in. It revived a few memories, that's all.'

'Don't be a bloody fool – you did superbly. How's Crabtree?'

'Badly shaken up. That's why I brought him back immediately.'

'In God's name, what happened?'

'There was an explosion, sir – in one of the sheds.'

123

A few hours later, Ogilvy and Crabtree, cleaned up but still very shocked, were able to tell Maxwell exactly what had happened. When they had finished he said: 'I sent Browning out there in the Sea King with the marines. He brought back the debris.'

'What was it, sir?' asked Crabtree.

'A small anti-personnel mine – Argentine origin.'

'So it could have been there since 1982,' said Ogilvy.

'Possibly.'

'And the fish boxes?'

'It's very difficult to say what was inside them. But I'm sure it wasn't fish. I'd like to hazard a guess they contained detonators, but as they're now in fifty million pieces that can only remain a theory.'

'What action can we take?'

'Not a lot. I'm putting in the usual report.' He swore softly and mimicked: 'Of course we mustn't react. Or be seen to.'

Later, on the bridge, Forbes ventured to ask Maxwell what he was going to do about his report. 'How much evidence do you need, sir?' he asked. 'They're obviously trying to scare us off. How can anyone at the MOD reckon this is a coincidence? That mine was planted.'

'It's six years old.'

'So they used an old mine.'

'Possibly.'

'How many of our blokes do Whitehall want killed before they take action? The whole fucking ship's company?' said Forbes angrily.

'You realize the implications if Whitehall did move?'

'I very much doubt if the Russians would go to the extent of putting their finger on the button,' he said with childish sarcasm.

Maxwell was silent. 'We're only assuming that was a Russian submarine – we can't be one hundred per cent certain.'

'And as it's vanished – '

But Maxwell didn't want to hear any more and interrupted impatiently: 'I'm going to risk a signal to the MOD – and see what happens.'

'And I hope it sends a squib up their arses, sir.'
'More likely they'll send one up mine, Commander.'

6 – The noose tightens

15 December 1989
11.40 p.m.
Gabriel stood on the rusty deck of the *Sante Fe*. She was anchored at the head of the group, in the lee of the spot-lit oil rig. Its gaunt structure loomed mournfully over a calm, dark sea, lit by a full moon that made the seascape almost as light as day. In the wan glow, the minor undulations of the ocean reminded Gabriel of the black lake that he had watched from his prison cell window in the Camino Barracks. Each morning he would stare into its depths, seeing it as the void he so passionately sought.

For a while Gabriel reflected on Maxwell, for he was becoming curious about his adversary. Maxwell should have been a typical product of British private education, Dartmouth, the Royal Navy. Instead he was a rebel, attacking the tradition that had raised him. But England was not Uruguay. Maxwell had not experienced even the smallest part of the price Gabriel had had to pay for his attacks on the system. Even though Maxwell's rebelliousness had not endeared him to his superiors, life had still gone well for him. He was rich, he was successful, he was publicly admired. Nevertheless, Gabriel considered, there are similarities between us. Both of us have upper middle-class backgrounds and wealthy families. But we have something else in common too: we are very single-minded men.

He went down below to talk to his KGB controller in Buenos Aires. Using the scrambler, he got through almost immediately. Gabriel was calling in response to an urgent request and he was apprehensive as the static-strewn conversation began. Much had gone wrong. Perhaps he was going to be replaced – and that was something he would not be able to bear.

'I want you to come back.'

For a moment Gabriel's worst fears were confirmed and he began to protest. But the distant voice brusquely cut across him.

'No, Gabriel. It is not that we are not satisfied with what is happening in the South Atlantic. There has been much incompetence, but we appreciate it is hard to recruit good operatives. Something has happened and you are needed for a briefing.'

A flood of relief suffused Gabriel and he almost shouted aloud in joy.

'I am preparing a better system of recruiting,' he began but the voice wanted no more.

'You can explain that', it said wearily, 'when you arrive.'

16 December 1989
10.45 a.m.
Whitehall

'You've seen Maxwell's report?' said Rear-Admiral Gardner, Assistant Chief of Naval Staff.

'Yes, sir.' Captain Hazelton, Director of Naval Operations, nodded.

'And what is your opinion?'

'I find it very worrying, sir.'

'You do apppreciate that if Maxwell's right we could be in the hell of a mess.'

'But *is* he right, sir?' said Hazelton, throwing the ball firmly into Gardner's court.

Gardner gave him an irritable look. 'Let's assume for a moment he is and look at the overall situation. After all, we've been contracting our naval surface units and reducing British naval strength operating in the South Atlantic.'

'You're certainly correct there, sir,' said Hazelton, trying to make amends. 'The Frigate Force alone has been reduced to forty hulls and most of these are either being maintained or refitted or are committed to NATO.'

'We just haven't got the ships.' Gardner sipped at a cup of tepid coffee with distaste.

'As you know, to keep one frigate on station four frigates are needed to be in the cycle – either on passage or being maintained,' said Hazelton, warming to his theme. 'We just don't have sufficient bite with so few ships at our disposal.'

'If we actually had to do anything, we'd need American or French help,' Gardner agreed.

'We couldn't count on that, sir.'

'You're so right, we couldn't. That's why a South Atlantic Treaty Organization is long overdue.' Gardner began to thump his soap box. 'If we have a treaty which included all the South American seafaring nations that could really defuse the aggravation over the sovereignty issues.'

'Yes, sir,' said Hazelton. 'But we're not likely to get a set-up like that, are we?'

'Not at the moment,' said Gardner sourly. There was a long pause then Gardner continued: 'Let's go on supposing Maxwell's right. He's our man on the spot and *Mercator* is ideally suited to the work she is doing. Let's get him to do some more investigative work – particularly in the Sandwich Islands where we were blind stupid enough to allow the Russians that fishing anchorage. If I had my way I'd kick the Russians out of Candlemas altogether.'

'Yes, sir.'

'Are you humouring me, Hazelton?'

'Not exactly, sir.'

'But you don't agree with me, do you?'

'I think Maxwell could be leaping to conclusions. I admit he's had a lot of trouble – and some of it stinks – but he's known to be the kind of chap who's inclined to jump the gun.'

'But even if he is, I see no harm in the *Mercator* having a closer look around.'

'It could be unfortunate if Maxwell stirred up a hornet's nest. The last thing we want, surely, sir, is a major confrontation with the Russians in the South Atlantic.'

Gardner went to the window and looked out over Whitehall. Then he swung round on Hazelton. 'Get me Dunhill,' he said.

'The system', said Gabriel, 'can be activated at any moment we choose. Providing the mines are laid by us – or unit two – well ahead of the tanker's course, we can blow her out of the sea. Detection would be impossible.' He was briefing the Ola Roja operatives in the grubby ward-room of the *Santa Fe*. Everybody else was excluded, the doors were locked and Morales had placed a guard on them. But the rest of the *Santa Fe*'s crew were not likely to be inquisitive – they were too highly paid for that. They just knew that there was a special project being conducted from the ship, that it was connected with oil exploration and that they had no part in it.

'How ready are we?' asked Sabini.

'We're ready to do the test run,' replied Gabriel. 'But before we make the experiment I have to return to Montevideo.'

They looked at him enquiringly and Gabriel smiled sardonically. How anxious they were – how afraid they were of their Russian masters. And how quick they were to assume there was trouble. But no wonder, after what has happened, he thought with more logic. Suddenly Gabriel realized how paranoid he was getting. He must be careful.

Gardner picked up the telephone, aware that the Whitehall system had done its stuff and the line was scrambled.

'How are you bearing up, Aubrey?'

'Fine, thank you, sir.'

'You're obviously coping magnificently.'

'Thank you, sir,' Dunhill repeated dully.

Gardner cleared his throat awkwardly and then rushed into speech. 'Now, I gather you've seen Maxwell's report.'

'Yes, sir.'

'What do you make of it?'

'I think he has some points, sir.'

'You do?'

'But I also think Maxwell is assuming too much.'

'Have you discussed the matter with Kenny and Tennant?'

'Of course, sir. Both are of the same mind.'

'I'm going to order Maxwell to carry out some further investigations in the Sandwich Islands. At the same time I'm telling him emphatically to keep a very low profile.'

'That's very wise, sir.'

'But I don't want to lose a tanker out of this.'

'I don't think the Russians would be fool enough to do anything like that, sir.'

'What if they have the kind of system Maxwell is talking about?'

'I just don't believe they'd risk being detected. There's too much at stake.'

'So you don't believe in the system Maxwell described.'

'I believe there could *be* a system,' said Dunhill cautiously. 'But if there is I'm sure it's being used for monitoring purposes, sir. My feeling is that we should try to disperse the Russian presence by working through the usual diplomatic channels.'

'That will take time.'

'I agree, sir. But I don't think any premature action is to be encouraged.'

'It's all a question of slowly, slowly, catchee monkey.'

'Yes, I believe that's exactly what's required.'

'Thank you. And Aubrey – do you think anyone is trying to scare Maxwell off? He's having a lot of trouble.'

'I honestly believe it's coincidental, sir.'

'I see. Well, thank you, Aubrey.'

'Thank you and goodbye, sir.'

Gardner turned back to Hazelton. 'Dunhill believes the Russians are monitoring – not planning to blow up our tankers.'

'Yes, I'd be inclined to agree, sir.'

'I'm just not so sure.' Gardner was silent. 'I'm definitely going to order Maxwell to investigate the Sandwich Islands,' he said at last decisively.

'It must be discreet.'

'It will be. If not, I'll bloody well relieve him of his command.'

The rig was dotted with a myriad of bright working lights and as Gabriel watched it he was reminded of Montevideo – the city that he loved and feared so much. They had not waited for the shadows of the night or the emptiness of an early morning. They had made their arrests in crowded daylight or on streets that were clearly lit. It had been unnecessary to be discreet for the crowds walked by, seemingly oblivious to the beatings and to the burnt bodies dumped out of cars.

'Bad memories?' Morales had come on him unawares, making him start. 'I'm sorry – am I interrupting you?'

'No.'

'I wanted to talk. Sometimes I wonder if you expect me to communicate by telepathy.'

'What did you want to talk about?'

'About what we are trying to achieve.'

'I would have thought it was very clear what we are trying to achieve. Why do you have doubts?'

Morales hesitated.

'Come – I can see you have doubts.'

'It's just that I'm wondering what we are meant to be. Soviet puppets – or revolutionaries in our own right.'

Gabriel sighed and then laughed gently. But there was little humour in the sound. 'My dear old friend, are you incapable of original thought? The world is grey – we are neither Soviet puppets nor independent revolutionaries. We are somewhere in the middle of all that. But don't you see how much we can achieve – despite the compromises?'

'Sometimes I see nothing.'

'Then you should at least see this. Once we have thoroughly disrupted any possibility of a South Atlantic Treaty Organization, the Soviets can move forward on the oil and the hydrocarbons. In exchange, they'll finance us elsewhere. In Chile, for instance – and in Bolivia and Brazil. We have to move against the Right – and go on moving.' He paused, turning back to the lights of the rig. 'There are several ways of ending a military regime,' he said eventually. 'Either by the suicide of the Generals brought about by a defeat – a national humiliation. That happened in Argentina and in Greece. Or by revolution, which would soon be crushed by the Americans. Or by a negotiated retreat such as happened in our own Uruguay. In other words we got the amnesty we had to have and the Generals got the amnesty they had to have. So we have the compromise government we deserve – the coalition that has no teeth.'

'But the deal with the Generals was worth it, surely, Gabriel?'

'Sure – it provided for the release of two hundred long-term prisoners, but that's just a transition.'

'And now we've had the referendum.'

'Democracy is on its way. What are you in Ola Roja for? Peanuts?'

'I am here because of my belief in you, Gabriel – and in what you believe in. That the Soviets will give us finance to fight all military dictatorships in South America.'

'And hold up to them the compromised democracy of Uruguay. You're a fool.'

'You cannot be too much of an idealist,' Morales replied angrily.

'With what we're risking you have to be,' said Gabriel.

7.15 p.m.
Off South Georgia
'Nick – '

'Yes, sir?'

'I've been nobbled.' Maxwell gave Forbes the signal. It read:

FROM MOD TO MERCATOR
R 141602z DEC 89
FM MODUK
TO HMS MERCATOR
CONFIDENTIAL
YOUR REPORT RECEIVED AND NOTED. PROCEED SOUTH
SANDWICH ISLANDS FOR FURTHER INVESTIGATION. KEEP A
MUCH LOWER PROFILE. INVESTIGATION MUST REMAIN

'My God!' said Forbes. 'Every Russian in Antarctica knows about us by now, don't they?'

'Probably,' said Maxwell. 'But we've got to convince them we've been frightened off.'

'At least they do want us to investigate. They could have put the mockers on the whole thing.'

'Mm. But it's going to be a damn sight more difficult in future. If my credibility had been higher, I'd have been taken more seriously. As it is, we've been asked to continue the investigation – but be an invisible ship at the same time!'

'But you've got a good reputation for sound common-sense. I don't see – '

'No – neither does the MOD. The point is – someone's destroying my credibility. And I won't give you three guesses to discover who.'

'They wouldn't take Tennant's word for it.'*

'Wouldn't they? They must have faith in him. He's handling most of Kenny's work now. But anyway, they didn't have to rely on Tennant's word alone. No doubt they have Dunhill's too.'

'But Dunhill wouldn't put the boot in for you, sir. Particularly after the way you've supported him.'

'I'm afraid he would, Nick,' said Maxwell quietly. 'But I tell you this – even if we *do* have to be an invisible ship, I'm going to get that evidence. *Somehow.*'

'The ship's company's a bit restless, sir.'

'What's the state of morale?'

'Rocky. They all want to have a go at something they can't see – and they feel it keeps hitting 'em.'

'Yes,' said Maxwell. 'And if the men start letting us down, we're finished.'

For the next two days *Mercator*, ostensibly carrying out their programme, searched every bay, every beacon and almost every blade of tussock grass along the coasts of South Georgia.

---

* Tennant was accredited to the British Embassy both in Buenos Aires and in Montevideo.

It was a long and laborious task with no let-up and no reward. They saw vast colonies of king penguins in Hound Bay, elephant seals by the score in Gold Harbour Bay and herds of reindeer by the shores of Royal Bay. There were albatrosses, petrels, terns and skuas by the million – but of any human presence, there was no sign.

19 December 1989
9.00 a.m.
Nearing the South Sandwich Islands
Morale amongst the ship's company of the *Mercator* continued to slip as the search continued. The men not only resented being kept in the dark but were growing increasingly uneasy about the ship's obvious vulnerability.

In an unenviable attempt to reassure them (whilst having to withhold most of the information they needed) Maxwell made an early morning broadcast.

'I won't attempt to minimize the difficult position we are in, although I cannot tell you exactly why we are in it for security reasons. Sufficient to say that we have been conducting an investigation into subversive activity in the Antarctic and that we shall be continuing to do this in extremely low profile. This does not mean to say that the importance of our investigations is in any way diminished. I realize you have already experienced considerable provocation, and I must ask you to be alert at all times in the future. I shall try to keep you well briefed on what we are doing within the limits of the security regulations imposed upon us. That is all.'

As Maxwell put down the microphone, he turned to Forbes and said: 'What do they think I've got as a ship's company – robots?'

'I know Dunhill would be very pleased if he discovered they were,' said Forbes.

Mercator's ship's company were in a sombre mood as they studied the sheer cliffs and cone-like profiles of Zavadowski, one of the more forbidding of the volcanic Sandwich Islands. Here the volcano was in constant eruption, and the stink of sulphurated hydrogen, combined with the smell of some nine million penguins, permeated every nook and cranny of the hull.

Maxwell, looking at the chart with Cunningham, commented with some amusement: 'They've certainly chosen some appropriate names.' He ran his finger over the main geographical features of Zavadowski. 'Stench point, Acrid Cove – '

'It's the main volcanic cone that's so well named, sir. Mount Asphyxia.' He shuddered slightly.

'You know – they used to call the old whaling station on South Georgia the gateway to hell,' said Maxwell. 'Now I think we've arrived at hell itself.'

Certainly the island seemed deeply sinister, with its all-embracing pungency and its black beaches. The still, brooding menace affected even the most unimaginative of men.

'It fair gives you the creeps,' said Dolly Grey, staring up at the dark cliffs and the beaches that teemed with chinstrap penguins and seals.

'It's a good pong,' said Taff Evans. 'Takes a bit of living with, that.'

'I can almost see them little devils, standing up there with horns, spittin' down at us.'

'Those aren't devils,' said Taff. 'That's the SAS, blacked up for Argie bashing.'

Grey drew his oilskin jacket more closely about him. 'There's nothing human up there,' he said.

'That's right,' replied Taff. 'I was talking about the SAS.'

Back on the bridge, Maxwell watched the silent peaks with apprehension. 'God – it gets you, doesn't it?'

'Yes,' said Cunningham, 'right in the guts, sir. It smells like that medicine the doc used to give out for diarrhoea.'

Maxwell laughed. 'One step on that shoreline and you'll get the shits anyway. I suggest we leave this to the aviators. Let's just do the necessary aerial photography, get the geologists out collecting soil samples, fix the position by satellite, and bugger off out of it.'

135

'Yes, sir,' said Cunningham, relieved.

The two Lynxes were launched, one for aerial photography and the other to take the senior hydrographer, known as (in the absence of any geologist) 'H Charge', Dick Cross, to collect his soil samples. Ogilvy, flying 983, the leading Lynx, with Crabtree as observer, climbed to one thousand feet and circled the volcano, staring down into the smoke-filled chasm surrounded by grey rocky outcrops towering above the snow-clad slopes. The stench made them feel desperately sick, so Ogilvy climbed to five thousand feet, but the smell was not much better. The cliffs and shores of the island were covered in guano, which was hardly distinguishable from the snow and ice, but as they were continuing to circle the island Ogilvy suddenly shouted:

'Dick, what's that thing down there?'

'Only a beacon. *The Antarctic Pilot* says there are a few beacons on the island.'

'Oh, well.' Ogilvy sounded bitterly disappointed. 'We got so used to looking for Russian installations on South Georgia that I thought we'd made another breakthrough. Bugger it!'

'Hang on.' Crabtree was staring down at the ground. 'Surely that structure's no ordinary beacon. It looks too new to have been put up by the *Discovery* in the thirties.'

Cross shrugged. 'Maybe you're right.'

The Lynx landed close to the beacon and they climbed out, scattering chinstrap penguins which stumbled over the rocks and ice in a frenzy, some on their stomachs and some waddling as fast as their stumpy little legs would carry them. But once the rotors had stopped they all closed in on the helicopter. Heads on one side, they gently tapped the wheels of the Lynx with their beaks until Crabtree climbed out and chased them away before they did some damage.

Ogilvy and Cross went over to the small lattice structure and examined it carefully. 'I'd say it was put up recently,' said Ogilvy. 'And it's got sockets for power supplies.'

'Why just a beacon?' Cross said, puzzled.

'I reckon they bring their own power supplies and then put up a satellite tracker on the top – similar to the one Browning and the old man found,' said Ogilvy. He turned and yelled at Crabtree, who was still trying to ward off penguins: 'Call up the ship, tell them what we've found and ask for some Greenies* to come over and check it out. I reckon there's a chain of these bastards all round the Southern Ocean, and I bet they're connected up to some sort of underwater detection unit system so that traffic can be monitored from a Soviet ship or even from Moscow.'

Then, just as Crabtree disappeared into the cab, Ogilvy called: 'On second thoughts, don't call up the ship on UHF in case that submarine's around. Let's fly back and report now.'

As the helicopter rose from the volcanic rock, all three men were ecstatic.

'The old man will be over the moon,' said Ogilvy. 'We've got his evidence now.'

But they were disappointed to find that Maxwell was by no means over the moon. To ease their sense of anticlimax he decided to tell them again how difficult his situation was, but when he saw how badly this was going down he added: 'What you've found only confirms my worst suspicions, but it won't necessarily change the MOD's mind. They feel very strongly that the Russians are setting up a monitoring system – not a way of blowing tankers to kingdom come. So we've *got* to find evidence of *that* before they'll take us seriously.'

Forty minutes later Ogilvy and Crabtree flew Cross and three electronics experts back to the island where they investigated the installation in minute detail, took numerous photographs and thoroughly searched the surrounding area. But nothing new was discovered. There was only the beacon.

When Maxwell was told the negative results he decided to buy some more time for the investigation by giving up some of the Life/Science work promised to the British Antarctic Survey base at Signy Island. He told Forbes to inform the ship's company that they would be calling in at Signy Island in a couple of days' time, to explain that future schedules were pressing and that the *Mercator* could only spare a short period for aerial photography of penguin colonies and seals.

* Electronic experts.

137

They arrived off Signy in the South Orkney Islands on 21 December and Maxwell went ashore to call on the Base Commander.

'You're just the man I want to see,' said Franks as Maxwell stepped out of the Lynx into the snow.

Surprised, Maxwell followed him back to his office, where tea and hot toast were produced. After some exasperating small talk and even more annoying tentative commiserations over past events, Franks finally came to the point.

'I'm getting really concerned about our relationship with the Argie Antarctic station on Laurie Island.' Franks paused, marshalling his thoughts, anxious to be concise. 'There's been a load of Russian fishing activity in the area recently which is pretty unusual. Obviously they'd found new grounds for krill and ice fish, but they were also frequently in communication with the Argentine stations at Laurie and Marambio on Seymour Island.'

'What were they talking about?' asked Maxwell.

'Medical advice or a supply of fresh water – small things really, but all this Argentine–Russian co-operation seems a bit worrying.' He looked at Maxwell, waiting for comment. Receiving no reply he went on: 'Since the war in 1982, we had been building quite a good rapport with the Argies, and we were even persuading them to do a bit of scientific research.'

'Don't they usually do research?' asked Maxwell mildly. He liked the Argentines and was irritated by Franks's racist approach.

'No, they use these bases as a military presence in what they consider to be Argentine Antarctica. They're all supposed to be scientific, in accordance with the Antarctic Treaty, but we know these stations are manned almost exclusively by the military as part of their sovereignty claim over this whole sector of Antarctica. We're used to it of course, but what worries me now is that I have the impression the Argies are getting over-friendly with the Russians.'

Maxwell suddenly realized that Franks was genuinely concerned and wondered if he should tell him about his suspicions. He hesitated – and then decided against it. Until we've got concrete proof, the fewer people who know the better, he thought. Particularly not someone as prejudiced as Franks. 'Look – I'd be most grateful if you would report anything else you find out to me – personally,' said Maxwell slowly. 'It's part of our function to keep abreast of any changes in the social climate here.'

'Sure, James. But what do you think? Do you get the impression things are hotting up in the South Atlantic?'

Maxwell looked at him enigmatically. 'The last thing I want is to give anyone the impression I'm an alarmist,' he said gently.

21 December 1989
1.45 p.m.
Montevideo

They met in the bar adjoining the central bus station in Montevideo. Gabriel felt drained and exhausted as he sat drinking. Opposite him, the other man looked rather like a down-at-heel travelling salesman in his badly cut suit and scuffed shoes. Later they took a bus to the beach and walked along the dirty white sand. The sea was an oily green and only a few boys played football in the sultry hour of the siesta.

'We have discovered there is to be American involvement,' he began.

'The oil?'

'That too. But they have other interests.'

'Yes?'

'Star wars.'

For a moment, Gabriel did not think he could be hearing correctly. He paused, kicking aside a plastic bottle. 'What?'

'There is a possibility the Americans are considering the Antarctic as a Bellisha Missile base. The South Atlantic would become a star wars control centre.'

'You mean the Western Alliance might set up a control centre for guided missiles?' Gabriel stared at him incredulously.

'A very complex system. And if anything went wrong – there

139

could be the gravest of consequences.'

'If anything went wrong,' said Gabriel quietly, 'it could melt the ice-cap. There would be a disaster – an incredible disaster.'

'Apart from that – which I grant you is a dire possibility – it would militarize South America. Uruguay and Argentina could become one big American base.'

Gabriel paused, watching the wavelets lap the dirty beach.

'You are finding it all a little hard to take in?'

Gabriel shrugged. 'I accept it as a possibility.'

'It's more than a possibility.'

'What am I to do? Is there alternative action I should be taking?'

'No. The campaign is to be continued. It must be made clear that the waters of the South Atlantic are dangerous.'

'That may deter the British. But if what you say is true, the Americans may have too much to lose to be deterred.'

'This has been taken into account.'

Gabriel looked up at the rumpled man. His face was puffy, unhealthy, and he wondered if he drank. Some Russians drink a lot – even those in vulnerable positions. 'I don't understand – '

'And I am here to enlighten you.' He put his arm round Gabriel's shoulder and steered him over to the rocky promontory that ran out to sea. They sat down on the dry, craggy surface and Gabriel watched the waves beating at the reef far out to sea. They set up a translucent spray, spiralling up to the cobalt sky. It was a splendid sight. 'Are you ready to test the sonar?'

'Yes.'

'After that you are going to be privileged – ' The man paused and looked out to sea. Then he said: 'You will be the first terrorist group to explode a thermal bomb.'

22 December 1989
6.00 a.m.
Off James Ross Island
It was a very dark Antarctic morning. The temperature was

140

minus 6° C and the *Mercator* pitched heavily from the wind on the starboard bow which was blowing Force 8 from the west.

Robertson, the Officer of the Watch, called Maxwell in his bunk. 'Captain, sir, Officer of the Watch.'

'Yes,' replied Maxwell, yawning.

'Sir, I have a large strip of pack ice on the radar at a range of eight and a half miles, and at the moment I can see little alternative but to plough through it.'

'Reduce speed to eight knots when we are two miles from the nearest edge of the ice,' snapped Maxwell. 'I'm coming up to the bridge.'

He turned over in his bunk and sat up. Maxwell had been called four times so far that night, and after each call he had plunged back into a deep exhausted sleep, until he was woken again by Robertson with fear in his voice. Sighing, Maxwell rolled out of his bunk, pulled his trousers over his pyjamas, lugged on an oiled sweater and climbed the ladder to the bridge.

'Where's this bloody ice?'

'You can just see it through the night vision aid, sir, but it's painting very clearly on radar and covers the whole horizon. I can't see any way round it.' He grew quieter towards the end of the sentence as if he doubted his assessment of the problem.

Maxwell took a careful look. 'Switch on the second ice light,' he said gently. 'You're right,' he said to Robertson. 'Well done.'

Robertson looked relieved and Maxwell felt momentarily impatient at his lack of confidence. Then he remembered that this was Robertson's first experience with pack ice. Patience, thought Maxwell, through gritted teeth.

Ten minutes later, the *Mercator* had reduced speed again to four knots and the pack ice seemed suddenly all around them. Maxwell stepped to the wing of the bridge and watched the fluorescent chunks of ice grinding down the starboard side. It was an extraordinary primeval scene, hauntingly beautiful yet terrifying. Most of the ship's company gathered on the upper deck to witness *Mercator*'s first encounter with the menacing beauty of the Antarctic. Maxwell watched them and was oddly touched; it was almost a shared mystical experience as they watched the rise and fall of the ice together.

Ogilvy came up to the bridge, looking apologetic. 'Mind if I have a squint from here, sir?'

'Be my guest,' said Maxwell, the spell broken.

'Here we go again, sir – just like it was in the *Endeavour*,' said Taff Evans, steering an erratic course through the pack.

'Good memories?' asked Maxwell.

'I loved it, sir – still do. Kind of gets me. Makes me think I'm on another planet.'

The *Mercator* shook as she jarred and jolted through the irregular chunks of ice.

'What's their density?' asked Forbes, yawning as he arrived blearily on the bridge.

'About seven tenths,' said Maxwell.

Robertson looked anxiously ahead through his infra-red vision enhancer and calculated there was just enough room for *Mercator* to push the ice away rather than breaking a path over the top as she was designed to do.

Maxwell turned to Robertson. 'There's a clear channel coming up. Are you confident of taking her through?'

'Yes, sir.' His voice was brisk.

'Right – I'm going back to bed. Is this your watch, Commander Forbes, or are you being over-zealous?'

'I can't sleep, sir.'

'You OK?'

'It's the ice – I can never sleep the first time we meet up with it.'

'Let's hope Shackleton's ghost approves of the new ship,' said Maxwell. 'I wouldn't like him to put a jinx on us.'

'No problem,' said Forbes. 'We've already got one.'

A few hours later a weary Maxwell broadcast again to the ship's company. Walking round the ship he had detected a heightening of morale and an uplifting of spirits among the men. It was as if the ice was what they had come for – as if they knew this was the *Mercator*'s real environment. So, despite his fatigue, Maxwell was able to deliver what he hoped was a more optimistic speech, untrammelled by the menace of the recent past.

'Gentlemen, we are scheduled to work in the James Ross Island area for ten days. We shall be carefully monitoring Argentine activity at their bases in Marambio, Petrel and Hope Bay. We shall also be transporting a small group of scientists from the Scott Polar Institute at Cambridge, who are doing a special study of the behaviour of large tabular icebergs.

'The area, as some of you may know, is not an easy one to approach as the passage from the north-east is blocked by an enormous iceberg which was originally seventy-five miles long . . .'

The iceberg was an incredible sight, shimmering opaquely in the sunlight.

'It's split into four main sections,' Maxwell told Cunningham who had not been to the ice before.

'It's amazing,' he said, staring ahead. 'That big part looks just like the white cliffs of Dover. How long do you think it is?'

'About twenty-five miles.'

The *Mercator* passed very close to the berg. 'You can see the light shade of green around the edge,' said Forbes.

'Always a sign of danger close to?'

As they passed under the lee of the berg, Sinclair stood with Ogilvy on deck, looking up at the towering white mass beside them. Penguins scattered as the *Mercator* cruised slowly past and snow petrels wheeled above them.

'That's about eighty metres high,' said Sinclair wonderingly. 'Bloody incredible.'

'There's about another three hundred metres under the water,' replied Ogilvy, watching the colours of the berg change from transparent light blue to deep sapphire, lit by the reflected light. Some parts of the great ice wall were completely smooth; in others there were deep cracks and occasionally they could make out a cavern. The silence, punctuated by the *Mercator*'s low throbbing engines, seemed to hang over them like a pall.

143

23 December 1989
12.30 p.m.
In Antarctic Sound
Next day, Maxwell returned from a reconnaissance trip with
Forbes and Carrington in one of the Lynxes. As they neared
the *Mercator*, Forbes said: 'Looks as if we've got visitors.'

A large trawler was anchored a few hundred yards from the
ship and a decrepit-looking motor boat was bouncing across a
heavy sea, heading towards the *Mercator*'s bows.

'Now, who the hell is that?' asked Maxwell irritably.

'I can't make out the name of the trawler, sir,' said Carrington, leaning forward.

'Ah – wait a minute,' said Sinclair. 'It's the *San Juan*.'

'I have a Christmas present for you, Captain,' said Petrowski,
striding into Maxwell's cabin. He stepped aside and the Kingsleys came in. Both Lucinda and Miles were wearing paper hats
and false noses and were blowing streamers – much to the
horror of Lynch, who was standing just behind them, a glacial
smile pinned to his lips.

Maxwell jumped to his feet, not knowing how to react. A
feeling of near-panic seized him. To see her – in his ship. Immediately he felt completely vulnerable.

She removed her false nose and smiled at him. 'I hope this is
a pleasant surprise.'

'You're very welcome,' said Maxwell.

'We thought we'd have a break,' Miles Kingsley explained.
'The islands can get very claustrophobic.'

'Jan offered us a week on board the *San Juan*,' added
Lucinda. 'We're living in great luxury, pampered by everyone
– especially Jan.'

Petrowski made a vague, embracing gesture. 'They need a
holiday – I give them a holiday – and I give to you, as promised, some excellent Patagonian hake. Enough for all your
men. I left it in the galley.'

'Well – I'm glad you didn't bring it in here,' said Maxwell,
trying to smile reassuringly at Lynch's raised eyebrows.

'Although, I'm delighted to have it,' he added hurriedly. 'What will you drink?'

Gloomily, Lynch began to move at a funeral pace towards the drinks cupboard. Clearly he did not approve of such sudden frivolity.

Lunch was very difficult for Maxwell, but the other three seemed to be in a jovial enough mood – and there was not the slightest hint of uneasiness in Lucinda's behaviour. Only Maxwell felt the odd one out – the man on the edge. Despite the frantic activity of the last few days Maxwell had still been conscious of Lucinda's presence in the back of his mind. Now, her sudden arrival was painful in the extreme. Did she have *any* idea of what he was feeling? he wondered. But of course she didn't, he reasoned. Why should she? She probably didn't give a damn.

The meal seemed endless, yet Maxwell broke his usual rule by offering after-lunch brandy, thus prolonging the agony. Why am I doing this? he asked himself. But he knew. However painful it was – he didn't want her to go.

'I'm even learning how to trawl,' Miles was saying, but Maxwell wondered if Kingsley had any news for him. There seemed to be no way of getting him on his own.

'What are you learning, Lucinda?' asked Maxwell, forcing jocularity.

'To be a sea cook. Oh yes – I'm not being some lady of leisure. I'm going to help on deck too.'

'I will show them the beauties of the Antarctic,' said Petrowski theatrically. 'We're going to trawl between Clarence and Elephant Island.'

'That sounds promising,' said Maxwell.

'Why?' asked Lucinda. 'Are there plenty of fish there?'

'Plenty of ice. You should see some spectacular scenery.'

'You love the ice, don't you?' Petrowski said, speaking directly to Maxwell for the first time since the meal had begun. 'You're at home here.'

'You're right,' replied Maxwell softly. 'I do feel at home here. I sometimes think I belong here. If I wasn't so wedded to the stud,' he said, 'I'd come back and live in the Falklands.

145

Run a sheep station.' Wedded, thought Maxwell ironically. Well – that's how it is.

'I can't imagine you doing that,' said Lucinda.

'And you'll die here?' asked Jan laughing. He was far more relaxed in the *Mercator* than he had been in the Kingsleys' home. Perhaps he only relaxes in ships, thought Maxwell.

'Yes – I wouldn't mind.'

'P'raps you'll be buried next to Shackleton,' said Lucinda.

'I'm not important enough for that.'

'You will be,' she said decisively.

'There's a message for you in the communications office, sir,' said Lynch, coming in on Maxwell abruptly, only to find him sitting at his desk, his head in his hands. Seeing Lynch, he jerked upright.

'Don't you ever bloody knock?'

'I did, sir.'

'Well, can't you knock a little more loudly, then?'

'Yes, sir. Sorry, sir.'

Maxwell rose stiffly to his feet. As he passed Lynch he gave him a friendly punch in the chest. 'It's me who should be sorry. I should never drink brandy after lunch.'

Lynch gave him a look that said – I told you so. Unexpected guests with false noses and streamers are bound to play hell with your liver.

Carrington gave Maxwell the message with a grin. 'Your luncheon guests, sir.'

It read:

FROM HMS SAN JUAN
TO HMS MERCATOR
THANKS FOR A WONDERFUL LUNCH AND A HAPPY CHRISTMAS
TO THE MERCATOR AND ALL WHO SAIL IN HER
PETROWSKI AND LANDLUBBER CREW

Maxwell was conscious that all the operators in the communications office were amused, but it didn't worry him. For the first time in days he felt a lifting of his spirits.

'We'd better send a message back.'

Carrington took out his pad and licked a pencil. 'Yes, sir?'

'Well – how about: THANKS FOR THE FISH – er – AND A HAPPY CHRISTMAS TO YOU ALL. That seems about right.'

Carrington went across to the radio and began to call up the *San Juan*, whilst Maxwell gloomily returned to the bridge. Dear God – how much he wanted her. Now.

24 December 1989

11.15 a.m.

Antarctic Sound

Maxwell had been warned about the fast currents through the Fridtjor Sound – the narrow gap between the Tabarin Peninsula and Anderson Island – but he had not expected the number of large icebergs that were either aground or jammed into the coast on either side. As a result, he decided to launch one of the Lynx helicopters for an ice reconnaissance mission.

It was mid-morning with a fresh breeze from the west, some snow showers and temperatures of about minus 4°C. The southern end of the Sound was enveloped in pack ice but the *Mercator* pushed her way through with ease, negotiating the first of the three large tabular bergs which almost blocked the entrance.

Ogilvy in the Lynx radioed in: 'There's a gap not much wider than the ship herself between the second and third bergs in the channel.'

'Is it possible?'

'Yes, sir – just a bit of a delicate manoeuvre.'

'I'm sure we're capable of that, Giles. Thank you. Out.'

Maxwell edged the *Mercator* up to the ominous gap between the towering bergs. The passage was so narrow that it looked almost impossible, and as the *Mercator* closed Maxwell could hear the bubbling, cracking noise that the bergs made as the ice expanded and contracted. The wind, glancing off the blueywhite surface, made an intense whistling sound and he could see it funnelling down on the water between the bergs, creating an eddying pattern that looked hostile, uninviting.

Then Forbes spotted a small iceberg bobbing up and down malevolently in the swell just short of the gap. Cunningham set a course to pass the ice very close to port, but as the bow of the *Mercator* came level Maxwell said calmly:

'You're going to nudge that.'

'Sorry, sir.'

The result of Cunningham's error swiftly became dramatic as the bow suddenly came off line. Maxwell hypnotically watched his navigator driving the *Mercator* towards the wall of a vast iceberg at a speed of five knots.

'Port thirty, stop port,' Maxwell ordered rapidly, but there was little reaction from the ship for the fast current running between the bergs was pushing the bow of the ship hard over to starboard. 'Full astern,' said Maxwell, the sweat beginning to run down his back, whilst Cunningham stood, gazing ahead, already visualizing his court martial. Pipes shrilled and Maxwell's voice was sharp as he ordered: 'Stand for collision for'd, assume NBCD state 1, condition Zulu.' Rapidly all watertight doors and hatches were closed and repair parties were on standby.

The entire ship's company braced themselves for the impact. Maxwell glanced at the wheel. It was hard over to port, but the swing had still not been checked as the current on the port bow was too strong. Then the bow swung aggressively to starboard.

'Midships,' ordered Maxwell sharply. 'Starboard thirty.'

Taff Evans, who was today's quartermaster, thought: Christ! The old man's gone barmy. He's finally cracked. We'll never get out of this one. He's going to swing us right into the fucking berg.

The Olympus engines roared into sixty per cent, seventy, eighty, full power, and then the way on the eleven thousand, nine hundred ton *Mercator* started to check. She was still a hundred and fifty yards from the berg, but it looked one hell of a lot closer, and she was still moving towards it at four knots.

Maxwell was very calm. He turned to Forbes and said quietly: 'Take every precaution for'd, Nick. We're not out of trouble yet.'

As he spoke the *Mercator* cannoned off a small flat piece of ice, which fortunately accentuated the swing to starboard. Now if they *were* going to hit at least it would not be head-on. But Maxwell was all too well aware that considerable damage could still be done. The engines continued to roar but the ship's way was checked and he felt some of the tension in his stomach relax. It was one of those situations where he had done all he could, and now in the few seconds remaining he just had to wait for the outcome. The suspense was agonizing. Closer and closer the *Mercator* came to the towering berg, with the seconds seeming like eternity. But nevertheless, with each second the way was coming off the ship.

Cunningham was standing beside Maxwell and Forbes, willing the ship to stop. Maxwell could hear him praying aloud:

'Please God no. Not this time. Please God no.'

Slowly the engines were winning. 'I think we're going to be all right, sir,' said Cunningham shakily.

'I don't,' retorted Maxwell curtly.

Seconds later the port bow hit the berg with a resounding crack and a deafening scraping noise. Most of the company were jarred off their feet and Maxwell watched sailors agitatedly running along the upper deck to the port side of the fo'c'sle to investigate the damage. Fortunately, the berg was slab-sided and there were no protrusions, but it towered above the ship menacingly, making the *Mercator* look like a toy boat in a bathtub. Ice split off the berg all over the forward part of the ship, but gradually the gap between the *Mercator* and the berg widened as the ship drew away. Now she was beginning to gather sternway and it was possible to survey the full extent of the damage.

Forbes went to investigate below decks with the For'd Fire and Repair Party, while Chief Petty Officer Brown, the Chief Bosun's Mate, and Chief Shipwright Crabb assessed the upper deck for damage above the water line. Beyond a few dented plates, they fortunately found little to report.

'It's all experience,' Maxwell told a still very agitated Cunningham. 'Even mistakes. Particularly making mistakes.'

149

Maxwell then stopped the engines, took the ship and went slowly ahead in a broad sweep to make another attempt at negotiating the narrow passage.

Forty-five minutes later, the *Mercator* slid through the gap between the bergs into the strange magic of a narrow Antarctic passage.

Large bergs were crowded against the banks of the shore at irregular intervals. Some of them were over fifty metres high, and many were deeply eroded at sea-level into a remarkable variety of shapes. These frozen relics of the last five thousand years gave the ship's company a sense of the supernatural. Like massive lumps of plaster of Paris wrought into unearthly shapes, with layered forms and eerily flat tops, the bergs were utterly still – resembling extra-terrestrial worlds. A few old glacier bergs had strayed into the Strait, and they had an opaque flat white colour containing soft hues of green and blue – or occasionally dazzling white, depending on the angle of the sunlight. Forbes even noticed one small black berg, looking dangerously like a rock, its colour caused by the mixture of moraine, stones and debris within the ice.

This sinister fairyland had the ship's company on the upper deck running off yards of film, whilst the *Mercator* pushed huge lumps of pack ice to one side, making an extraordinary sound – rather like the grinding of some giant's teeth.

Eventually, the *Mercator* emerged clear of the ice into the gloomy dark weather of the Antarctic Sound, where the sun seldom shines and the weather changes with dramatic, elusive speed. Rounding the coast of the Trinity Peninsula, the ship anchored in Hope Bay, off the Argentine base Esperanza.

They were safe, thought Maxwell. Then he laughed aloud, startling Forbes.

'What's up, sir?'

'I was just thinking – we seem to have staved off natural danger. If only our real enemy was the ice.'

Forbes nodded. For the first time he looked drained.

2.15 p.m.
Antarctic Sound
'They're magnificent,' said Lucinda, watching the icebergs. 'I could never get tired of them. Each one seems like a world of its own.'

She and Miles were on the bridge of the *San Juan* with Jan Petrowski.

'No wonder Captain Maxwell loves the ice,' said Miles suddenly. 'It must be like a refuge.'

'Does he need a refuge?' Lucinda's voice had a slight edge.

'Oh – I should think so. He strikes me as a rather lonely man. Wife far away running a stud farm in the home country. An attempt made on his life. Two of his senior officers missing. Under pressure from the MOD. Oh, yes – he's a lonely man all right.'

Petrowski cleared his throat, conscious of the unexpected sneer in Miles's voice. Had he had too much brandy? he wondered. Or was he simply up against his own suspicions? Lucinda was not taking it well and her tone was even sharper when she replied:

'Don't be absurd, Miles. James is surrounded by people. Isn't he, Jan?'

'Oh, yes. But you can be lonely amongst people, too. Besides, the Royal Naval Captain – he's an isolated figure. He has to be invited into the ward-room, you know.'

'And I'm sure he's invited many times,' she said warmly.

'Yes,' said Miles. 'I'm sure he accepts every invitation. Some more than others.'

There was a very long, very tense silence, during which Petrowski wondered if matrimonial problems were about to explode on the bridge of the *San Juan*. They were forestalled by a call from the radio room. 'Sir – we're getting some rather strange-sounding readings.'

'Strange?'

'We're unable to make them out.'

'Don't be a fool.'

'I'm sorry, sir. It's very erratic.'

'Then work on it.' He slammed down the receiver. 'They

151

ring me for such trifles.' Petrowski took a covert glance at the stony faces of Miles and Lucinda. So Maxwell had not been able to resist the temptation. He had wondered. It was a temptation he had found difficulty in resisting himself.

Petrowski looked ahead at the windless sea with its scattered grey-green bergs and the troops of penguins, ranged in sober, enigmatic ranks. 'I must go below and sort those idiots out,' he said abruptly.

A few minutes after he had disappeared Miles Kingsley's expression softened as he saw the seal cubs basking on the ice floe and he involuntarily put his hand round his wife's waist.

A shudder ran through the trawler before the explosion came, right up the decks to the bridge. As the massive heat seared them, Lucinda Kingsley saw her husband's puzzled expression, a cigarette half-way to his lips. He was staring at it bemusedly as the flames leapt towards them.

3.00 p.m.
'Yes?'
'There's a mayday call, sir.'
Maxwell was in his cabin writing a letter to his son when Forbes interrupted him on the intercom. It lay before him now:

> Dear Robin,
>   I suppose you'll have opened my present (silly question) and found it to be the right micro-computer. I know how –

'Identified?' he snapped.
'Yes, sir. I'm afraid it's the *San Juan*.'
'Holy shit!'

7.00 p.m.
Lucinda had no idea how long she had been in the rubber dinghy – nor who had put her there. She felt numb, her body

152

weightless, as she lay staring up at the dark canvas above her with its pinpricks of stars. Suddenly, she realized it was night and that something had happened. But what? All she could remember was the heat. She moved and looked at her hands. They were black and for a moment she felt irritated. How had they got so dirty? Then she noticed that it was not so much dirt, but an ingrained something or other that she could not make out. It was all too much of an effort to worry about and she lay on her back again, looking up at the stars. She felt soothed by their brilliance and relaxed by the slapping of the swell against the rubber sides of the dinghy.

Letting her mind wander, Lucinda thought of James Maxwell – and the way they had made love. Even if they had been very drunk, she had never found anyone to excite her as much as he had. He had been clumsy, not very gentle, almost gauche, but that was the way she had liked it – the way she had wanted it. Even now, she could feel him again and she felt desire – an urgent desire that made her tense and conscious of pain in her hands and legs. So sharp was it that she cried out his name – again and again into the cold vastness of the Antarctic night.

'She must have gone down immediately, sir,' said Ogilvy as the Sea King swooped over the black water, its searchlights picking up a motley flotsam of pathetic debris – beer cans, clothing, food, papers, books, spars, table tennis bats and other unidentifiable objects that bobbed hopelessly in the increasingly heavy swell.

The *Mercator* had arrived on the scene ninety minutes after the *San Juan*'s mayday call and had picked up twelve survivors from a probable crew complement of twenty-eight. But of Petrowski and the Kingsleys there had been no sign. Now, for some four hours the Sea King and both Lynx helicopters had been sweeping the area for more survivors – but there was no trace of anyone on the water.

'They had a few minutes,' replied Maxwell. 'But most of them would have been blown to hell.'

'What do you think it was, sir?'

'I *know* what it was,' said Maxwell grimly, 'although I doubt if we can prove it.' He felt empty, devoid of any emotion but rage. And that burnt fiercely.

8.30 p.m.

The pain kept coming and going in great waves and Lucinda, who had not had children, wondered if this was like the drawing pain of childbirth. In between bouts, she rested and saw James's face. It was comforting and helped her withstand the agony. She was still unaware of what had happened – it was as if a part of her mind had closed up.

She did not hear the roar of the helicopter above her – it seemed to blend in with the sound of the sea that had become her world. The spotlight hit her, flooding the dinghy with sharp, pale light. She looked up at the metallic belly above her and, frightened of something she could not understand or recognize, began to cry out in a high keening wail, like a child seeing a menacing crack on the ceiling of a darkened bedroom.

The Sea King hovered over the dinghy, the spotlight picking out the blackened figure inside. A crewman was winched down and directly he was in the violently bobbing craft he began gently to wrap a blanket and a hawser around the survivor. Then he signalled the helicopter pilot and the winch bore the pathetic bundle aloft. A few minutes later, the Sea King landed back on the *Mercator*'s deck and the survivor was rushed to the sickbay.

'It's a woman, sir – badly burnt,' said the MO.

Maxwell bent over the bundle of charred flesh.

'She's breathing, just.'

'Yes,' said Maxwell.

'Any idea who she might be, sir?'

'She's from the *San Juan*. Her name's Lucinda Kingsley.'

25 December 1989

Julia Mendoza wandered along the rocky beach of Sparrow

154

Cove, mingling with the penguins and the elephant seals. The former accepted her completely but the latter gave her baleful stares and made trumpeting, belching sounds while their young floundered around them, so she kept her distance. It was cold and the wind tore at her as she picked her way over the slimy boulders.

She wanted to spend the day on her own but had phoned the Gilletts who had invited her to dinner that evening. Diana told her about the *San Juan*. She had been in tears.

'The Kingsleys were such *good* people. We'd been friends ever since we arrived. And poor dear Jan – he was a marvellous character.'

'But she'll live? This Lucinda.'

'Who knows? They've flown her to a special unit in BA. She's very bad – the burns. Apparently – '

'Do you really want me to come tonight?'

'Oh, yes please. Dear Julia. You must come.'

She had agreed but Diana had seemed reluctant to ring off. 'These awful terrorists,' she had said. 'I know it's these Ola Roja people. But Bernard says there's no evidence so far. That's the devil of it.'

Julia gazed out to the grey-green anger of the lashing South Atlantic and wondered how long she could bear it.

On board the *Sante Fe* Morales found Gabriel in his cabin. He had his head in his hands.

'Why don't you join us? There's going to be some drinks to-night.'

'I'm busy.'

'You should be celebrating. The system has been fully tested – now we're ready for the tankers.'

'There's still the problem of the *Mercator*,' replied Gabriel.

Is he up to all this? wondered Morales suddenly. He looked particularly old tonight. Why had he been recalled to Monte-video? Was he going to be relieved of his post?

As if reading his thoughts, Gabriel said: 'Go back and get drunk. I have planning to do.'

'There's something wrong.'

'No.'

'Will you talk to me?'

Gabriel looked up at him impatiently. 'Oh, yes,' he said, 'I'll talk to you. But this is the wrong time.'

7 – Change of heart

26 December 1989
9.00 a.m.
Antarctic Sound

> FROM HMS MERCATOR TO WHITEHALL
> 261032 Z DEC
> CONFIDENTIAL EXCLUSIVE
> AS A RESULT OF THE SAN JUAN ATTACK MY EARLIER
> SUSPICIONS CONFIRMED. INTEND TO PLACE SHIP ON WAR
> FOOTING UNTIL FURTHER NOTICE. MEANWHILE WE
> CONTINUE SEARCH FOR SURVIVORS.

'That's what's called taking the initiative,' Maxwell told Forbes.

'Give 'em hell, sir. They deserve it. I've just heard from BA. Mrs Kingsley's still alive but her burns are very serious and it'll be a long job. The Argentine Navy are thinking of calling off the search.'

Maxwell stared through the bridge window into the thick fog that had descended suddenly, a quarter of an hour ago. He shrugged. 'They're right. We're not going to find anyone now. I'm going to give it another couple of hours – and then head back to Stanley.' At least she was alive, he thought. But would she ever really recover? All he could feel was anger – a deep, hard anger, that felt like an immovable object in his guts. Like Gabriel, Maxwell wanted revenge – and he didn't care how long it took him to get it.

Maxwell slapped the MOD signal down on Gillett's desk.

FROM MOD NAVY TO HMS MERCATOR
YOUR 261032 Z DEC
CONFIDENTIAL EXCLUSIVE
CONSIDER SAN JUAN INCIDENT IS EITHER ACCIDENTAL
EXPLOSION OR ISOLATED OLA ROJA TERRORIST INCIDENT.
ARGENTINA NOW INVESTIGATING. YOUR SUSPICIONS
NOTED, BUT CONSIDER YOU MAY BE OVER-REACTING. DO
NOT PLACE MERCATOR ON WAR FOOTING. RETURN TO LOW
PROFILE INVESTIGATION.

'Damn,' said Gillett inadequately.

'They're blind,' raged Maxwell. 'What else do they want? It'll be a tanker next.'

Gillett's face was expressionless. 'Of course, Jan was never careful about maintenance – '

'Come on,' said Maxwell, 'you know damn well they were blown out of the water.'

'But why should anyone want to blow up a trawler?'

'Dummy run – for me.'

Gillett looked at him unbelievingly and Maxwell felt a lurch of indecision. Then his confidence returned.

'We're becoming a nuisance,' he said, 'an expendable nuisance.'

Gillett frowned. 'I'm not disbelieving you, James.'

'You are, but it's quite understandable. You probably think I'm paranoid.'

'Lucinda and Miles.' Gillett's voice broke. 'And Jan. They were my friends.'

'They were beginning to be mine,' returned Maxwell.

She was on the side of the iceberg, dressed in jeans and an anorak, casually watching the *Mercator* slide past. Penguins cavorted about her and sea-birds gathered on a ledge above her head, watching, watching, with little black eyes, hard nuggets of hatred. He stood on the bridge. 'Happy New Year,' she said as the ship steamed past. 'Good luck to all who sail in her.'

Then, behind him, he saw the *San Juan* – a coffin ship, painted black, draped in black with black funeral ponies champing in the stern. Petrowski was on the bridge, a scythe in his hand. 'No,' said Maxwell, as she jumped from the berg on to the prow of the *San Juan*. 'No.' But she didn't seem to hear – not to hear at all. Then, with terrifying speed, the *Mercator* slipped over an oily sea, leaving the *San Juan* a speck on the moonlit ocean. The bergs were closing in, the penguins were dancing, the sea-birds were diving. There was a bang. And the ocean was empty. Maxwell woke screaming.

29 December 1989
8.00 a.m.
Off Port Stanley
Lynch brought him coffee with brandy.

'Are you all right now, sir?' He was all concern, his hand shaking slightly as he passed Maxwell the cup.

'Rotten dream.'

'You've had a bad shock, sir.'

'Any more news from BA?'

'Yes, sir – two more of the crew dead. But Mrs Kingsley – they say she's going to come through. They're flying her to England – special place there.'

Maxwell lay back in his bunk, feeling as if he hadn't slept at all. 'Any other news?'

'No, sir.'

'Where's Commander Forbes?'

'Gone ashore, sir. Said he wanted fresh air.'

9.15 a.m.
Port Stanley
Julia Mendoza drove the Land Rover at a furious pace over the humps and pot-holes down to the government jetty at Port Stanley. A combination of rain and wind was blowing great gusts of water over the windscreen and buffeting the vehicle with considerable violence. Nevertheless, she continued to

159

drive at speed until she screeched to a halt at the jetty.

'Commander Forbes.' He was coming out of the harbour-master's office and looked up, bewildered.

'Julia Mendoza – what are you doing here?'

Thank God, she thought, I've caught up with him at last. She had spent hours watching the *Mercator* through binoculars, checking on who was coming ashore.

'I rented the Gilletts' cottage.'

'And their Land Rover?'

'They lent it to me.'

'You must be very persuasive.'

She shook her head impatiently. 'How long have you got?'

He looked at his watch. 'Couple of hours.'

'Why not come for a drive?'

The blustering wind and rain had abated to a misty drizzle as they stumbled over the wet tussock grass. They reached a small, sandy beach, strewn with mounds of kelp. To their right, a rocky point shot out a forbidding craggy finger into a tumultuous grey sea.

For a while they sat watching the waves break on the point, spray hurtling up into the still-gathering wind. Then they walked down to the water's edge to watch the penguins waddling about the rocks.

'Are you sailing tonight?' she asked.

'No – tomorrow.'

'Will your Captain Maxwell allow you to come ashore?'

'I should think so.'

'I thought shore leave was cancelled.'

'Not here. The Captain reckons Stanley's safe. And we can't keep an entire ship's company in mothballs. So, what have you in mind?'

'Dinner at my cottage,' she said.

Forbes returned her gaze steadily. 'I'd like that,' he replied. It was extraordinary – he had never experienced anything like this before. What was it about her that he found so compelling? But he knew before he had asked himself the question.

160

Julia Mendoza had built a fortress around herself and she was inviting him in.

As if in reply to his thoughts she said: 'I need the isolation here. I've never asked anyone to share it with me.'

'Then I'm privileged.'

She looked at him, smiling in a way that he had never seen. 'I don't think so,' she said.

That afternoon Forbes talked to his fellow officers in the wardroom. He knew that Maxwell had no objection to them knowing the full story, and he had asked him if he could put the latest developments to them. Maxwell had agreed, hoping that he could convince them they had been given all available information.

After Forbes had told the gathering that Whitehall were refusing to take their Captain seriously, there was a short, tense silence.

'I just can't see *why* they should take it all so lightly,' said Carrington.

'Perhaps they really *do* believe the old man is over-reacting,' said Crabtree.

'Maybe he is,' Sinclair put in.

'Why?' asked Forbes sharply, realizing too late how defensive he sounded.

'Well – his argument is that all these episodes are linked and there's a Commie plot against us.'

'It's not as crude as that,' replied Forbes.

'Isn't it? Let's look at each of the six incidents. The attempted assassination of the old man – they could have been running a vendetta against any British officers. The murder of Rosemary Dunhill? The same. Then the explosion – in the *Escuardo*. Oh, we found a few Russian documents. The oil rig ships, well, maybe it's possible that Arrowsmith and Lucas did go overboard. Then you find the old bomb in the shed – it could have been there for years. Finally, that old wreck of a Polish trawler goes up, which could have been any kind of technical fault. They don't necessarily all have to be linked.

After all, the Russians are everywhere, aren't they? Always stirring it up. It doesn't mean they're out to get us personally.'

'You know the Captain thinks the Soviets have got a plan to blow tankers out of the water with a satellite system which can't be detected. We've already found evidence of that,' said Forbes. 'Well, that's what *we* think it is. But Whitehall won't take it seriously. They say it's a monitoring system and the old man's over-reacting. And here we are, floundering about in the South Atlantic, neglecting our programme and chasing an enemy we can't see.'

'It would make the MOD a bit sceptical, wouldn't it?' said Sinclair.

'But there's obviously more to it than monitoring,' said Ogilvy, who had not spoken before. 'And we'd look pretty damn silly if we didn't investigate the possibility. I suppose what the MOD are saying is that the monitoring – as they'll have it – is nothing to do with either Ola Roja trying to stir it up between us and Argentina – or Argentina itself having a go and blaming Ola Roja. I mean – either way, we're under attack.'

'And the MOD reckon we're bringing it on ourselves. If we drop the investigation and go back to the programme – then we won't get bruised.'

'Maybe that's what we should do,' said Sinclair slowly.

Much the same arguments were put forward on the mess deck. Taff Evans was loud in his defence of the Captain, against ABs Mick Strang and Jimmy Allen, who felt they were being deliberately left in the dark.

'We can't break security,' Evans asserted, 'or every Argie or Commie bastard will suss out our next move. The more people who know, the quicker it spreads. You know what happens on every bloody run ashore – it's all mouth with certain people I could name.'

'Speak for yourself!' Allen was livid.

'It strikes me the Skipper's got a thing about the Commies,' said Strang. 'It's the reds under the beds scare all over again.'

Evans swung round on the mess deck in general. 'Why don't you bastards try thinking straight? There's something going on in the South Atlantic that bloody well stinks – and we're gonna sort it out. Not sit on our arses and do sweet fuck all like Whitehall.'

'The only problem there,' said Strang, 'is what're we gonna do if you're wrong and the Captain's wrong? We'll look right wallies.'

9.30 p.m.
Port Stanley

Forbes was horrified when she took off her sweater. The burns on her breasts had left great cavities in them, craters that were surrounded by wrinkled scar tissue, some of it livid, the rest fading into the normal dark colour of her skin. The remainder of her body was firm and lithe, but her breasts were horrendous. Try as he might, Forbes could not take his eyes away from them.

'There's no reason why you shouldn't know, I suppose.' Her voice was very calm, controlled, making Forbes feel cruelly insensitive.

'Look, I'm terribly sorry. There's absolutely no need to say anything. I'm such a – '

'You've seen my breasts. You need an explanation.'

'I don't *need* one.'

'You're going to get it all the same.' She smiled at him. 'Ten years ago I was a journalist in Uruguay. The Government didn't like what I wrote and I became a political prisoner. They tortured me until I was released. That's all I've got to say – and I don't want to talk about it.'

'There's no need to. I'm just so very sorry.'

'Don't be. There are some things I'd like to tell you – things that happened when I was a child.'

'Why do you want to tell me?'

Julia paused for a long time. Then she said: 'Because I think I could love you.' Before he could interrupt, she rushed on: 'I was born in a shanty town near Solis – that's not very far from Montevideo.'

'So you're Uruguayan.'

'Not entirely – my mother was Uruguayan and my father

163

was from the Argentine. They were very poor. My father was a labourer and she was a whore.'

Forbes was shattered. She certainly didn't give the impression that she had come from that kind of background. He tried to put his arm around her, but she pushed him away.

'Let me finish,' she said.

'I keep telling you, you don't have to – '

'I have started now,' she said brusquely. 'It was a filthy hole. I had no affection for it whatsoever – or for my parents. I was one of six but I haven't seen my brothers and sisters since we were children.' Julia's voice died away and then she continued more slowly. 'My uncle had some money and he would come round quite a lot. We never went to school and he would take us back to his house because he said he wanted to educate us. But instead he took us into his bed. If I didn't do as he said, he'd beat me.'

Forbes said nothing, wondering why she had decided to tell him all this.

'He screwed us. My uncle screwed us. The girls anyway – I'm not sure what he did to the boys. I was terrified of him. It was no use telling my parents. My father was a violent man and would only have said I was making it up. And I would have been beaten. So in the end I ran away.' Her voice was no longer controlled and the tears coursed her cheeks.

'Julia – '

'I don't make a habit of telling people this, you know,' she said, the pain in her voice making Forbes wince.

Forbes took her in his arms.

'I needn't have told you, I suppose. But I wanted to be honest with you.' There was a long silence and then she continued: 'I ran away and kept running until some nuns put me into a convent school for a while. It was so different from anything I'd been used to and I hated it, but it civilized me, I suppose. Soon after I left school I met this man. He was much older than me, quite wealthy. He bought me clothes and introduced me to people – so I married him. Then he died. Later, I married a Uruguayan journalist, Juarez. He was older than me again, but this time only by a few years. He was good to me and

164

introduced me into journalism.'

'What happened to Juarez?'

'I left him.'

'Why?'

'He wanted children.'

Forbes gazed at her uncomprehendingly.

'I wasn't prepared to have any.' Her voice was cold. 'I couldn't face the thought of confronting childhood again. To face the possibility of re-living all that.'

'But your children could have been happy. They had every chance.'

'I told you – I couldn't bear childhood. Anyone's.'

'And what has happened since then?'

'Oh – I have a lot of friends,' she said evasively.

They lay on their backs, staring up at the ceiling. Then she said: 'I love you, Nick.'

'And I love you, Julia. I really love you.'

She closed her eyes, hoping the lies she had told him were enough. Certainly, they should match the lies she had told everyone else.

30 December 1989

2.30 p.m.

Off Port Stanley

The next afternoon the *Mercator* sailed from Stanley *en route* to Punta Arenas to pick up scientific equipment. As she carved her way across the choppy seas north of Drake's Passage to the Magellan Strait, Maxwell knew he was being watched carefully by Argentine aircraft. Although she was destined for Punta Arenas, the *Mercator* had to pass through Argentine territorial waters and her every movement was monitored as a routine precaution.

Two days later she arrived off the Argentine coast at first light and was immediately overflown by a Mirage aircraft based at Rio Gallegos. This heightened the already electric atmosphere on board and Forbes reported the growing tension amongst both officers and ratings to Maxwell.

165

'They need something positive to happen,' he said.

'How about being blown up?' asked Maxwell. 'Would that help?'

Maxwell's responsibilities now weighed more heavily on him each day. Looking for evidence, expecting an attack, unsupported by his superiors – all combined to work him into an increasing state of tension. Forbes, on the other hand, felt an extraordinary sense of bewilderment. He had been so surprised – and flattered – after Julia had confided in him, had said she could love him – that he found it very difficult to analyse his own emotions. He was very drawn to her, he thought he loved her. But he didn't know, couldn't tell. Her ravaged breasts, her grisly background made him admire and respect her, yet Forbes felt himself on the edge of a precipice, pausing before the drop.

As the *Mercator* closed Dungeness Point at the extreme east of the Magellan Strait, Argentine military helicopters hung overhead until the British ship was safely into Chilean territorial waters and with Chilean airspace overhead.

A few hours later, the *Mercator* berthed alongside the main jetty at Punta Arenas. A Chilean officer of the guard greeted the ship, a small band played and a visitor for Maxwell was announced.

'Who is it?' asked Maxwell.

'Symons,' replied Forbes. 'British Embassy.'

'Perhaps he's come to relieve me of my command,' said Maxwell.

'My chance for glory,' said Forbes, unsuccessfully trying to lighten the atmosphere.

'Whitehall think I'm over-reacting,' Maxwell said, determined to be as frank as possible.

'Tell me about it.' Maxwell found Symons unexpectedly reassuring, but he suspected him of role-playing. So it was time for the Father Confessor, was it? So he could report back on how paranoid Maxwell had really become. Nevertheless, he told him the whole story, underlining the lack of credibility he felt he had with Whitehall.

Symons nodded briskly when Maxwell had finished. Strangely he did not seem in the least surprised. 'You could be right in your assumptions, Captain Maxwell. Whitehall may well have been persuaded that the situation is less serious than you and I believe.'

'Who by?'

'That's just what we don't know. But we *do* know a little more about Ola Roja. They're financed by the Soviets and made up of Cuban cells which have penetrated Argentina, Uruguay and Chile. But the current operation is being organized by someone who's inexperienced.'

'What do you think I should do?'

'I want you to carry on, accepting Whitehall's instructions without question.'

'But if you're right – if there is a mole in the MOD – then I shall simply be drawing Ola Roja's fire.'

'But this is what you thought all along, Captain Maxwell. What you've been doing, in fact.'

'Yes, but the MOD thought – thinks – differently. That took away the reality of it – to some extent.'

'You must have confidence in your own opinions.' Symons sounded even more schoolmasterly and despite himself Maxwell smiled.

'I am. But I'm also human – and when the MOD makes light of my warnings – ' He deliberately did not finish the sentence. 'Do I get any protection?' he added abruptly.

'We can have a SAS unit standing by.'

'Where?'

'Ascension.'

'Thanks for nothing,' said Maxwell bitterly.

Directly Symons left, Maxwell rang through for Forbes and asked him to come straight to his cabin. As he recounted the conversation Maxwell wondered just how much Miles Kingsley had influenced Symons – if he had at all.

'It vindicates you, sir,' Forbes said triumphantly when he had finished.

'No it doesn't, Nick. It simply means that MI6 feel there's

maybe something in what I'm saying. Just maybe.'

'But the mole? That's an interesting new theory.'

'It's a speculation – a possibility. What I'm worried about is we're on our own without any official back-up at all.'

'In other words, they could knock us out any time.'

'Oh yes – and we wouldn't stand a chance.'

'What about the ship's company? How much are you going to tell them?'

'As much as I bloody well can,' snapped Maxwell.

'If we can't tell the men,' said Forbes slowly, 'they'll be totally unprepared.'

'We can't tell them,' said Maxwell. 'But I'll be damned if I'll leave them unprepared.'

1 January 1990
9.30 p.m.
On the *Sante Fe* in the Antarctic Sound

'I gather your sister has befriended the Commander.'

Gabriel looked at Morales with hostility. 'She has slept with him, yes.'

They were dining alone. The food, as was the custom on board the *Santa Fe*, left a great deal to be desired, but for once the ship was not wallowing in a heavy sea and Gabriel had temporarily lost the nausea he had been fighting ever since he had come aboard.

There was a long uneasy silence during which Morales wondered exactly what was the relationship between Gabriel and his sister Julia. Superficially they seemed wedded to the cause. But what had it been like before the cause, before their imprisonment and torture?

'Of course,' said Gabriel impatiently, 'she has had no sexual relationships since she came out of prison. It will be very difficult for her.'

'Just what is she hoping to gain with Forbes?'

'A guide to Maxwell's thinking.'

'Is that all?'

'She wants to work,' said Gabriel. 'At the moment it's the

only way she can be of use.'

Perhaps this was a clue, thought Morales. His sister is an appendage, dependent on him to be part of the campaign. But why? Then he knew – or thought he knew. Julia Mendoza was a person who had lost everything – except Gabriel. She was no part of anybody – or anything – except him. And that, thought Morales, was her tragedy. 'Sleeping with Forbes could be absolutely useless,' he said, knowing he was goading Gabriel.

'That's very likely.'

'The cause is everything to her then?'

'She has nothing else.'

Morales cut at the tough veal and then gave up, pushing the food to the side of his plate and drinking more wine. 'We will be ready in six days for the first target.'

'We have to be certain of every detail. Our goal is ambitious – and we are inexperienced. Everything must be double-checked.'

'It is always,' replied Morales defensively, but Gabriel brushed his reassurances aside.

'So far we have made many mistakes. The system is perfect – it is us who are not. If we succeed we know we have Soviet backing for other operations. If we make any more mistakes – '

'You'll be relieved of command,' commented Morales, 'but with greater repercussions than if Captain Maxwell is relieved of his.'

'He will only lose his job,' agreed Gabriel.

'Is it time for you to talk to me?'

'Talk?'

'You have something to tell me. Something connected with your visit to Montevideo.'

Gabriel shook his head. 'Not yet.'

'But when? Why are you keeping me out of the picture?' Morales was becoming angry and Gabriel put a hand on his arm in attempted pacification.

'You must wait. But not for long.'

'But what am I waiting for?' he demanded.

'The submarine,' replied Gabriel quietly.

11.00 p.m.

Port Stanley

Julia Mendoza sat in front of a peat fire. The inside of the cottage was still and for once there was not a breath of wind outside. For the first time since she had arrived she felt at peace –
and this was because she had now made the decision.

Despite all she had been through in prison, and the long preparation she had shared with Gabriel, she was not ready –
and would never be ready – to be a part of his campaign of death. Hundreds of ordinary men and women were going to die, whether they were in the tankers, in the *Mercator* or in anything else that got in the way of the great, hopeless ideal that her brother had so determinedly embraced. What had happened already was bad enough. The list of the dead was already long and they had barely started.

She stood up, shivering despite the fact that the room was warm. By renouncing her part, she was renouncing Gabriel. She knew that. As Julia walked towards the telephone she wondered what her brother would do to her.

2 January 1990

3.00 p.m.

Punta Arenas

Maxwell had no notice of Peter Kenny's arrival by helicopter and therefore had little chance to prepare the ship. But Kenny quickly made it clear that he was not interested in ceremony.

'I wanted to come down here and see you, James. I know you're in a bit of a dilemma.'

'That's an understatement, sir. I take it you know about the MI6 visit?'

'Symons has seen me, too. What I'm saying is that if you don't continue a low profile investigation we're going to be in very great trouble. If we make *any* accusations based on so little evidence a really big incident could be sparked off between us and the Soviets. And that's something we just can't afford.'

'If I'm right,' said Maxwell, measuring his words and trying desperately not to show his anger, 'then we'll – possibly inconveniently – be blown right out of the water. I don't know how big an incident you consider that.'

'They wouldn't do it.' Kenny sounded confident.

'Why not?'

'Because of the repercussions. Come on, man – there'd be a second task force down here.'

'I doubt it. We couldn't run the risk of causing a third world war. I mean – getting the Argentines off the Falklands is one thing, taking on the Russians is another.'

There was a knock at the door and Maxwell looked up irritably as the Yeoman of Signals hesitantly appeared.

'I'm sorry to interrupt you, sir, but the Navigating Officer is ashore and we have a highly classified signal to decode. It's marked "Immediate", and as none of the officers cleared for this sort of traffic are on board I shall have to ask you to decode it personally.'

'All right, Yeoman,' said Maxwell, exasperated. 'Set up the machine for me and I'll come down right away.'

Leaving Lynch to serve Kenny with coffee, Maxwell hurried into the wireless office. A few minutes later he read the decoded message on the teleprinter.

FROM HM AMBASSADOR IN SANTIAGO, COPIED TO FCO, WHITEHALL, MOD.

1. MRS JULIA MENDOZA SUSPECTED PASSING INFORMATION TO OLA ROJA. SHE MAY HAVE ACCOMPLICES IN PUNTA ARENAS.

2. REQUEST YOU PASS ALL KNOWN INFORMATION OF MRS MENDOZA, TOGETHER WITH ANY KNOWN ASSOCIATES IN MONTEVIDEO, TO THIS EMBASSY SOONEST.

3. UNDERSTAND THIS LADY IS WELL KNOWN TO AT LEAST ONE OF YOUR OFFICERS. CONSIDER THIS LIAISON SHOULD BE ENCOURAGED WITH VIEW TO FINDING OUT NAMES OF OTHER MEMBERS OF HER CHAIN/CELL.

WINTERBOTHAM

Maxwell was considerably shaken as he hurried back to the

Ambassador, but Kenny was furiously angry. 'She's one of my secretaries,' he said, as if commenting on a social solecism. 'She's been with me for five years.' He hurried on, anxious not to let Maxwell speak. 'Still, that's what they said about Burgess and Maclean and Philby – and all the others. They knew them so well.'

'What are you going to do now, sir?' asked Maxwell.

'Get on to the MOD – and tell them that the British Ambassador feels they're making a mistake by undervaluing MI6 intelligence – as well as the constant warnings of the Captain of HMS *Mercator*.'

'Thank you, sir.'

When Kenny had left, Maxwell sat and thought about the sudden, dramatic turn of events. As he did so, his respect for Kenny grew. At least the man had the grace to admit when he was wrong.

'Sit down, Nick. I'm afraid I've got some bad news.'

'Not to do with my mother – '

'No – it's Julia Mendoza.'

Forbes stared at Maxwell incredulously.

'She's suspected of passing information to Ola Roja, although there's no firm proof as yet.' He tossed the signal from Santiago on to his cabin table and Forbes read it quickly. Then he threw it down.

'They've got it wrong.' He searched desperately for words but could find none.

'You can see that my instructions are that you should keep the relationship going as normally as possible, find out what you can about her friends. Obviously that will be difficult for you – ' Maxwell could see that Forbes's bewilderment had now become anger and, when he spoke, his voice was barely controlled.

'She occasionally mentions the names of British friends in Uruguay – mostly from the Embassy. Then of course there's the Gilletts. They even let her borrow their cottage. Perhaps they're under suspicion too?' Forbes spat out the words.

Maxwell continued: 'Thinking back, Nick, can you recall any associations these people may have with Aubrey Dunhill's wife?'

'Everybody in the diplomatic set knows the Dunhills,' said Forbes contemptuously. 'You know that as well as I do.' He lit a cigarette.

Maxwell tried another tack. 'Does Mrs Mendoza give you the impression that she has quite a lot of money?' he asked.

'Yes – she married into it.'

Maxwell poured Forbes a whisky. 'I'm really desperately sorry that you've been put in this situation, Nick.'

'So am I, sir.'

'But you must remember that however bad you feel you mustn't be tempted to discuss any of this with anyone else.'

Forbes nodded dully.

'It seems inhuman to ask such a thing, but I would be most grateful if you could continue your – friendship – with Julia Mendoza and not reveal that we have been tipped off that she is a suspect.'

Forbes glared at him venomously. 'As a naval officer I don't want to be involved in intrigue or international politics.'

'I accept your view entirely, Nick. Neither do I. But that's the situation, unfortunately.'

'I'm in a really filthy position, sir.'

'I know – but so is the *Mercator*.'

Forbes was silent. Then he said: 'There is one thing, sir.' His voice was expressionless. 'She has a friend in Buenos Aires called Abel Dumas.' He paused.

'Yes?' prompted Maxwell.

'He's a businessman of some kind – travels around South America. Point is – he spends a lot of time in Havana.'

'I see.'

'He's a close friend.'

'How did she come to mention him?'

'I asked her – if there was anyone else. She said, only him.'

'How close are they?'

Forbes stood up and his voice was very clipped as he said: 'I don't know – I'll try to find out.' He walked towards the door.

'Nick – '

'Yes, sir?'

'I'm very sorry.'

'So am I, sir.'

5 January 1990

10.00 a.m.

Off the Falklands

At 10.00 the *Mercator* arrived off Pembroke Point Light and started the short passage up through Port William towards Port Stanley. As the ship steamed briskly towards the anchorage, steamer ducks scattered before the icebreaking bow, penguins bobbed about on a nearby beach and some British soldiers on shore waved enthusiastically as the *Mercator* went past. Only the houses high above Stanley were in a position to view her entry, and as usual people were there with flags. It was at times like this that the weary Maxwell realized how important the *Mercator* was to the Falklands. Picking up the microphone, he addressed the ship's company:

'Captain speaking. As we make our approach to Stanley, please be on your guard at all times. We're doubling sentry duty on arrival, and I'm afraid I have to tell you that there will be no leave during this short visit. That is all.'

Maxwell turned to Forbes. 'That doesn't apply to you.'

'You want me to see Julia?'

'Please.'

Forbes turned away, his hands trembling as he picked up his cap. He felt completely indecisive. He still had the same compulsion for her – it had never diminished and he could not imagine it even beginning to falter. Yet here he was, about to put her under some kind of amateur surveillance. It was absurd, but horribly painful.

That evening, Julia Mendoza collected an inhibited Forbes from the jetty and drove him up to the cottage at Rocky Point. She had cooked a very hot lamb curry and they ate it by candlelight, accompanied by a Chilean red wine. Then they had a tinned Christmas pudding Forbes had miraculously found in

174

Punta Arenas.

They made love again after dinner but Forbes was unable to make it work. After a while they lay apart.

'I'm sorry.'

'What's the matter, Nick?'

'Nothing – I'm just under a lot of pressure.'

'I won't ask what.' The atmosphere between them was electric and Forbes felt inadequate and depressed.

'Nick.'

'Yes?' He looked hopeless, lying on his back, smoking.

'They say Ola Roja is not out to destroy the *Mercator* – but to discredit its Captain. Tell Maxwell to be careful.'

Forbes sat up, almost unable to believe what he had just heard. 'Where did you hear these rumours?' He was alert now, distrusting her, wishing that he didn't.

'On the grape-vine.'

'What grape-vine?'

'I can't tell you that – but you should take what I have told you seriously, and tell your Captain Maxwell.'

'Julia – what the *hell* are you talking about?'

'I want you to go now.' There was a dull finality in her voice as she got out of bed and began to put on her clothes.

'Where did you get all this information?'

'Will you please go?'

Forbes still lay on the bed.

'I shall be leaving Port Stanley tomorrow,' she said, rather pathetically.

'Where are you going?'

'Europe.'

Forbes sat up. 'Why?'

But she simply finished dressing without answering him. 'I don't want to see you again,' she said after a long silence.

Forbes said nothing and she went on talking, too quickly. 'I shall be leaving the job at the Embassy – I've been there too long.'

'And the rumours – these extraordinary rumours – '

'Please take them seriously.'

'Someone will want to know where you got hold of them.'

'Are you threatening me?' Suddenly she was bitterly on the defensive.

'I'm warning you.'

'I thought *I* was warning *you*,' she said, sitting on the edge of the bed to put on her shoes.

When Forbes returned to the *Mercator* and reported back to Maxwell, he was shaken and depressed by the extraordinary finality of it all, the unbelievable finality. It was as if Julia had been spirited away to another planet. But it was entirely of her own volition and a growing feeling of emptiness yawned inside him. Nevertheless he repeated what Julia had said, word for word, and then sat on the edge of the bunk, his head in his hands.

Maxwell, unable to bring him any comfort, said: 'I'll have to signal the MOD and tell them she's about to leave the country.'

Forbes looked up and his eyes met Maxwell's. 'I've been put into the shit of a position,' he said. 'I feel – I've never been involved in such a filthy business.'

But Maxwell was not sympathetic to his self-pity. 'Can't you understand – the lives of the whole ship's company are at stake. All you've done is your bloody duty.'

There was a moment of crackling confusion before Gabriel came on the air.

'Julia?'

'Gabriel – I must talk to you.'

The static returned and she lost his reply.

'I didn't hear that.'

'I said – is this a crisis? Over.'

'Yes. I want to get out.'

'Get out?'

'I've had enough – I can't do it any longer.' Her voice was shrill with fear and anxiety but his only response was to laugh. It came out like a sharp bark over the air-waves.

'You're tired – go and get some rest. Talk to me later.'

'Gabriel, please understand.' She was angry that he was not

176

taking her seriously.

'Listen, Julia – ' His voice took on a note of sudden, new urgency and she could hear that some of his former confidence had drained away. 'We can't talk over the air like this. I'll come ashore and – '

'No.' She was completely emphatic for she knew that if she saw him he would overrule her and make her stay with him – as he always had.

The static returned, and then cleared.

'What?' he asked. 'I didn't hear.' But she knew he was playing for time now.

'I said no. I don't want to meet you. I'm going to Europe.'

'What about your job?'

'I'm owed a holiday.'

'And then?'

'I shall write to Kenny.'

'Julia – this is absurd. Calm down. Think.'

'My mind's made up, Gabriel.'

'You realize they'll not let you do this.'

At last, she thought, almost in relief. It's come. Now I know where I am. 'I can't help that,' she said woodenly, as Gabriel was saying:

'I just want you to give yourself time. Think about your commitment to the struggle. Think about what they did to us.'

There was a pause, then he said very slowly, very angrily: 'Don't you realize how much is at stake?'

'I know how much there is at stake. That's why I can't take it any longer.'

FROM MERCATOR 051558 Z JAN
TO COMMANDER IN CHIEF FLEET
COPY: MOD
IMMEDIATE
SECRET
1. JULIA MENDOZA LEAVING EMBASSY FOR DESTINATION UNKNOWN.
2. SHE IMPLIES MERCATOR IS NEXT TARGET.
3. WHAT IS OUR NEXT COURSE OF ACTION?

A few hours later Maxwell received the most satisfactory response from his superiors he had received so far:

FROM COMMANDER IN CHIEF FLEET 052054 z JAN
TO MERCATOR
IMMEDIATE
SECRET
1. WE WILL PLACE MENDOZA UNDER SURVEILLANCE.
2. TAKE ON EXTRA CONTINGENT MARINES PORT STANLEY.
3. AIR COVER IS BEING IMMEDIATELY SUPPLIED.
4. CONTINUE ROUTINE TASKS AS PER PROGRAMME.

6 January 1990
10.00 a.m.
Maxwell read out the signal to his assembled officers in the ward-room with something akin to glee.

'We didn't get an apology,' he said. 'But the marines and air-cover are our real vindication.' His mood was infectious and, for the first time in days, Maxwell knew that his officers were behind him. But the tension was still there – and increasing. Ogilvy expressed it.

'With respect, sir, I don't see that additional marines and air-cover are going to help us much – not in a sophisticated mine-field.'

Maxwell shrugged. 'There's nothing anyone can do for us. We just have to proceed with caution.'

His officers looked back at him with expressions ranging from obvious apprehension to uneasy determination whilst his bleak phrase, 'There's nothing anyone can do for us', hung relentlessly in the air.

'What happens if we draw their fire?' asked Cunningham. 'We're blown to bits. Is anyone the wiser?'

'No,' said Maxwell. 'What we're going to do is to find the centre of operations. And bloody fast.'

'Under guise of "continue with routine tasks as per programme", sir?' asked Forbes.

178

'Exactly.'

'But what are we looking for?' Ogilvy was clearly frustrated and Maxwell could see the alarm in his eyes.

'We're looking for an island base – somewhere where the mines can be activated. I'm pretty certain we're not going to find it in coastal waters.'

'Then – '

'It's somewhere in the ice. And that's where our routine tasks are being carried out for as long as it takes.'

'Just one point, sir.' Ogilvy's voice was not entirely steady. 'Does the activation centre have to be an island?'

'What are you getting at?'

'Couldn't it be a ship?'

Maxwell was silent, considering. 'You mean – a ship like the *Santa Fe*?'

'Yes, sir.'

'It's been searched. And it's clean. The whole group was searched.'

'They may have other ships – '

'Whatever it is,' said Maxwell, 'we'll have to find it. Quickly.'

That morning, Maxwell broadcast a warning to the ship's company. He spoke frankly, trying to win the confidence of every man. 'Gentlemen, I must make it absolutely clear to you that I have been reliably informed the *Mercator* is now the number one target of the terrorist group, Ola Roja. We are to pick up an extra detachment of marines this afternoon from Port Stanley and the RAF are providing air cover. Nevertheless, none of this will prevent us being caused maximum damage by the sophisticated mine system I believe Ola Roja are operating. Therefore, our immediate objective, under guise of routine tasks, is to find the centre of those terrorist operations. My belief is that this centre is somewhere in the Antarctic Peninsula. We shall now go on to a war footing. Thank you for your support.'

Maxwell's speech was greeted with amazement by the majority of the company and, once they had recovered, considerable tension began to manifest itself, in different ways, within

179

each man. Taff Evans articulated everyone's fears when he said:

'Nice of the Captain to tell us – whatever support we get, nothing can stop our arses being blown in.'

7 January 1990
4.00 p.m.
Drake's Passage, east of Cape Horn

In previous Antarctic seasons, *Mercator*'s predecessor, HMS *Endeavour*, had been strictly limited to the northern extremity of the pack ice and to a time when there was no likelihood of her being crushed. But *Mercator* was an ice breaker and the seasonal limitations were nothing like as critical. Therefore she began to steam south, beginning a careful search, disguised as a routine work period, whilst the continuous droning of the overhead Nimrods heightened the tension. Much of the Antarctic 'routine tasks' work was hydrographic, which meant mounting two survey teams and considerable aerial photography on the western side of the Antarctic Peninsula. There were also a number of geological samples to be collected from outcrops of rock high above the Lemaire Channel, Paradise Bay and areas on the western side of the Peninsula, as well as other operations for the Life/Science Division of the British Antarctic Survey. The *Mercator* was plunging her way across Drake's Passage in a Force 9 gale from the south-west. Heading into a very large swell, she was pitching and rolling heavily and the forward part of the ship had already been placed out of bounds as the sea continuously crashed over the fo'c'sle. Meanwhile, sailors worked below decks, trying to prepare the new survey equipment, and maintain the aircraft and much of the associated electronic equipment – never easy at sea but rendered virtually impossible in the wilds of Drake's Passage. Luckily, these arduous tasks made them temporarily forget the real danger that was with them every hour. But directly the work was over, the tension returned, both on the mess decks and in the wardroom. It showed in all kinds of different ways: old friends would find previously tolerated mannerisms no longer

180

bearable; old enemies would find more excuse to argue. A fight had already broken out in the stokers' mess, the Chinese laundryman had been punched for burning a shirt and, in the wardroom, the helicopter pilots, observers and aircrew were exhausted by the flying hours that Maxwell insisted they put in despite the Nimrods continually circling overhead.

'I'm sorry, Giles,' he explained to Ogilvy. 'But you're our eyes. I've got to have you on patrol.' Maxwell knew that the helicopters were fulfilling a dual role: they were still his main defence against the underwater threat, but they were also the best kind of advance search party he could ever wish for.

The extra twenty-four marines he had taken on board at Port Stanley did little to ease the situation, for their presence over-crowded the living quarters and the fact that they were strangers increased the general tension.

'Ever felt you were a sitting duck?' asked Dolly Grey.

'I was in the Falklands War,' replied Evans, 'so I got used to it.'

'At least you could see the buggers coming,' put in Grey dourly. 'This way we haven't got a chance. They could get us any time. All we're doing is living for the day.'

'More like the minute,' said Taff Evans.

Chief Petty Officer Bruno Brown, the Chief Bosun's Mate, appeared on the bridge at 16.50, asking permission of Robert-son, the Officer of the Watch, to take five sailors out on to the upper deck, starboard side forward. His object was to secure the gangway which had broken away from stowage and was likely to be lost over the side.

'Very well,' said Lieutenant Robertson. 'Inform the Com-mander on your way down and make certain that the men are wearing life-jackets and are secured to a lifeline.'

'Of course, sir,' said Brown wearily, indicating that he would have had the initiative to think of these precautions without being reminded. The weather, if possible, was getting worse and Maxwell, who hated putting his men at any extra risk, would rather have lost the gangway. Suddenly he turned anxiously to Robertson and said:

'Alan, make sure those sailors keep clear of the upper deck

until you've turned the ship to the east and given the starboard side a lee from the sea and weather.'

The pipe shrilled out: 'Chief Bosun's Mate ring one.'

'Buffer,' said the OOW, 'I'm turning the ship to port to a course of zero-nine-zero to give you some shelter in case you have to hang someone over the side when securing that bloody gangway.'

'Aye, aye, sir,' said Brown.

Soon the *Mercator* had begun to swing to port and was being plummeted in a corkscrew motion, for by now the sea was on the starboard quarter, beginning to lift the stern of the ship and throw her forward.

Maxwell told the OOW to come further round to port until the sea was under the port quarter. 'I think zero-two-zero will be about right,' he added.

'Aye, aye, sir,' said Robertson.

Maxwell then ordered Brown to take his men out on to the sea-lashed upper deck, where minutes before green water had been rushing through the scuppers.

'Tug Wilson,' said Brown, 'we'll have to lower you over the side to recover the gangway securing bracket. It's broken adrift, so off you go. Take Shiner with you.'

'That platform at the top of the gangway is buckled already – must have taken some sea to do that!' observed Taff Evans.

'It would have taken the whole gangway as well if the chef hadn't heard it banging away by his pit,' said Brown.

Tug and Shiner were lowered carefully over the side with the sea boiling a few feet below them.

'Don't think I like this job,' said Shiner. 'Let's sort the bastard out and get back down the mess.'

'OK. You take this end of the bracket and pass it up to Taff.'

'He'll have to lash it in place – the securing hinge is buckled.'

'Taff,' shouted Tug above the wind, 'the fucking lifeline is going! It's chafing on the jagged edge of the gangway and we'll both be in the oggin' in a minute.'

Taff grabbed the inboard end of the lifeline and passed it over the side to Wilson.

'Get it round your waist.'

'My bloody hands are so cold, the fingers aren't working properly,' said Tug.

Suddenly there was a splitting sound and the lifeline parted. Shiner grabbed Tug and for a moment they were suspended below the gangway against the ship's side.

'I knew this bastard was a pension trap!'

'I think the Skipper did too,' said Shiner. 'At least he turned the ship round for us. We'll have to hang on while they lower another rope.'

Brown struggled to get another line over the side of the heaving ship. Eventually he managed to swing it underneath the still unsecured gangway where the two ratings were suspended.

'Just made it, lads!' he yelled. 'Secure the inboard end and then keep the slack in hand.'

Soon they were safe again but too cold to continue the work. Brown hoisted them up and over the side and lowered Able Seamen Dolly Grey and George Varey to take their places.

By this time, Forbes, who was already in a filthy mood, was impatient. 'What the bloody hell's going on, Buffer? We'll be back in South Georgia at this rate.'

'Sorry, sir, but we've had a bit of trouble with this job. It's not easy,' Brown protested and Forbes tried to control himself.

'I know – but try and get it secured as soon as possible. The Captain's getting worried,' Forbes said guiltily, in an attempt to cover up his bad temper.

George and Dolly worked quickly and efficiently and within ten minutes the gangway was firmly lashed back into its stowage and the two ratings recovered without further incident.

Maxwell ordered: 'Starboard twenty – midships steer zero-six-five, and the *Mercator* was heading once more for the Antarctic.

On the bridge Maxwell said discreetly to Forbes: 'Careful, Nick, you're pushing the men too far.'

'Sorry, sir,' he replied, gazing straight ahead into the worsening weather.

183

The gangway episode seemed to have put at least some of the ship's company into a more positive frame of mind and Maxwell realized that the challenge of physical activity – something they were all used to – was the welcome appearance of normality. They had battled against the sea – not something indefinable – and they had won. But Forbes remained aloof, efficient but uncommunicative, and Maxwell felt his own position, his own chain of command, becoming more and more isolated.

In an attempt to divert his men, Maxwell told Robertson to lay on an intensive programme of social activity and this he did, organizing games of tombola and miniature horse-racing with a generous nightly diet of films on closed circuit video. Gradually over the next fortnight tension de-escalated and a slightly calmer atmosphere began to spread throughout the *Mercator*. But the underlying fear remained.

On 19 January a number of icebergs were sighted off the starboard bow and Maxwell knew the mountains of the Antarctic Peninsula would soon be in sight.

The Yeoman of Signals looked through his binoculars and called Carrington. 'Officer of the Watch, sir: land on the starboard bow.'

Trinity Island was now fully visible and the snowy peaks of the Peninsula were easily definable in the cloudy distance. The *Mercator* altered course to port into the Gerlache Strait before negotiating the tricky waters to the south of Trinity Island.

Able Seaman Robens was at his Special Sea Duty Station, manning the precision depth recorder, and was making routine reports:

'One hundred and eighty metres shoaling rapidly,' he said.

'Report every half-minute and on reductions in depth by twenty metres,' said Carrington.

'Nonsense. Report continuously – this is going to be tricky,' interjected Maxwell brusquely.

'Aye, aye, sir. Ninety metres shoaling. Fifty metres shoaling.'

'Stop both engines,' said Maxwell.

184

'Fifteen metres steady.'

'Half astern both engines.'

'Thirteen metres steady,' said Robens.

The *Mercator* gathered sternway as the minimum depth remained at thirteen metres. Maxwell breathed a sigh of relief and altered course to starboard to take a longer, deeper route to the south of Trinity Island. The *Mercator* then made her precarious passage amid the pack ice and rocks just north of the Christiana Islands and into the Orleans Strait. After that the Palmer Coast with the Wright Ice Piedmont were clear to starboard and Cape Andrews lay ahead.

The pack ice was well dispersed and the weather looked moderately fine. Maxwell could see some killer whales playing amongst the ice floes, and penguins bobbed about in the bay. It was Antarctica at her majestic best, thought Maxwell, but how long would the peace last?

Survey parties were dispatched each day to complete the sounding runs of the inshore areas and two of the *Mercator*'s boats were used for this purpose. Sophisticatedly fitted out, the boats were able to do the same job as the ship herself. Three survey teams, two in the boats and one in the *Mercator*, then worked flat out from dawn to dusk, sounding and mapping the whole area.

While the surveyors were hard at work, Maxwell organized a special series of courses to follow the survey plan. Meanwhile, the helicopter crews were still strained to breaking point as they undertook aerial photography and ferried stores, food and equipment ashore, as well as continuing their main undercover operation – the search for the mining control station.

The remainder of the ship's company either worked in support or were landed in small groups. Led by Royal Marines with mountain-leadership experience, they took samples of rock and lichen and photographed the wildlife in an area that was virtually unexplored.

Maxwell found surveying one of the more tedious activities, particularly as it left him with too much time for introspection.

185

His sense of isolation increased, his relationship with Forbes remained arid, he wrote regularly to Susan – and he kept thinking of Lucinda. The latest news from England was that she was still very ill – but was slowly improving. Maxwell would watch the icebergs for hours at a time, staring into their translucent depths, seeing her again and again. Sometimes she was animated; other times still, watching him, meeting his eyes, never out of his mental sight.

28 January 1990
10.30 a.m.
Off Trinity Island, Antarctic Peninsula
The *Mercator* had now been surveying for over a week and Maxwell was pleased that an estimated ten-day job had been completed in only seven. The weather had been remarkable, the blizzards and gales mostly taking place at night.

Then, suddenly, routine was shattered again. Sinclair, piloting one of the Lynx helicopters, reported sighting a small camp of scientists in the vicinity of Detroit Plateau and Maxwell took immediate action, summoning Forbes to the bridge for a briefing.

'I want you to take a look.'

'I'd be delighted to.' For the first time in days Forbes looked purposeful.

'Launch 86,' said Robertson, the Officer of the Watch, having manoeuvred the *Mercator* to obtain maximum wind over deck.

The Sea King set a course of a hundred and twenty degrees and flew forty-five miles down the track to the area in question, but as bad weather was approaching Maxwell recalled it. By 12.00 hours conditions had cleared and the helicopter set off again.

When they arrived at the site, Forbes could see that it was composed of three separate encampments, all of which were crowded with a large number of insect-like personnel. As the Sea King circled the area Forbes saw that both Argentine and

186

Russian flags were evident and most of the men were wearing the orange jackets worn by the Argentine military in Antarctica. There was a mass of excavating equipment, a helicopter landing pad, numerous pipes, small lifting trucks, snow cats and skidoos.

Suddenly, there was a blast of air and the Sea King bounced about in its wake, shaking horribly, and for a moment Forbes wondered if it was going to break up.

'We're being shot at!'

'But we haven't been hit,' replied Sinclair, as he wrestled with the controls.

'Climb to height three thousand feet,' said Crabtree sharply, and the helicopter soared upwards and slowly began to stabilize. 'That was close,' he said.

'Too bloody close.'

'There's smoke coming from the side of the mountain.' Forbes was shivering and he suddenly realized what poor shape his nerves were in. He looked around him covertly, wondering if the others had noticed. But they were too preoccupied.

The smoke was clearing and Sinclair suddenly burst into relieved if slightly hysterical laughter. 'They're using explosives – blowing up the rock face. No one's shooting at us at all.'

But Forbes still found he could not control the trembling. With an effort he said: 'Let's go in and see what they're up to.'

As they clambered out of the Sea King, Forbes wondered what their reception was going to be. He did not have long to conjecture as an Argentine Wing Commander ducked under the rotors, grasped his hand in a determinedly friendly grip and greeted him in almost perfect English.

'Base Commander Gallo.' He was short, somewhere in his late thirties, with a warm, urbane manner. 'Welcome to Peron Base.'

After introductions and much handshaking, Gallo led the way to the accommodation block. 'How did you find us?' he asked *en route*, apparently delighted that the Royal Navy had dropped in and wishing they would do so every day.

'We were doing a survey,' said Forbes, wondering how lame

187

the explanation sounded, but Gallo seemed more interested in giving them all a lecture.

'As you can see, this is an Earth/Science experimental base, but with an emphasis on hydrocarbons,' he said crisply.

'How do you supply this base?' asked Crabtree, falling into line as the intelligent questioner.

'By heavy lift helicopter from Hope Bay or Marambio. Sometimes the Russians use a helicopter from one of their ships or bases,' he said in the same matter-of-fact tone.

'Have you found much oil or gas in the area?' Forbes sounded more like a nervous pupil.

'Limited so far, but it looks promising.'

Looking round him, Forbes was becoming increasingly aware that Peron Base had little or nothing to do with hydrocarbons. He had become familiar with the trappings of oil exploration and this looked very different. He could see a stream, for instance, that was clearly in constant use and there were a large number of perimeter pipes melting the snow. Forbes also noticed that quarrying machines were parked in a special enclosure and a few hundred yards away he was sure he could see an explosives pound.

'Do you find much in the way of hard rock minerals?' asked Crabtree as they arrived outside the accommodation block.

'No, we've not had much luck there.' Gallo opened the door and they walked into the steamy atmosphere of an inner office. 'Coffee?' he said. 'Or something stronger?'

They all asked for coffee, conscious of three other men in the cramped space, and for a while a halting conversation was held about Antarctic oil.

'If you find oil up here, isn't it going to be a bit of a problem piping it down the coast in these temperatures – and in this terrain?' asked Forbes.

'We've already found it,' said a man in what sounded to Forbes like a Russian accent. 'But not in great quantity. We are using this station for field work elsewhere.'

'I see,' said Forbes, wondering if he did and hoping the others were taking in more than he was.

'Who knows what we shall find here,' said the man. 'But as

long as it can be used by everyone we shall be well pleased.'

How generous, thought Forbes as he nodded and smiled. The hollow ring of this flat propagandist statement hovered uneasily in the air and Gallo's offer of a tour of the base was greeted with considerable relief. He began with the accommodation block, moving on to a sophisticated radio room, a meteorological laboratory and a recreation hut. Then he led them through the littered packing cases to a small hut. 'In this area we are using a number of chemicals on copper,' he lectured. 'The deposits of both lead and copper are quite large here, and so we are using Russian experience to carry out a variety of experiments. This is a course we are allowed to take within the terms of the Treaty, but if we had Russians openly helping us in Argentina, then the Western countries would come to all sorts of unpleasant conclusions.'

'Yes,' said Forbes, 'I expect they would.' Once they were in the laboratory Forbes realized that it could be Doctor Frankenstein's for all he knew about the scattered test tubes and pipes lying on the benches. He looked at his watch. 'We should be getting back.'

'I do hope your Captain will visit us,' said Gallo with great enthusiasm.

'Thank you,' said Forbes. 'I'll ask him.'

Once in the air everyone visibly relaxed and there was an air of near-hilarity as they joked about Gallo and his open-handed tour.

'What did you make of it?' Forbes asked Sinclair as Crabtree completed a rather over-long imitation of Peron's Russian visitors.

'God knows, sir,' said Sinclair. 'But I'm damned sure it's not within the Treaty. What I can't understand is why they're so bloody friendly. It's almost as if they're crying out to be investigated.'

'They're not exactly low-profile,' said Crabtree. 'It's a real little Moscow on Sea.'

'There is one possibility,' said Forbes slowly.

'What's that, sir?'

'It's a pretty crazy notion, but it did cross my mind that they might be mining uranium.'

Back on the bridge of the *Mercator*, Forbes further explored his crazy notion with Maxwell.

'It's a possibility one can't ignore.'

'But it's a remote one, isn't it, sir?' Forbes was almost alarmed to see how seriously Maxwell was taking him.

'I can't be certain, of course. But if I took Cooke with me he might be able to give us a more positive answer.'

'Do you think you should go, sir – in the circumstances?'

'It would look almighty suspicious if you went back – and I've got the invitation.'

'It's damned risky – it could be a set-up. Can't you send someone else?'

Maxwell shook his head. 'Cooke's a bloody good scientist and if they're all concentrating on the Royal Navy Captain he'll have more of a chance of a productive look-see. I can be very overbearing when I try.'

Before he went, Maxwell sent a signal to his Commander in Chief at Northwood:

FROM MERCATOR 290955 Z JAN
TO COMMANDER IN CHIEF FLEET
IMMEDIATE
SECRET
1. DURING ROUTINE HELICOPTER PATROL AN ARGENTINE BASE WAS DISCOVERED CALLED PERON IN POSITION 64° 10′ SOUTH 59° 45′ WEST.
2. BASE WAS VISITED AND ESTABLISHED AS CENTRE FOR ARGENTINE AND SOVIET GEOLOGICAL FIELD WORK.
3. FIELD WORK MOSTLY CONCERNED WITH EARTH EXCAVATION.
4. NORMAL SUPPLY ROUTE ARGENTINA (USHUAIA) – MARAMBIO – PERON.
5. CAUSE FOR CONCERN IF THIS BASE NOT OFFICIALLY

DECLARED TO ANTARCTIC TREATY COUNTRIES.
6. WRITTEN REPORT FOLLOWS.

The Yeoman took the signal down for transmission and when he had gone, Forbes said. 'If the Russians have found uranium couldn't they handle it much more secretly and easily if the South Atlantic was in chaos?'

'Yes,' said Maxwell. 'You're damn right they could. The ground mines could be used to produce a hostile situation – particularly if Argentina is in on it.'

'Then why the hell did Gallo take us round so easily?'

'There could be one reason,' said Maxwell. 'They want me.'

'Then you mustn't go.'

'Oh, yes,' said Maxwell. 'It's about time I drew their fire – instead of setting up the whole ship's company for it.'

10.00 a.m.

As the Sea King flew back towards Peron Base, Maxwell tried to squeeze as much information as he could out of Cooke. The process proved to be more fruitful than he had imagined.

'What exactly are we looking for?' asked Maxwell.

'It's not easy to spot, sir,' said Cooke, who was in his twenties, dark, with a beard and a precise, convincing personality. 'All sediments contain trace elements. They're not necessarily present as distinct minerals but they're found in small quantities in the spectrum of common minerals. These trace elements include strontium, vanadium – and uranium. Now, I expect they've found lead and copper, but suppose they had found uranium too.'

'What would they do if they had?'

'Pack if off to Russia, to see what kind of uranium it was – 235, 238 or 239.'

'Why can't they determine it here?'

'All uranium atoms behave the same way chemically and there's no way of separating them by simple chemical sorting. They have to be taken to a special unit.'

'What do the numbers mean?'

191

'If it doesn't contain 235, it's still possible to create plutonium – and plutonium contains the same fission characteristics as uranium 235.'

'You mean they could use the plutonium to build power stations?'

'Yes – in Argentina.'

'And weapons?'

'Oh, yes,' said Cooke, 'very easily. I'll need to take a look at their laboratory techniques and their packing station – and I'm pretty sure they won't let us see those.'

'I don't know,' said Maxwell. 'Either we're walking into a trap, or they've completely underestimated *Mercator*'s role.'

'You mean they think we're a bunch of ignorant sailors, sir?'

'That would be too much to hope,' said Maxwell. 'But if you want to pray – pray that's what they do think.'

Gallo was as welcoming as before when the Sea King landed and Crabtree, whom Maxwell left to guard the helicopter, was greeted as an old friend. Cooke, who did not introduce himself as a geologist on Maxwell's instructions, surreptitiously absorbed as much as he could on the tour. Then, in the communications room, Ogilvy came to grief, falling heavily over a stool and knocking down a tray of telex numbers. He picked himself up, looking extremely embarrassed. 'God – how clumsy. I really am sorry.'

'Are you hurt?' asked Gallo solicitously.

'Not at all. I'm very sorry.'

'You have kept your men at sea so long, Captain, that they can no longer walk on land.' Gallo laughed uproariously and the British contingent joined in uneasily.

At the end of the tour, drinks were passed round, light conversation was maintained and, after a decent interval, Maxwell suggested they return to the Sea King.

'It was a pleasure to meet you, Captain,' said Gallo, shaking Maxwell's hand yet again.

'You must come on board.'

'That would be delightful.'

'Shall we say tonight at about eight o'clock for dinner?'

Gallo smiled happily. 'That would be a great pleasure,

Captain.'

As the Sea King rose above the base Maxwell asked Ogilvy: 'What was the knock-about slapstick in the communications room in aid of?'

Ogilvy was busily writing down a sequence of numbers. 'I thought it would be interesting to discover which frequencies were used from their radio sets, sir. I wouldn't claim to have a photographic memory, but I can remember numbers – particularly if I really get close to them. That's why I had my little accident. Look, sir.' Ogilvy handed him a list of five sets of numbers. They were: 0423162, 1490122, 3614981, 9239004, 21313112.

'Hidden talents,' said Maxwell admiringly. He turned to Cooke: 'Well, Paul?'

'It's still very difficult to say for sure. They obviously didn't show us any labs involved in the process – I mean, they'd be pretty crazy if they did. But I did see something in the packing station that might be significant.'

'What was that?' Maxwell was barely able to conceal his impatience.

'I spotted some boxes with the international radioactive symbol on them. Mark you – they were tucked away right at the back and I only glimpsed them very fleetingly. But they wouldn't need that symbol for anything else – only uranium.'

'But even so – it's not a lot of evidence, is it?'

'Not a lot, sir. But it could begin an investigation. I mean – you can't just mine uranium at a flick of the finger. There should be plenty of evidence around if the place was thoroughly searched.'

Maxwell looked at his watch and saw they were about thirty minutes' flying time from the *Mercator*. Leaning forward, he called up the ship: 'Foxtrot Hotel, this is 982.'

'982, this is Foxtrot Hotel.'

'Foxtrot Hotel, this is 982, Captain speaking. Request Commander.'

'Message received 982. Out.'

In a few seconds Forbes came through.

'Any reply to my signal?' said Maxwell.

'Yes, sir. They want more information.'

'Too bad – we haven't got it yet. Send this signal: SUSPECT URANIUM MINING IN PROGRESS AT PERON – ' Maxwell broke off as the static on the line increased sharply. Then it went dead. 'Foxtrot Hotel, this is 982.'

'What's up, sir?' asked Ogilvy.

'Everything's gone dead. I can't raise them. Foxtrot Hotel, this is 982. Come in Foxtrot Hotel.'

But despite constant repetition of the call sign there was nothing, and the four men sat bewildered in the Sea King as they roared over the icy wastes of the Peninsula.

'You don't think anything could have happened to the ship, do you, sir?' asked Crabtree, voicing everyone's thoughts.

'No,' said Maxwell. 'There must be some freak weather.'

'Or we're round a – '

But Maxwell did not wait for further speculation and began the call sign all over again. 'Foxtrot Hotel, this is 982. Foxtrot Hotel, this is 982. Come in Foxtrot Hotel.' Maxwell turned to Ogilvy. 'You give it a try,' he said.

Ogilvy did, but there was the same disturbing silence.

Waiting on the bridge of the *Mercator*, Forbes reflected on the hardening of his attitude, not just to Maxwell but to the Royal Navy in general. What had begun as a much-needed adventure had ended in disillusion. Even if Julia was mixed up with Ola Roja, her appalling background made its self-evident excuses and, like every other man in her life, he had deceived her. And then, at the last moment, because she thought he cared for her and because she thought she could trust him, she had given him that invaluable warning – a warning that Maxwell was clearly paying no heed to at all.

He always was an insensitive bastard – they all are, these grand masters of the sea, confusing duty with morality and blimpish patriotism with perception. It was all no good. He would get out, resign his commission, team up with some little upmarket tart with a bit of money and start yacht-chartering. He was finished with big ships – and those who drove them, whether they sat in the Captain's chair or behind some White-hall table. Bugger them all.

Five minutes later Ogilvy reported: 'It's a funny thing, but I'm sure we've got a list.'

'What the hell do you mean?' asked Cooke, considerably dis-concerted.

'It's just that we're slightly overweight to the starboard.'

Maxwell felt the sweat break out on his forehead and he caught Cooke's rising alarm. He had a vivid recollection of those smiling faces at Peron Base – waving, waving goodbye. He saw Gallo, hearing him say again: 'You have kept your men at sea so long, Captain, they can no longer walk on land.'

'What does that mean?' he asked.

'It means we could have something attached to us, sir,' said Crabtree quickly.

'Like – '

'Like a small explosive device, sir.'

There was a shocked silence during which Cooke began to shake and Maxwell said to Crabtree: 'I thought I left you on guard.'

'I didn't move, sir,' said Crabtree. 'They must have shoved it on as we took off.'

Maxwell turned abruptly to Ogilvy whose hands were steady on the controls. 'Any ideas?'

'I wouldn't like to put her down, sir.'

'You think it's timed to go off when we land on the deck?' asked Crabtree, an edge of hysteria in his voice.

'It might be. If it's what we think it is, sir. Of course there may be some other explanation.'

There was a short, unpleasant silence in the vibrating cock-pit. Then Ogilvy suggested: 'If I hover someone could open the door and have a squint.'

'I'll do that, sir,' said Crabtree. He edged forward and Ogilvy put the helicopter into a hovering position. Slowly Crabtree slid the door open and a blast of searing cold air shot up. Leaning over, Crabtree stared down and at first could make out nothing. Then he shouted: 'There is something – near the rear wheel.'

'How is it attached?' yelled Maxwell.

'Difficult to say, sir.'

'Can you get at it?'

'It would be very tricky. It's a long way from the door.'

Maxwell turned back to Ogilvy. 'Can you get her down in a hovering position so we can all get clear – including yourself?'

'It's possible, sir. But where?' Ogilvy looked around him desperately.

Maxwell gazed down at the inhospitable, snow-capped landscape. 'Check out on the ship again,' he said sharply.

'Yes, sir.'

They tried several times but from the *Mercator* there was complete silence.

'How far are we from the ship?'

'About twenty minutes, sir,' said Crabtree.

Maxwell again looked down, seeing miles of snow-covered mountainous terrain, crevasses, slopes – and ice. Although there were some rocky outcrops there was still no obvious landing place. He thanked God, however, that they were all wearing heavy protective clothing.

The weather was clear to the east but with cloud increasing. Maxwell knew the wind was becoming fresher every moment, gusting up to between twenty and thirty knots, and sporadic snow showers were beginning to obscure visibility.

'OK,' said Maxwell, feeling the sweat running down the front of his shirt despite the cold. 'There's an outcrop – try and get her down.'

Without warning the Sea King suddenly lifted and Maxwell felt intense heat round his feet. Then it was all fire and pain and Cooke screaming like an animal in the seat beside him. He looked round at him as he felt the helicopter plunge towards the ground, and for a moment he saw Cooke in a hazy red cloud of flame. Then the darkness came.

Julia Mendoza sat in a small Parisian bistro sipping Pernod and wondering what would happen to her. It was strange to be alone – although she had been alone for a large part of her life. But it hadn't felt like it for she had always been in Gabriel's shadow. Permanently waiting – waiting for the results of his mockery of a trial, waiting for him to come out of prison, waiting for him to fulfil his plans. And why? Because she loved him and because he needed her, and would go on needing her. Sometimes his need, she knew, was greater than his love. But either way she had been bound to him. Until she met Forbes and saw who Gabriel would kill. There were thousands of Forbeses – innocent men, bound to their duty as she was bound to Gabriel. That's why she had gone, because she suddenly saw the hopelessness of all the torture and carnage that any belief, any system could inflict. She could no longer be part of it.

What was she to do? Suicide had seriously preoccupied her recently, but it was not in her nature. She had always been a survivor. But now, to what possible purpose? At forty-three her life must be at an end and over the last few days she had felt increasingly helpless. She had cast herself completely adrift. Nick Forbes often filled her mind and she would spend hours tramping the Parisian streets, thinking about him in a circular way. Sometimes she saw herself being romantically married to him in a sunlit church in some pastoral English village. But even these waking dreams ended in a hail of assassin's bullets as she walked down the aisle.

8 – Survival

29 January 1990
4.00 p.m.
Maxwell woke to find himself lying beside something warm. He snuggled up to it, but the pain was so great he opened his eyes into blinding whiteness and dark fur – fur that was covered in a spreading redness that he began to recognize as blood. His own blood? Maxwell gradually realized he was lying beside a seal. He tried to move but the pain drove him back into unconsciousness.

Later he surfaced and, stretching out a hand, felt more indescribable pain and the absence of the moist fur. Forcing himself to turn over, he looked up at the dark grey Antarctic sky. He turned over slightly, the pain seemed to ease fractionally and Maxwell discovered he was lying in a snow-covered valley between two mountains which led down to a beach. Unrecognizable bits of the helicopter were scattered around in the snow and he could see the outline of a man lying a few yards away.

Experimentally, Maxwell moved again, and found that the pain seemed diminished. Stiffly he staggered to his feet and then leaning on his arm felt the pain return, shooting through him in a hot rush that made him realize his arm must be broken. It was the same arm that had been brushed by the assassin's bullet in Montevideo – which now seemed an eternity ago.

Maxwell felt blood on his forehead, crusted now and no longer flowing. His back ached intolerably but that was all. Keeping his injured arm to his side Maxwell staggered towards the pile of clothes. Reaching it he looked down and immediately began to vomit into the snow. It was Crabtree, but he was missing his arms, legs and lower jaw – all that remained was

198

part of his face and torso. Stumbling away from him, Maxwell found Cooke and Ogilvy lying near each other. Cooke was hardly touched but was clearly dead. Ogilvy had blood seeping from his head and his mouth. But he was alive.

Maxwell bent over him and Ogilvy's eyes flickered open. He tried to say something but his speech was slurred and the words unrecognizable. Then he tried again and this time Maxwell could just make out what he was trying to say.

'Numbers,' he whispered. 'Numbers.'

Perplexed, Maxwell knelt down in the snow beside him and took his hand. It was deadly cold.

'Numbers,' he repeated. 'Numbers.'

Then Maxwell saw that Ogilvy had a scrap of paper clenched in his hand. 'What's that, old man?'

'Numbers.'

Suddenly, Maxwell realized that these were the codes Ogilvy had memorized at the Peron Base. The telex numbers he had knocked over in the communications room. Gently he took them from him and put the scrap of paper carefully in his inside pocket.

'Thank you,' he said, rising and standing beside Ogilvy whose breathing was now becoming laboured. 'I'll see if I can make you more comfortable.'

He started to search the wreckage for any blankets and for the survival pack. After a while he discovered a blanket and two jackets, which he took over to Ogilvy, jarring his broken arm painfully in the process. He laid them over him and then gently detached the regulation issue radio beacon that was strapped to Ogilvy's waist. He returned to Crabtree, but could only find parts of the beacon in his muddled remains.

Maxwell took Ogilvy's beacon down to the beach and set it pointing seawards. It began to bleep and he knew that at least he was doing something practical, although he gloomily realized that its range was only the snow-covered horizon. Painfully he went back to the survival pack and spread its contents out on the beach. As he did so the wind increased until he knew it was nearing gale force.

Awkwardly, using one arm, Maxwell weighted down each

item with stones and rocks, checking them off as he went. Surveying them, he found he had sleeping bags, a tent, extra food, a rucksack, an extra first-aid kit, an axe and a knife. The tent of course would be useless – he'd never pitch it one-armed, on ice or shingle, in this wind. For a moment he almost laughed aloud for the challenge presented to him was like a manic version of the survival exercises he had undertaken at Dartmouth as a cadet.

Ogilvy was still conscious when Maxwell returned to him. But the blood was fresh on his lips and his breathing was more rasping than before.

'I'm going to make a shelter,' said Maxwell. 'Then we'll both be able to get into it.'

Ogilvy shook his head. 'Mustn't move,' he muttered.

'I'll be gentle.'

'Stomach.'

Maxwell lifted the blanket but saw nothing. Then, slowly pushing aside Ogilvy's flying jacket, he saw, for the first time, a dark mass of blood and intestines.

'I've fixed up a beacon.'

'No *Mercator*?'

'We only lost radio contact.'

'Die.'

'No one's dying around here,' returned Maxwell sharply, but Ogilvy closed his eyes. 'Do you want any water?'

Ogilvy shook his head, the blood at his mouth bubbling, crimson against the snow.

Maxwell picked up the axe from the survival kit and began to dig into the ice under a rocky outcrop as hard as he could with only one working arm. As he dug, his broken arm began to throb painfully. He knew he should stop and strap it up but he wanted to get Ogilvy under cover first.

Half an hour later he walked through a rising wind to Ogilvy. 'I'm getting on with the shelter.'

No reply.

'Soon have you in.'

Again Ogilvy shook his head and, unreasonably, Maxwell felt an overwhelming desire to hit him. He went away quickly, and continued digging.

Hours later he had dug down just deep enough into the ice to create a shelter for two. He felt exhausted and the pain in his arm was now unbearable. As soon as he had seen to Ogilvy he would try to strap it up.

Somehow, unbelievably, Ogilvy was still alive when he returned. 'I've made the shelter,' said Maxwell.

Ogilvy looked at him with glazed eyes. Again he shook his head. Poor sod, thought Maxwell. Very gently he uncovered him and began to pull him, inch by inch, towards the outcrop. Terrified of what damage he might be inflicting, Maxwell dragged him to the shelter. As he was doing the dragging one-armed, the whole process was not only incredibly slow but particularly painful with the gale force wind an added torture. At last he got Ogilvy into position and half pushed, half levered him down. Then he dragged the sleeping bags across and piled them around him.

'Well – you're here now,' said Maxwell. 'Better make the most of it.'

For a moment he thought Ogilvy had slipped into unconsciousness but then his eyes flickered open.

'Are you in pain?' asked Maxwell.

Ogilvy's lips opened slightly then closed.

Maxwell tried again. 'Are you in pain? There are some pain-killers in the first-aid box.'

The reply came so softly that Maxwell could barely hear. 'No.'

'Good. We'll be picked up soon – don't worry.'

Ogilvy closed his eyes. Then he said: 'The bastards have done for us.'

'Not yet they haven't.' He clambered into the hole, dragged the sleeping bags around them and huddled up to Ogilvy's recumbent figure.

Maxwell lay beside Ogilvy in the shelter for another ten minutes. It was bitterly cold but at least it was out of the wind. He looked down at Ogilvy, knowing there was nothing more he could do for him. Tentatively Maxwell wondered if he could start a fire. It was getting dark now and anything he wanted to find he would have to find right away. Matches! He went through Ogilvy's pockets, but with no success. Extricating himself from the shelter again he struggled across to the bodies of Crabtree and Cooke. Didn't Crabtree smoke? He thought he did but now couldn't be sure.

Both the bodies were nearly frozen as Maxwell searched their pockets. He was almost in despair when he found a box in Crabtree's back pocket, bent out of shape, damp, but matches all the same. Stumbling back to the wreckage he made a pile of anything he thought might burn – and a lot more besides. Then he tried to light it, but the matches were too damp and he wasted a dozen before he decided to return to the shelter and wrap them in the sleeping bag in the hope they might dry out.

Lying again beside Ogilvy, listening to his rasping, erratic breathing, Maxwell gave in to despair. He had taken a damn fool risk and was responsible for the deaths of Crabtree and Cooke. And soon, no doubt, Ogilvy. Perhaps the radio silence meant they had also attacked *Mercator*. Both the Lynx helicopters had been on board and there was a slim possibility that one of them might have escaped from the ship and begun a sweeping search for him. They would have had him logged in the wireless office, but suppose the *Mercator* had gone down so quickly that – Maxwell closed his eyes against the grim possibility and, cruelly, Lucinda appeared in his mind's eye.

Ogilvy moaned beside him in the searing Antarctic night and Maxwell tried to dismiss his own thoughts. He knew that Ogilvy was dying, but suddenly he felt a movement beside him. Ogilvy's eyes were open and he was speaking with far greater articulation than before.

'Sir?'

'Yes, Giles.'

'I can see.'

'What do you mean, old man?'

'I can see everything.'

'What can you see?'

'I can see outside this shelter – the bits of the helicopter and the bodies and the snow – and the sea. The sea, with those enormous bergs. It's lapping at the ice.'

202

A feeling of hopelessness came over Maxwell.

'Am I dying, sir?'

'Of course not – you've just got a bit of a fever, that's all.'

'There's blood in my mouth, sir.'

'Yes – but that's to be expected. You've been injured.'

'There are figures moving about, sir.'

'Where?'

'Outside. Look – there's Cooke and Crabtree. They're building a snowman. They've got a Christmas tree.'

Maxwell said nothing.

'There's something in the sea, sir.' Ogilvy's eyes were wide open now and his voice was gratingly hard. His lungs wheezed horribly and his hand gripped Maxwell's. It was soft and sweaty. Pulp, thought Maxwell. He's pulp.

'What's in the sea, old man?'

'Something bright.'

'Can you – make out anything more?'

'It's bright,' said Ogilvy. There was a rattle in his throat and the slimy hand gripped Maxwell's ferociously. 'Am I dying, sir?'

'Lie still.'

'Tell me –' His voice rose to a shrill, high note. 'Am I dying, sir?'

'Yes, old man,' said Maxwell sadly. 'I think you are.'

'I can't feel anything.'

'Good.'

'There's brightness – such brightness – on the water, sir.'

Ogilvy's vision was so strong that Maxwell could almost see that frigid, unearthly glow himself.

'It's an iceberg,' said Ogilvy. 'It's floating towards us.'

'Hang on.'

'No – I can't breathe, sir. There are colours in it, sir. Hundreds of colours. I can see –' His throat was rattling harshly and Maxwell wondered how long he could bear the sound.

'God bless you, Giles.'

'Sir –' The rattle came again and then Ogilvy gave a kind of sigh.

203

Maxwell sat holding Giles's hand for some time. It didn't feel limp or slimy any longer. It felt warm and enduring – a link with humanity. Perhaps his last.

Eventually Maxwell fell into an uneasy sleep. When he awoke Ogilvy's hand was rock hard and he kept hearing his voice saying: 'Something bright – something bright on the sea, sir.'

Stiffly Maxwell clambered out of the shelter, his injured arm shooting blinding pain through him. Dazzled by the whiteness and seared by the blasting wind, Maxwell looked for relief towards the sea. Then he saw the helicopter.

For a few moments Maxwell tried to make out the markings. Then he saw there weren't any. It hovered over him, its black body looking like some kind of flying insect. Straining his eyes upwards Maxwell waved desperately, the hope surging over him whilst, at the same time, his brain registered bewilderment. Why the hell didn't it have any markings? As with the *Mercator*'s helicopters, the door had been taken off for easy escape, but he could only make out the dim outline of the pilot and observer. Still waving, Maxwell saw the helicopter reduce height. Gradually his optimism swamped his doubts. He was going to be rescued, he was not going to die. He would live. The joy surged through him as Maxwell looked up, waving at the pilot. Then he saw the machine gun and, idiotically, he continued to wave. It was only when the bullets began to rain down in the snow and ice around him that Maxwell turned into a hopeless, gasping run.

The black helicopter was being buffeted by the steely wind but still the machine gun chattered. Maxwell felt a sharp pain in the shoulder and then his whole arm began to hurt so excruciatingly that he whimpered as he stumbled over the ice. The helicopter followed him, making for a ridge about fifty yards ahead whilst the penguins scattered, falling ludicrously on their stomachs, emitting raucous croaks.

Panting, gasping, the pain searing at him, Maxwell struggled on, knowing that he was going to die. The helicopter followed, with its noise and spitting death. Just as he was nearing the ridge Maxwell fell heavily and the intense agony overcame him. He rolled awkwardly on to his side.

For a few seconds Maxwell blacked out, but then, unmercifully, he regained consciousness. Turning over on his back, he watched the helicopter's belly while it hovered above him. He saw the observer leaning out, lining up the machine gun. Maxwell closed his eyes, knowing that it was now only a matter of seconds. Lucinda's face briefly swam into his mind's eye. She was smiling and he could almost hear her saying something, but the helicopter rotor blades were making such a ferocious noise that they dominated everything. Still he lay there, still the appalling noise continued, still nothing happened. He couldn't even hear the sound of the bullets hitting the ground. But they must be coming and very soon they would reach him, putting a stop to all this senseless agony. Please, Maxwell prayed, to a God he had not addressed since childhood, please let it happen now. But it didn't – and the noise increased to such a volume that he imagined the helicopter was just a few feet above him. Then he opened his eyes and saw there were two helicopters.

The black helicopter was gaining height, its noise diminishing as it spiralled into the cloud above. To his amazement, Maxwell then saw one of the Lynxes circling above him. It was unbelievable, it couldn't be happening, thought Maxwell, as he saw the marauding black helicopter fly out of view. Meanwhile, the Lynx was gradually descending towards him as he still lay flat on his back on the snow-covered rock. Feebly Maxwell tried to rise, but the pain was too great and welcome unconsciousness overtook him.

30 January 1990
10.45 p.m.
Vicinity Temple Glacier on board the *Mercator*.
Racked by pain-dominated dreams, Maxwell saw Ogilvy standing on the iceberg as it faded on the horizon, the colours glowing as blood red as the liquid that flowed from his mouth. Then the black helicopter flew out of the berg and roared towards Maxwell, the machine gun pumping bullets into his

205

chest. He screamed, thrashing his body hopelessly against their dull impact. He felt hands pressing him down, and he thrashed again, the pain like a hot knife plunging in. It was never totally withdrawn and he longed for the blackness. Then he felt a needle in his arm and a sweet all-consuming relief filled him as the pain receded. Again he plunged into blessed unconsciousness – and the berg headed back towards the beach. Ogilvy had gone. In his place stood Lucinda. But she had Ogilvy's eyes.

Maxwell stirred, felt pain, the needle and relief. But this time he did not plunge into welcoming darkness. He opened his eyes and to his amazement saw Forbes and the MO. Then he realized he was lying in the sickbay of the *Mercator*. It was impossible, of course, all part of the nightmare. Soon the helicopter would be back, chattering death. He tried to sit up but Forbes gently pushed him back.

'Sorry, sir. You must lie down.'

'The ship – ' Maxwell tried to pull himself up again.

'A VHF black-out, sir. We're fine.'

'No,' muttered Maxwell. 'It's not possible.'

'You should take it easy, sir. The doc said not too much talking.'

'Rubbish,' said Maxwell, suddenly coming to. 'What kept you?'

'There's a lot of ice to cover, sir. We searched through the night and then heard the beacon just as we spotted that unmarked chopper hanging about.'

'One of those cavalry rescues,' said Maxwell. 'You came up over the horizon.'

'I thought we'd lost you, sir.'

'I thought I'd lost everybody,' replied Maxwell. He closed his eyes and suddenly slept.

It had taken over an hour to board the submarine in severely choppy seas and by the time they were all assembled, Gabriel felt at his most exhausted. The Maxwell operation had clearly gone wrong at the last moment but quite what its implications

206

were going to be was difficult to say. On one hand it showed they meant business, on the other it once again proved how incapable they were of carrying anything through effectively. But there was no time for explanation. His controller was sitting, drinking coffee, seemingly impervious to the claustrophobia of the mess-room. Of the captain or any of his officers, there was no sign.

'To quote the American entertainer, Mr Sinatra – "and now the end is near", Gabriel.'

Gabriel sat down heavily on the opposite side of the table. 'For me?'

Unbearably, his superior did not answer directly. 'For Ola Roja. But first we have our final warning.'

His clothes looked even drabber, even more tent-like in this sub-human light, thought Gabriel. And he had neglected to shave himself properly. There were two bloodied nicks on his chin and above these he was growing a wispy moustache. Hair didn't seem to grow well on his pale features.

Gabriel said nothing, his spirits sinking even further. He no longer had the initiative – if he had ever had it in the first place. And Julia was constantly on his mind. What would they do to her? Where was she?

'We intend to carefully monitor the explosion. Once it's over, I don't think the Americans will risk their investment. Their Government will draw back.'

Gabriel shifted uncomfortably.

'You do not share my confidence, Gabriel?'

But he had not been thinking about what was going to happen. Julia was still on his mind. 'I'm sure you're right.' He stumbled into speech. 'They will not take that kind of risk.' There was a pause, then Gabriel continued: 'So there will be no further need for Ola Roja.'

'The organization will go into cold storage.'

'And *Mercator*? We will let her run free?'

'I am told she is being withdrawn.'

Gabriel started. He looked across the table unbelievingly. 'So – ?'

'So your work has not been in vain. However fumbling.'

There was another pause. 'Gabriel, you have a job. You will return to it. There is only one problem that remains.'

He knew what it was and the dull fear seemed to swamp him.

'Obviously your sister cannot be allowed to roam at will. She is in possession of a very great deal of dangerous information.'

Gabriel tried to pour confidence into his voice. And failed. 'I really don't think she – '

'Nonsense. If you *have* failed us – it is here. We have always appreciated your difficulties in recruitment – and been sympathetic. But this is a different matter. You should have known her better, predicted her weakness. As it is – '

Gabriel looked into his eyes for the first time, but he already knew what he would find there.

'As it is – we shall locate her quickly.'

'Am I to stay on board?' he asked.

'No you will be returned to the *Santa Fe*. We can't afford you, Gabriel.'

Next morning Maxwell was allowed to sit up. Taking stock of his injuries he discovered his right arm was broken in two places but his shoulder had only received a flesh wound. He was also suffering from exposure. Forbes, who had assumed temporary command of the *Mercator*, came into the sickbay after lunch with a large scotch.

'That's more like it,' said Maxwell.

'How do you feel, sir?'

'Bloody awful.'

'The Doc says you'll be OK.'

'That's gratifying.'

'I naturally signalled Whitehall directly we brought you on board.'

'And what did they have to say this time? More low prcfile investigation?' said Maxwell sarcastically.

'Oh, they've got their knickers in a terrible twist now. Diplomatic protests are flying about everywhere and Britain's sending two frigates and a guided weapon destroyer down.'

'What's the betting they'll have dismantled everything at

Peron by the time they get there?'

'I've no doubt they will, sir, but they won't get started again that quickly.'

'Depends on how much they get out.'

'Well, yes. But they'll be watched much more effectively from now on, I should think.'

'What are Peron saying?'

'Oh, Whitehall accused them of sabotaging the helicopter.'

'What did they say to that?'

'Well, naturally they told a different story. They claimed you'd arrived at the Base, made aggressive noises about their "perfectly innocent prospecting" and that your helicopter had crashed on the way back to the ship.'

'Bastards,' said Maxwell.

Forbes looked at his watch. 'If you like you can hear all about it on the World Service. It's been top of every news bulletin.' He switched on the wireless.

Whilst they were waiting Forbes said: 'I'm very sorry about my attitude over the last few days, sir.'

'Forget it.'

'I expect you realize – '

'I *said*, forget it. Hang on – '

'This is the BBC World Service at 16.00 hours. Here is the news. An incident involving an Argentine Antarctic base and a helicopter from the Royal Navy ice patrol ship HMS *Mercator* has resulted in diplomatic protests being sent to Moscow from London. The Prime Minister has dispatched two frigates and a guided weapon destroyer towards the Antarctic to – '

'My God!' Maxwell snapped off the radio.

'Whatever's the matter, sir?'

'The numbers,' he said. 'Ogilvy's numbers.'

'What numbers, sir?'

'He memorized some authentication numbers in the Peron communications office. I think that's why they tried to get rid of us.'

'*Did* they suspect him then?'

'He did it crudely. He wanted to remember as many numbers as possible so he knocked them all on to the floor.'

'Did he remember them?'

'Yes, that's what I'm trying to tell you. He gave them to me on a piece of paper. Where the hell are my clothes – the clothes I was wearing?'

'In your cabin, sir. I'll bring them.' Forbes darted out and returned with Maxwell's bullet-torn, bloodstained clothes.

'Lynch says he's had no time to – '

'Bugger that!' Maxwell said impatiently. 'Go through the pockets. There should be a scrap of paper with about five sets of numbers on it.'

Carefully Forbes went through the pockets but to Maxwell's fury he drew a blank.

'Try again.'

He tried again but still there was nothing.

'Shit!' Maxwell stared angrily ahead. 'Wait a minute. The small inside pocket.'

Forbes tried and emerged triumphant with a tiny scrap of much-folded paper. 'This it?'

'Yes, that's it. Now get down to the communications office and try them out. Fast!' Maxwell leant back exhausted, weakness stealing over him as the doctor came in.

'Tiring ourselves out, are we?' he said.

Maxwell told him to go away.

An hour later, Forbes returned from the communications office to confront a feverishly impatient Maxwell.

'What the hell took you so long?'

'Sorry, sir. Took a bit of time.' He looked slightly dazed.

'What's the matter?'

'Well, sir – when they got to the fifth authentication number, they raised – it just doesn't seem possible.'

'Spit it out, man.'

'They raised Peter Kenny, sir. There must be some mistake.'

The ice island had incredible beauty, with its sheer translucent sides and the magnificent cavern that indented its northern flank. The sun radiated the colours, filling the ice with subtle hues that Gabriel would never have believed possible.

210

The submarine was on the surface, dwarfed by the magnificence of this gradually melting berg. To destroy it seemed the greatest act of sacrilege anyone could commit. Slowly they cruised around it, until they swung round its southern tip. On a sparkling ledge stood sentinel groups of penguins. There were thousands of them. Waiting to be blown to kingdom come.

The sea was very still in the fading afternoon light, and the penguins also seemed immovable. The circling conning tower of the sub did not seem to disturb them in the least. They're waiting for execution, thought Gabriel. He had been told that when the island exploded, it would make a tidal wave. Any shipping in the vicinity would be destroyed. Bergs would collapse. It would not go unnoticed. There was to be comment, no responsibility taken. Just the warning. Of what would happen if the ice-caps melted. A very small example – but effective. No sensible government could possibly afford to ignore it.

The submarine continued to circle the island, and the light continued to fade. Now the ice was dark green, glowing in the gathering darkness like a crystal. Gabriel looked at his watch. A few hours – and then it would be shattered. The sea would rise up and take it. He looked at his watch again. They were unable to calculate whether *Mercator*, in its present position, would receive the full thrust of the wave. But there was a chance. And Gabriel prayed that chance would be fulfilled. If Maxwell was dead, there was no one to fight for *Mercator* – and if there was no one to fight for her, then there could be no future for her. He did not know how his controller could be so sure the *Mercator* was being withdrawn. But even if orders had gone out, with Maxwell still alive, those orders could be countermanded. For Maxwell was a survivor and, because of this, his ship would survive with him.

Bells clanged, indicating imminent submersion, and Gabriel took one last, lingering look at the immaculate beauty they were so soon to destroy.

31 January 1990
7.00 p.m.

Maxwell sat in his cabin with Forbes, drinking coffee and trying to come to terms with the unbelievable. They both still clung to the hope that some incredible mistake must have been made. Yet the authentication number had been checked and re-checked and the same name had come up each time. Also, to compound the situation, there was the appalling logic of it all, so well expressed by Forbes.

'No wonder you weren't taken seriously, sir. Not with someone as influential as Kenny putting the boot in.'

'But he *personally* led me on. That's what's so incredible.'

'It's not the first time a stereotyped English diplomat has worked for the Russians.'

'No – but we need more back-up than an authentication number.' Maxwell paused, passing a hand over his eyes. He felt desperately tired and despite her stabilizers the *Mercator* was rolling heavily, continuously jarring his arm. 'Anyway, I've probably finally shot my bolt with the MOD by telling them Her Majesty's Ambassador is working for the Soviets. If by any chance he *is* in the clear, I'm finished.'

'Yes,' said Forbes meditatively, 'I think you're right there, sir.'

The telephone rang, they both started and Forbes grabbed at the receiver as if it was a wild animal. He turned to Maxwell. 'It's the communications office, sir. They've got a signal from the MOD.'

'Then for God's sake get down there. I'd like to know whether it's my death warrant or not.'

Maxwell waited for six unbearable minutes until Forbes returned. During this time he felt a total loss of confidence. This was it then, the finish of his career. But just as he was picturing details of his court martial, Forbes threw open the cabin door and shouted: 'They're shitting themselves, sir.' He thrust the signal into Maxwell's hands and with sheer terror in his heart Maxwell read:

FROM: COMMANDER IN CHIEF FLEET   311205 Z JAN

212

TO: HMS MERCATOR
IMMEDIATE
TOP SECRET
1. YOUR 301755 Z JAN – EVIDENCE DISCOVERED BY YOU IN
PERON BASE CONFIRMS EARLIER SUSPICIONS BY MI6.
2. RECOVER YOUR SURVEY PARTIES. PROCEED FORTHWITH
TO MONTEVIDEO VIA STANLEY TO EMBARK HM AMBASSADOR
FOR PASSAGE ASCENSION.
3. HMA IS A POLITICAL PRISONER AND WILL BE CHARGED
WITH TREASON. HE IS TO BE KEPT UNDER OPEN ARREST
THROUGHOUT PASSAGE AND WILL BE INTERROGATED BY
SECURITY PERSONNEL WHO WILL ACCOMPANY YOU.
4. REASON FOR NOT FLYING HIM TO ASCENSION IS THAT WE
FEAR SABOTAGE.
5. FOR YOUR INFORMATION TENNANT, EX COUNSELLOR
BRITISH EMBASSY, BA, HAS BEEN RETURNED UK TO FACE
CHARGES.
6. PRESS WILL ONLY BE INFORMED ON ARRIVAL IN
ENGLAND.

'Tennant too – that explains a thing or two.'

'I wonder how many more of them there are? And I still
can't believe in Kenny.'

'You'll have to start trying,' said Maxwell. He felt a surge of
elation. To scream, shout, or even cry would have been a tremendous release – a necessary release. But decades of Royal
Navy training told on him and he picked up the microphone
with a studied calm.

'Gentlemen, we have been given a new job and, for political
reasons, we've got to do it as soon as possible. This means that
we shall be curtailing the survey programme this evening and
proceeding to Montevideo to embark a political prisoner. We
shall be paying a short visit to Stanley on the way where mail
will be collected. I feel I should tell you that there has been considerable political intrigue between Argentina and Russia
during the last few months.' He paused, wondering how much
he should tell them. 'We will arrive at Portsmouth on about
10 April instead of mid-May as previously programmed.

213

I should also like to say how much I have appreciated your support during the recent incidents that have affected our operations. However, I'm sure I don't have to tell you that we shall need to be continuously alert.' Maxwell paused again and then said slowly: 'During this operation we have lost five men – Lieutenant Arrowsmith, Captain Lucas, Lieutenant Ogilvy, our geologist, Dr Paul Cooke, and Lieutenant Crabtree. The bodies of the last three men have been recovered and there will be a short service in the dining hall tonight. Thank you again, gentlemen.'

Just as Maxwell finished his broadcast the Yeoman of Signals arrived on the bridge. 'Sir! There's another long signal coming through and the P.O. Tel* suggests that you might like to see it as it comes off the teleprinter.'

'I'll come down immediately. Incidentally, neither you nor the Radio Supervisor should be looking at that signal. Is the Navigating Officer there?'

'Yes, sir. He's decrypting it. Neither I nor the RS have been reading anything, I can assure you.' His tones of injured innocence amused Maxwell as he set off towards the wireless office with its urgent atmosphere of vital activity. Tapes were spewing out of machines, banks of electronics winked red and green lights and the operators fed the transmitters with coded messages.

Lloyd, the Radio Supervisor, said quietly: 'The navigator is over there, sir, at number three bay, cracking a Gold Text Signal.'

'Thank you,' said Maxwell and walked over to Cunningham.

FROM: COMMANDER IN CHIEF FLEET 010953 Z FEB
TO: HMS MERCATOR
PRIORITY
SECRET
PARA ONE
INTELLIGENCE SOURCES REPORT ORGANIZATION KNOWN AS
OLA ROJA HAS OBJECTIVE TO DISRUPT SOUTH ATLANTIC

* Petty Officer Telegraphist (Radio Supervisor).

SHIPPING AS COVER FOR SOVIET ACTIVITY. CONSIDER MANY
INCIDENTS EXPERIENCED BY MERCATOR DURING 1988-89
SEASON PART OF OLA ROJA ACTIVITY. RUSSIANS ACTIVELY
ENCOURAGING ARGENTINA TO OBTAIN AND EVENTUALLY
MANUFACTURE NUCLEAR WEAPONS.
PARA TWO
SOVIETS SEE ANTARCTIC AS IMPORTANT AREA FOR
EXPLOITATION BY WESTERN COUNTRIES. THEIR PURPOSE TO
OBSTRUCT WESTERN SCIENTIFIC PROGRESS THROUGH
ANTARCTIC TREATY AREA HAS FAILED HENCE RECENT ACTS
OF FORCE.
PAGE THREE
ARGENTINA VERY CONCERNED ABOUT COMMUNIST
INFILTRATION IN ARMED FORCES. FEAR MUTINIES IN
SEVERAL UNITS. EQUALLY CONCERNED ABOUT URANIUM
MINING AT PERON.
PARA FOUR
YOU ARE TO ARREST OIL RIG SUPPORT VESSEL SANTA FE AND
THEN PROCEED TO MONTEVIDEO WHERE YOU WILL ANCHOR
IN INNER HARBOUR. FULL UNDERWATER MEASURES ARE TO
BE TAKEN. NO SHORE LEAVE MAY BE GRANTED AND
PERSONNEL GOING ASHORE ON DUTY MUST BE KEPT TO A
MINIMUM. MARINE OFFICER AND FOUR MARINES WILL
ESCORT AMBASSADOR WHO WILL BE CHARGED WITH
TREASON IN ASCENSION. WE HAVE HIM UNDER HOUSE
ARREST.
PARA FIVE
JULIA MENDOZA MISSING IN FRANCE. POSSIBILITY SUICIDE.
PARA SIX
CONSIDER SOUTH ATLANTIC AREA VERY TURBULENT.
WOULD WELCOME YOUR VIEWS ON FUTURE NAVAL FORCE
LEVELS FOR FALKLANDS AND DEPENDENCIES.

Maxwell laughed.

'That sounds very hollow, sir,' said Cunningham.

'"Consider South Atlantic area very turbulent"! My God,
how they've got the nerve to pronounce judgement like that.'

'But at least they welcome your views, sir.'

'And by God they're going to get them!'

10.00 p.m.

After the service, Maxwell went to his cabin and called for Forbes. When he arrived he knew at once that there was something wrong. Maxwell passed him the signal and he read it through slowly while Maxwell waited in grim anticipation. Forbe's reaction was unpredictable.

'Ballocks – she's not the type to kill herself. If anything's happened to her it's the work of those Ola Roja bastards.' Forbes turned to face him and Maxwell could see there was a new bitterness to his eyes. 'Don't forget that she tried to warn us, sir.'

'She must have been in it up to the neck.'

But Forbes did not give him time to continue. 'Don't you think we could call it quits there, sir?'

'No,' said Maxwell, 'I don't. We're all lucky to be alive – bloody lucky. And don't you forget it.'

'I won't forget it,' replied Forbes savagely.

9 – Presumed dead

1 February 1990
7.00 p.m.
'And if they don't surrender, we'll take them by force.' Maxwell was on the bridge, giving his officers a detailed briefing on how they would put the *Santa Fe* under arrest, having already outlined the situation to the ship's company. His mood of elation was still with him, but he knew that Forbes was agonizing over Julia Mendoza's plight. I hope to God he doesn't lose his grip now, he thought.

Maxwell turned to Sinclair. 'What's the *Santa Fe*'s monitored position?'

'Approximately forty-three and a half miles south-southeast, sir.'

'Right – we'll go in with the Lynx and the marines.'

Diego, winched down by helicopter on to the deck of the *Santa Fe*, was met by Morales.

'We are already destroying equipment,' he said.

At once Diego could sense the building panic on the ship and he could see the fear in Morales's eyes. They're going to bungle it unless I slow them up, he thought. Men scurried over the deck, hauling unidentifiable machinery from below. Diego gripped Morales's arm. 'For God's sake – this is chaos. Who's checking what's going overboard?'

'Caterino.'

'Then where the devil is he? He should be up here doing an inventory. And what about documents, read-outs, papers? Their Lynx will be arriving soon. Now where is Mendoza?'

'In his cabin – opposite my own,' said Morales stiffly. 'And

217

if I may say so, we are well organized.'

'That would be a miracle,' said Diego, hurrying away.

As Morales continued to supervise the ripping out of the remote control detonation equipment, Diego found Gabriel Mendoza. He looked as if he had not slept for days and there was a beaten look in his eyes. Diego took his hands and kissed him on the cheek. The cabin smelt hot and musty and forcibly reminded him of a cell – a prison cell.

'No, my old friend,' he said quickly as Gabriel began to speak. 'Don't say you've failed.'

'What else can you call it?'

'The system has been tested and found workable. That is your achievement.'

'You seem to forget this ship is about to be put under arrest.'

Diego looked around him contemptuously. 'This hulk? A casualty of progress – like Kenny.'

'Will the Soviets see it that way?' He laughed softly, ironically.

'I saw Kenny just before he was arrested. He assures me the Soviets agree we should beat a tactical retreat.'

'And leave the Antarctic to the British Navy? The system can hardly be effective now they know how it works.'

'They can't afford to keep a presence here, Gabriel. In a matter of months we can be operating again. They may know how it works, but they would need a task force to track it down.'

Gabriel shrugged. He seemed totally uninterested. But Diego persisted. 'I have been instructed to tell you that you have served us well. You will return to Montevideo via Cuba.'

'How long will I wait in Cuba?'

'I can't tell you that.'

Gabriel looked at Diego cynically. 'You realize my sister is in Europe?'

'We regret that,' said Diego. 'But we don't intend to pursue her.'

For the first time Gabriel looked at him with something approaching gratitude. But he did not thank Diego. 'And what of our present position?' was all he asked.

'You have overlooked how strong our bargaining power is,' replied Diego. He looked at his watch. 'It will not be long now.'

8.30 p.m.

Despite the failing light, the flurried activity on deck was clearly obvious to Maxwell as the Lynx flew towards the *Santa Fe*. Great gouts of water went up as machinery was hurled over the side and sea-birds hovered aloft, hoping food might follow.

'We can't have this,' said Maxwell. He picked up the microphone. 'Captain Maxwell of HMS *Mercator* calling *Santa Fe*. The Royal Navy are placing your ship under arrest and wish to board. We note that you are jettisoning equipment. This must cease immediately. Over.'

Maxwell repeated the message and told Sinclair to maintain the Lynx's height as it hovered out of range of the *Santa Fe*. Spotlights, set up in the launches carrying the marines, probed its neglected superstructure. A pale crescent moon rode over the spectral scene and the night was clear, with no traces of the day's mist.

The *Santa Fe* was quick to reply.

'This is Captain Morales of the *Santa Fe* calling Captain Maxwell of the *Mercator*. Over.'

'Captain Morales – this is Captain Maxwell receiving you. Over.'

'We will continue to dismantle redundant equipment and cannot give you clearance for boarding.'

'Then we shall have to use force.'

'I don't think so, Captain Maxwell. We have two hostages here.' The note of triumph in Morales's voice was resoundingly clear.

Maxwell looked at Sinclair in disbelief and then said: 'Identify the hostages.'

'They are Lieutenant John Arrowsmith and Captain, Royal Marines, Henry Lucas.'

The crew of the Sea King were rigid with shock as Maxwell, trying to control his voice, demanded proof.

219

'They are coming up on deck now. Over and out.'

A few seconds later two figures emerged. Both were emaciated and neither looked much like Arrowsmith or Lucas.

'They could be anybody,' muttered Maxwell.

Morales came back on the air. 'We will hand over these hostages in return for your co-operation.'

'What co-operation?'

'We are taking a passenger off the *Santa Fe* and wish him to be given safe conduct to Cuba. The hostages will travel with him. Once he arrives safely in Cuba, the hostages will be released.'

'How do you intend to get him there?'

'He will be taken to Ushuaia airport. We want a plane prepared for him.'

'What is the deadline?'

'You have two hours to make the necessary arrangements, Captain Maxwell.'

'I would like to properly identify the hostages.'

'I'm afraid that is not possible.'

'It must be,' said Maxwell. 'Otherwise there's no deal.'

'I will have to consult.' The tension in the Sea King increased until it became unbearable, particularly as Morales seemed to be off the air for an eternity. 'One of your officers will board the *Santa Fe*,' he said eventually. 'But he will arrive and depart by launch and will be the sole occupant.'

'Message understood. I'm returning to the *Mercator* and will contact you from the bridge.'

As the amazing news of Arrowsmith's and Lucas's return from an assumed grave spread around the *Mercator*, Maxwell conferred with his shocked and bewildered officers.

'So they hung on to them for bargaining power,' said Cunningham. 'That really demonstrates their lack of confidence.'

'Yes,' said Maxwell. 'They must have known it was likely we'd track them down sooner or later.'

'We can't send anyone else over, sir,' said Cunningham. 'We'd simply be playing into their hands.'

220

'I'd like to volunteer to go, sir.' Forbes was insistent.

'But why does anyone have to go on board?' asked Sinclair. 'We've seen them – isn't that enough?'

'No,' said Maxwell. 'It's not. We *must* double-check that it really *is* them, and if it is we must try to find out where they were concealed for so long.'

'They'll never let them talk, sir.' Sinclair was adamant.

'Nevertheless we have to try. Who knows? The *Santa Fe* may not be the only command ship.'

'I'd very much like to go, sir,' said Forbes again but Maxwell looked doubtful.

'I'd rather send someone less senior.'

'Nevertheless, I'd still like to go, sir.'

Maxwell considered the situation carefully, trying to evaluate the possible dangers. Eventually he gave up. There were too many of them, but all things considered he felt Ola Roja were in no position to try and kidnap any more Royal Navy officers. Maxwell turned abruptly back to the radio and called up the *Santa Fe*. Morales was on the air at once.

'We are sending Commander Forbes across, but he's going to be covered by a Lynx helicopter which will be loaded with marines. I must warn you that, if any harm comes to him or them, you will be held personally responsible.'

To Maxwell's surprise, Morales did not try and prevaricate. 'I understand you. Commander Forbes is to begin his journey immediately. Please make sure your helicopter keeps its distance or we shall shoot our hostages – and Commander Forbes.'

'Understood. Over and out.'

'Jarvis says they're still jettisoning equipment, sir.'

But Maxwell was not interested. 'I'd rather have my men back alive – if they are my men. And tell Jarvis to get back here.'

Maxwell explained developments over the telephone to an appalled and increasingly querulous Hazelton.

'And you say you can't be certain *who* they are?'

'No, sir. Not absolutely certain. That's why I'm sending Forbes in.'

'Yes – well – ' Hazelton began to show his customary lack of decision. 'It's not like you, James, to be so cautious,' he said curiously.

'No, sir.' Maxwell almost laughed aloud at the other's discomfort. 'I just wouldn't like to be in the position of over-reacting again.'

Hazelton emitted a sound somewhere between a snarl and a snort of derision. 'I'll get back to you in ten minutes,' he snapped.

Whilst he waited, Maxwell spoke as reassuringly as he could to his ship's company.

'Gentlemen, as you may be aware, we have tracked down the source of Ola Roja's activities in the South Atlantic to the oil rig support vessel *Santa Fe* which has been functioning as an operational headquarters. But we are now faced with a new situation for, as you may know, we have discovered that Lieutenant Arrowsmith and Captain Lucas – originally missing presumed dead – are being held captive on the *Santa Fe* and will only be released if safe conduct is given to a passenger who wishes to be flown to Cuba. I am now awaiting the MOD's reaction. Commander Forbes is at this moment *en route* to the *Santa Fe* to assist negotiations. You will be kept informed of all developments. That is all.'

Taff Evans was quick to pronounce judgement: 'Let's give those bastards what they want – and get back our blokes.'

Thomas, however, was more cautious. 'Depends who that passenger is, doesn't it?' Most of the lower deck agreed with him.

But when Hazelton contacted Maxwell again, dead on his promised deadline, he brought discomforting news.

'James, we are in a very difficult predicament.'

'Why?' Maxwell was anxious to allow no further prevarication from Whitehall.

'This passenger they talk about is almost certainly Gabriel Mendoza – Julia Mendoza's brother.'

'How do you know this, sir?'

'Tennant.'

'I see. Well – who is he, sir?' Maxwell was impatient.

222

'He was a brilliant left-wing journalist who was barbarically tortured in Uruguay. Gabriel's been used by Ola Roja to test the mining operation.'

'But how important is he?'

'Not very. But he has contacts we'd like to get hold of.'

'Then what do you suggest I do, sir?'

'We are flying in an SAS team from Ascension.'

'But that will take hours. We only have – '

Hazelton cut in on him impatiently. 'You will have to negotiate – get the deadline extended.'

'That may not be possible.'

'You must try.'

Knowing there was no point in arguing, Maxwell came off the phone in a blind rage.

Forbes arrived on board the *Santa Fe* without incident, leaving the launch with its outboard engine running below. He was met by Morales and two crewmen who frisked him nervously. The atmosphere on the unkempt deck was chilling and, for the first time, Forbes felt the nearness of death. Even the stars above him seemed cold and menacing, and the sound of the Antarctic sea below was like the cry of some hostile force. He felt completely alone – despite the Lynx hovering overhead – with only the night and the quiet sea and his gathering fear. It would be easy enough for them to kill him now – to push him overboard, to slit his throat, to do anything. His thoughts turned haphazardly to Julia. These were the men she had worked with, she had known. With an effort Forbes regained control of himself.

'I would like to see my two officers immediately.'

'That was the agreement,' replied Morales stiffly. 'Naturally we shall honour it.'

'And it is important that I see them alone.'

There was a long pause. Morales also sounded afraid as he broke the tense silence. 'That will not be possible.'

A group of men suddenly detached themselves from the shadows around the fo'c'sle. The two in front looked familiar.

They were escorted by four armed seamen. 'I think you will agree that these men are Lieutenant Arrowsmith and Captain Lucas. There can be no doubt of that,' said Morales.

Once they were a few feet away from him, Forbes agreed. Yes – there was no doubt at all. But their physical condition was appalling and Forbes was shocked by their emaciation and something far beyond that – a kind of trapped animal-like aura that was pitiful, even horrifying, to see. Forbes stepped towards them but Morales intervened.

'There must be no contact.'

It was Arrowsmith who spoke first and the desperation in his voice was so intense that Forbes had difficulty in not backing away. His face was pale and gaunt and his uniform hung on him like a scarecrow. 'You've got to get us off, sir. You've got to get us off. For Christ's sake – ' His voice broke on a high whine and his lips moved wordlessly.

Forbes tried to sound both convincing and authoritative at the same time. 'Of course we'll get you off, John. Just hang on a bit longer, old boy, while we finish negotiating.'

Arrowsmith began to mutter something unintelligible but Lucas cut in. His face was badly bruised and there was a dirty bandage round one of his hands. He seemed to have lost less weight than Arrowsmith and although his voice was hoarse it was very controlled. 'John's ill, sir.'

'And you?'

'I'm OK.' He suddenly began to speak very fast. 'They took us by launch to a Soviet submarine – ' He got no further for Morales stepped forward and hit him round the mouth, while one of his men turned a revolver on Forbes.

'Piss off!' said Forbes. 'And leave him alone.'

'I have to tell you, Commander, that your visit is over. I assume you're satisfied with the identification.'

Forbes ignored him. 'Keep hold, Harry. It won't be long now.'

As he was escorted to the ladder by Morales and his entourage, he wondered how long it would be before Arrowsmith cracked up altogether.

'That bloody submarine – I should have guessed.' But Maxwell was more concerned about Arrowsmith's mental condition than his past whereabouts.

'Lucas will do all he can to keep him together, sir.'

'Yes, but the poor little sod can't take much more – no doubt about that. And we've got problems the MOD end.'

'What problems, sir?'

Maxwell told him and Forbes swore. 'They don't stand a chance now.'

Maxwell picked up the radio telephone. 'This is Captain Maxwell of *Mercator* calling Captain Morales of the *Santa Fe*. Over.'

The response was immediate. 'You have thirty-two minutes left. Over.'

'I've spoken to the Ministry of Defence. They cannot, repeat cannot, make the arrangements in that time.'

'Nevertheless, Captain Maxwell, they will have to.' Morales sounded crisp and confident and there was no trace of the fear Forbes had seen in him.

'That is impossible,' returned Maxwell with equal calm.

'Then one of your men will be killed when the two-hour deadline is up. Tell that to your Ministry of Defence. Over and out.'

Looking at his watch and feeling a vast emptiness in the pit of his stomach, Maxwell contacted Hazelton again. 'They refuse to comply, sir, and say they'll kill one of the hostages in half an hour unless the procedure goes ahead as originally planned.'

'Then I'll have to get back to – '

'We're running out of time, sir.'

'I know that, James. But the Prime Minister is adamant that we should not allow this man to get away. We *have* to use delaying tactics.' There was silence and then Hazelton rushed on: 'But what I think he may well be prepared to do is compromise and divert the SAS to Ushuaia.'

'How much longer will they need?'

'Another six hours.'

'Six hours! I don't think they'll wear it for a moment.' Maxwell paused, trying to control himself. 'Get clearance on that then, sir. But you must come back to me quickly.'

'I'm aware of the urgency, James.'

Maxwell looked at his watch again and turned to Forbes. 'Twenty-eight minutes,' he said. The bridge was crowded with the *Mercator*'s officers. Most were silent, staring at the dark shape of the *Santa Fe*, wallowing clumsily in the swell, picked out about half a mile away by wan moonlight. Many of the ship's company stood silently on the lower decks, watching the hulk of the *Santa Fe* as if she was some magic talisman. It was 10.45 p.m. and the cold, windless night was as bleak as it could possibly be. The unbearable waiting seemed to cast a chill round every man's heart and Cunningham was reminded of the night before a battle, the armies in their tents, waiting for the bloody carnage of sunrise.

Then Hazelton came back.

'The Prime Minister's agreed and they're on their way to Ushuaia. Try and persuade Morales to hold his fire.'

Morales sat in the radio room, chain-smoking, accompanied by a rigorously calm Diego and a silent Mendoza. The three of them were undergoing the kind of vigil that was stretching their nerves almost to breaking point.

When Maxwell came back on the air, the deadline had only eight minutes to run and even Diego was noticeably agitated.

'The arrangements will take another six hours – that is the fastest possible time and the British Government's last word on the subject.'

'Then we shall be forced to carry out the execution.'

'I would strongly suggest that you reconsider that decision. It will have very serious international repercussions.'

'Nevertheless, we shall be forced to carry out the execution.' Morales looked up to Diego for guidance and he nodded quickly.

'You understand the consequences?'

'The consequences are not our concern. They should be

yours, Captain Maxwell.'

At 10.57 precisely an arc light was lit on the deck of the *Santa Fe*, Lucas was marched to it, a revolver was put to his head, there was a single shot and he went down.

A howl of rage broke out on HMS *Mercator* and it glanced over the water like some primeval anger.

'Why can't we just blow the bastards out of the water?' said Taff, this time representing the main body of the ship's company.

'Because John Arrowsmith's still on board,' said Grey hopelessly. 'And while there's a chance for him – '

On the bridge there were much the same thoughts in mind when a grey-faced Maxwell turned to his officers and said: 'Pray to God they won't put a deadline on John.'

They didn't, and for the next five and a half hours there was complete silence from the *Santa Fe*, although every moment Maxwell, his nerves screaming, thought Morales would come on the air. In the end it became slowly evident they had accepted the MOD's deadline but had made their point. Of course, Maxwell thought cynically, if they killed John they would then be open to attack from the *Mercator*. But they were so unpredictable they could decide to do anything.

2 February 1990
5.00 a.m.
As the grey dawn light filtered on to the decks of the *Mercator*, the mist began to return, and Maxwell felt a chilly trepidation.

Morales came over the radio, sounding very agitated. 'The situation is as follows: one, an unmarked Chinook helicopter will shortly arrive to lift off a number of personnel, including myself. If any attempt is made to obstruct or to follow this aircraft, the final hostage will be shot. Two, a smaller unmarked Bell helicopter will arrive at the same time and will lift off the colleague who wishes to fly to Cuba, the remaining hostage and an armed escort. If this second aircraft is obstructed or followed, the same will apply. Over.'

After Maxwell had acquiesced to his instructions, there was a short, almost ceremonial leave-taking on board the *Santa Fe* between Morales, Diego and Gabriel Mendoza.

'And I repeat,' said Diego, 'there must be no self-recrimination, Gabriel. You have served us well in overpoweringly difficult circumstances. What must be remembered is that you have laid foundations.'

But Mendoza had little to say. He shrugged. 'I would not have put it like that.'

'And you, Morales – much has been achieved in the *Santa Fe*.' He laughed. 'When they come here, they'll find very little to help them.'

'Everything is overboard – acquisition of evidence is now a diving operation.'

They all laughed companionably and Diego clapped his hand on Gabriel's shoulder.

'Come, my friend. It is time.'

The two helicopters arrived almost immediately. The Chinook hovered above the *Santa Fe* and began to winch up a number of men. Maxwell counted sixteen. Then it rose and began to hover above the Bell, which landed on the deck. Maxwell, his binoculars trained, watched a small man with long white hair duck under the blades and clamber aboard. He was followed by Arrowsmith, who waved up at the Sea King, and two armed guards.

The Bell began to rise from the pad and Maxwell said: 'Shouldn't be so difficult to knock them out.'

He felt a sudden surge of hope. 'If only we hadn't had to sacrifice Lucas. But Arrowsmith – '

Just as he said this the Chinook opened fire on the Bell.

Cunningham was shouting: 'God Almighty! They're firing on their own people.' He sounded incredulous. The entire ship's company stared in amazement as the machine gun continued to chatter while the Bell flew on, seemingly regardless of the bullets pumping through its superstructure. Then suddenly, a sheet of flame sprang from its nose and the helicopter plunged towards the sea. As it hit the surface, the Bell bounced and exploded in a ball of bright orange-coloured flame.

For a moment they were all too stunned to react. Then Forbes said: 'Shall I tell the Lynx to open fire, sir?'

The Chinook was swooping away now and Maxwell said quietly: 'No – tell them to reduce height to sea-level. Arrowsmith is the priority – if there's anything left of him.'

As Maxwell ordered two boatloads of marines to storm the *Santa Fe*, the Sea King hovered over the swell, looking for survivors. But there was no sign of anybody – just a mass of human and mechanical flotsam.

'But why the hell should they shoot their own people?' asked Forbes, bewildered.

Maxwell stared across at the *Santa Fe* and the boats that were heading towards her. She looked like a ghost ship, hung about in swathes of mist.

'Because they failed,' he said.

Whilst Maxwell gave a shattered Hazelton the extraordinary facts of the denouement on the *Santa Fe*, Forbes led the search. It revealed little – just two small control rooms stripped bare of equipment. In the hold, however, Forbes made a startling discovery.

'They've done our job for us then,' crackled Hazelton's voice.

'Ola Roja obviously believe in making a clean sweep.' Maxwell felt a deep sense of failure as he spoke and this seemed to communicate itself to Hazelton, so many thousands of miles away.

'There was nothing you could have done for Arrowsmith, James.'

Nothing, thought Maxwell, while I was acting under HM Government's orders. What he should have done, he knew, was to have created some kind of radio breakdown and acted on his own initiative. If he had sent in his own marines, perhaps much could have been averted.

'You're plastered over every headline and screen over here,' said Hazelton.

'Yes, sir,' replied Maxwell. 'We're now making a thorough

search of the *Santa Fe*.'

'Well done, James.' Hazelton's voice was vigorously encouraging. 'I deeply regret the loss of Arrowsmith and Lucas but, believe me, there was nothing anyone could do.'

Wasn't there? thought Maxwell when Hazelton had gone off the air. There was a lot we could have done, if I'd had the guts to take the initiative.

Forbes came on from the *Santa Fe*, breaking into Maxwell's self-condemnation. 'Something pretty odd has happened, sir. I think you should come over straight away.'

A few minutes later, a Lynx had ferried Maxwell over to the deck of the *Santa Fe*. There he was met by Forbes.

'We've put the crew in the hold, sir, but I reckon they took off anyone who knew anything. There's something you should see, though.'

Forbes took him down through the battered passages below until they came to the engineers' mess. It was hot and smelt of oil and stale food. A bulky form was lying sprawled across a bunk. It was Jan Petrowski. He had been shot several times in the chest and in the stomach and had bled very profusely. Much of his blood lay in pools on the cracked lino beneath the bunk.

'So it was Petrowski who was Kingsley's lead,' said Maxwell.

'You don't think they took him prisoner, sir?'

'Why should they? No one's going to bargain over the life of a trawler skipper. The *San Juan* must have been another Ola Roja operations ship.'

'I can't see him as a political idealist.'

'No – I would have placed Petrowsky as a mercenary. They must have blown up the *San Juan* when they no longer had any need of her.'

'They certainly believe in destroying their own,' said Forbes. 'But how could he have got away?'

'Careful preparation. An immersion suit and an inflatable dinghy with an outboard would have got him a fair distance before we came on the scene.'

'So they must have killed quite a few birds with that

explosion. The evidence, a first test – '

'And Miles Kingsley,' finished Maxwell. But he was thinking of Lucinda, thousands of miles away, so badly burnt.

'I wonder why they didn't take Petrowski with them – if they went to the trouble of saving him from the *San Juan*? I suppose they must have picked him up.'

Maxwell shook his head. 'God knows what they did – or how they think. But I can't see Jan Petrowski in Cuba, can you?'

10 – Victor's spoils

3 February 1990

The explosion came at 7.13 a.m. on a cold, bright dawn. It could be heard over a range of some twenty miles and brought Maxwell thundering to the bridge.

'What in God's name – ?'

'I don't know, sir. They're trying to monitor it now.' Forbes looked grey with fatigue and there was such an atmosphere of alarm and trepidation amongst his other officers that Maxwell was stopped dead in his tracks, looking round him in amazement at their uncertainty. Suddenly, he realized they had all been through too much for too long. There was bound to be a breaking point. Could this be it?

Cunningham was beginning to shake and he quickly stepped over to him, taking his arm firmly. 'It's all right, old chap – we're coming up the straight.' But Cunningham only stared back at him, a little muscle working relentlessly in his cheek. The despair was deep-rooted in his eyes and Maxwell knew that he wasn't going to be of any use – not for a very long time.

'The ops room report a massive explosion, sir. Somewhere to the north-east of Elephant Island. An explosion on a landmass – not the mainland. They think an island.'

'What island?' snapped Maxwell.

'They don't know. It's not there any more, sir.'

There was a short impenetrable silence; then Maxwell said: 'Christ – what the hell is going on?'

'They also report considerable water disturbance, sir.'

'How're they getting their information?'

'Sonar – and they're trying to raise the American research ship, the *John Hardy*.'

'I'm going down there. I'd like to speak to the skipper.'

'You'll have to hurry, sir.'

There was something else, Maxwell realized. Something that Forbes had on his mind.

'Well?'

'An explosion of that size, sir – couldn't it cause a tidal wave?'

'Yes,' replied Maxwell quickly, 'it could.'

Julia Mendoza shivered in the wintry Paris morning as she walked through the grey streets of the suburb. She had been staying in a dingy, modern hotel opposite a small park in which she would walk for hours – particularly when she couldn't sleep, which was most of the time. At first she had been the object of some curiosity – this middle-aged, deeply sun-tanned, lonely woman, pacing the gravel paths that wound round the arid, empty flower-beds. A living cliché. It was her only source of humour – the woman from the Orient Express. But slowly she merged; people stopped looking at her and the joke soured. She was no longer conspicuous.

Julia gradually built up a routine and, because of this, she began to feel safe. She tried not to think of the past and never the future. Often Gabriel edged into her thoughts and then life became unbearable. But, gradually, over the last few days, he had drifted in much less and she found herself locked into her routine. She would rise early from a dozing sleep and walk in the cold and often misty park. Then she would thankfully go back to the hotel and sit in the tiny and rather squalid breakfast room where she would voraciously consume a considerable quantity of croissants and coffee – the walking gave her a tremendous appetite. A lone commercial traveller or jaded business man would often share the room with her but, thankfully, they never made any attempt to communicate with her.

Later she would walk again, this time through the streets of the suburb, until she knew every shop, every street, every square. She would watch with pleasure the children trooping to school and would stand, drinking in their games in the playground, feeding off their vitality.

233

Sometimes Julia would take the Métro and travel into Paris. Often she would go to the Sacré-Coeur, sitting in its dark, shuffling silence, smelling the incense, at peace with herself. Afterwards, she would go to a bar, have a glass of wine and perhaps eat cheese or ham in bread. Then, depending on the weather, she would either walk again or go to a museum. Mostly she went to the Musée du Jeu de Paume, wandering amongst the feverish Van Goghs, keeping her mind, as always, on what she was doing or seeing. Later on she might go to a film or, as she had done on one particularly warm evening, walk under the bridges. Eventually, Julia would return to her hotel, as late as possible, to have a meal and go to bed. Lying sleepless throughout the night, she would permit her only indulgence of the day: a return to the childhood she had shared with Gabriel. She saw it in pastel tones, an easy nostalgia that only brought tepid warmth, but, thankfully, never pain.

Now, this morning, the park seemed at its most still, its most bitter. The frost crackled around her and the clarity of the chilling sun made her bones ache.

So used to being alone, she was therefore immediately conscious of a presence, but it was some time before she was able to identify it. Julia stared round the park, standing very still, scanning each path, each formal hedge, the empty fountain, the wired bandstand. Then she saw the man, standing beside a boarded-up café, watching her with resigned patience.

Maxwell's contact with the American skipper of the *John Hardy* was horrifyingly brief. Amongst the dim shadows and bright, flickering technology of the ops room, he at last managed to get through on a line that crackled fiercely as if on fire.

'This is Captain Nicholls. Over.'

'Captain Nicholls – this is Captain Maxwell of the *Mercator*. Are you reading me? Over.'

'I read you. But – ' his voice was temporarily lost ' – problems.'

'What are these problems? Over.'

'Severe weather, mountainous seas. Bearing down on us. Over.'

'The explosion. What do you know of the explosion? Over.'

'Very little, Captain. Almighty bang – very clear. Sounded – bomb – some kind.' Again his voice faded out into raging static. Then it returned, more flurried than before. 'We're in trouble – real trouble.'

'What's happening? For Christ's sake, what's happening? Over.'

But the static was there, roaring away, twice as dense.

'What's happening, Captain Nicholls? Over.'

His voice returned on the ragged air-waves, more fractured than before. 'The wave – there's a wave. Big bastard. Never seen – it's on us – there's no way – ' What sounded like a tremendous blasting sound joined the static. Then the air-waves were dead, leaving Maxwell numbed. Around him, radio operators desperately tried to re-establish contact. But he knew they would fail.

Julia walked rapidly down the gravel path, all too aware that she was walking away from the entrance, towards a peeling conservatory and the high walls of an apartment block. Slowly, the man began to saunter after her. She increased her pace with a pounding heart, knowing that she should break into a run, but knowing too, that she could not. Was he just another early morning walker? Or had he come for her? As she increased her galloping walk, Julia could not be sure of anything.

Now she was hurrying past the conservatory, taking another wide frosty gravel path that led back towards the entrance. Still the man strolled after her, making no attempt to increase his pace or to cut her off. Panting a little, her heart still pounding, Julia reached the half-way point. Still he ambled behind her.

Minutes later, she reached the empty street. Then a dust truck began to crawl down the road, men hanging on its back in donkey-jackets, grinning up at her. She had never been so pleased to see human beings in her life and, as she walked briskly past them, Julia smiled gratefully at their whistles and

235

at one rather feeble cat-call. Looking round her, she saw the man leaning up against the park railing. He was watching her unguardedly as she broke into a jog, heading for the Métro with a surge of returning panic.

'God help us.'

Back on the bridge, Maxwell stared ahead incredulously at the mass of heaving ice that was bearing down on them. It was shattered pack ice but beyond this there was a berg that looked as if it had suddenly been split in two.

'We're going to have to swing around, Nick. Bloody fast.'

Whilst Maxwell gave a rattle of orders to the engine room, Forbes said to Cunningham: 'For Christ's sake, snap out of it, man.' But Cunningham was staring straight ahead with a trans-fixed gaze and Forbes knew he would be wasting his time. As for the others – they were carrying on as normal, any panic allayed by the precise routine of the emergency drill Maxwell was carrying out. His voice was controlled and his manner confident. But in front a berserk South Atlantic bore down on them, a maelstrom of roaring water and huge chunks of broken ice.

Down below, Taff Evans and Dolly Grey were off duty and *Mercator*, her engines screaming, began to swing round in a seemingly impossible arc. Tumbling out of their bunks, they rushed to the restricted vision of the scuttle.*

'Christ – look at the bastard!'

The broken berg was in clear view, thundering down on the *Mercator*, the water boiling around it.

'What the hell's pushing it?' asked Grey, his voice climbing to a register that would have caused Taff considerable amusement anywhere else. But not here. Then they saw the wall of water behind the berg.

'That's not possible!' shrilled Grey.

'Then we're dreaming,' replied Taff Evens sardonically. 'Shall we start pinching each other?'

* Porthole.

236

As Julia Mendoza boarded the Métro and rode into the centre of Paris, she knew they would be waiting for her if she returned to the hotel. She was far too much of an old hand at pursuit to fail to recognize the man in the park for what he was. They were biding their time but would soon close in. Even now, as she looked round at her fellow passengers, she could not be sure she was not being followed.

For some minutes her sense of desolation increased. Clearly, they would not bother to take her alive – there was no need. But there was no doubt in her mind of one thing: she didn't want to die. Not now – not after Forbes.

As the *Mercator* completed her near ninety degree turn, Forbes suddenly saw the logic of Maxwell's manoeuvre. Coming up on the starboard side of the ship was a small tabular iceberg.

'If we can get behind it in time,' Maxwell said softly, 'it'll take the full force of this lot. If we don't – '

Engines racing, the *Mercator* ploughed her way to shelter, but as they forged ahead Cunningham began to gabble in a monotone: 'We'll not fucking make it. We don't stand a fucking chance.'

Before Forbes could move, Maxwell went over to Cunningham and hit him across the face. The blow cracked out across the bridge, and everyone turned away, unable to witness Cunningham's breakdown. For there, but for the grace of God, they all knew – But Cunningham continued to babble and Maxwell hit him again, more sharply than before. This time, he relapsed into a kind of petrified silence. Maxwell helped him to a chair. 'Sit down. It'll be over soon.'

Yes, thought Forbes, the fear churning in his stomach viciously. It'll be over soon. One way or the other. He glanced quickly outside. The broken berg and the wall of water were behind them now but still travelling at an astounding rate. It was as if an angry child were pushing them across a bath-tub.

'So this is a tidal wave,' he said bleakly to Maxwell. 'I've never seen one before. Have you?'

'Yes – in the Roaring Forties. And it was bigger, much bigger. This one's running out of steam.'

'Steam enough to sink us.'

'Oh, yes.' Maxwell sounded slightly uninterested. 'If we don't outrun that lot, we're finished.'

Julia Mendoza ran out of the Métro and stood on the Champs-Elysées, desperately trying to flag down a taxi. For what seemed like hours they hurtled past her, triumphantly full. As she waited, Julia kept glancing around her, identifying every single man on the boulevards as a significant threat. Now that she had made up her mind, now that she was really sure what she was going to do, Julia felt an agony of apprehension and abject fear. They would take her before she even got near her destination. They were bound to.

The taxi lurched to a halt beside her, taking her almost by surprise. Almost falling, she wrenched open the door.

'*Au Consulat Anglais*,' she said and sank back trembling into the hard leather of the interior.

> 'When the snows begin, and the blasts denote
> I am nearing the place.
> The power of the night, the press of the storm –'

The words repeated relentlessly in Maxwell's mind, reduced to monotony by the idiotic rhythm he gave them. In fact, the ice seemed to be gaining. For the first time in years, Maxwell silently prayed. His God had always been the God of muscular Christianity. The Protestant God chaps worshipped on brittle mornings in the raw chapels of British public schools. The God who was a chap's chap, the God who was omnipresent on the rugby field, the God who frowned on the unseemly, the masturbators, the cowards. Never an ostensibly merciful God. But it was that merciful God he wanted now – so hungrily.

In the hard, bright morning light, the elements were picked

out in the grimmest clarity. Behind them the ice had been forced up by enormous pressure into the strangest and most demonic shapes. And amongst the jumbled pack was a translucent grey-green ice monolith, standing in stark isolation above the rushing, jagged landscape.

'It looks just like a conning tower,' whispered Maxwell and Forbes asked:

'What was that, sir?'

'Oh, nothing. Just musing aloud,' muttered Maxwell.

In front of them, the tabular berg had caves in it and he could see an ice grotto, hollowed out by wind and sun. Silver fingers hung from the roof and the interior was a mass of green hue, ever changing, ever sparkling in the sunlight.

Down below, Evans and Grey were only able to see part of the ice mass rushing towards them and they had the illusion that the *Mercator* was stationary, awaiting the relentless collision that was about to take place.

'We don't stand a bleeding chance,' said Taff, sitting down heavily on his bunk. 'Not a bleeding chance.'

As the taxi dropped her outside the British Embassy, Julia Mendoza's resolution almost failed. She stood on the pavement, blinking in the glancing cold sunshine, suddenly feeling foolish, even perverse. The mood was very temporary – and abruptly broken.

They were running across the tree-lined road towards her. Two men, their hands in their pockets. Julia knew what they were going to do – and how quickly they would cut her down. Screaming, she ran the last few yards to the security guard at the front of the building. Those yards seemed like eternity – and, as she ran, she imagined she could feel the bullets ripping into her. But once the security guard moved forward – once she was past him – Julia knew she was safe. She did not look behind her, only continued to scream and shout and scream again as the guard moved back towards her, his face a mixture of alarm and derision. He thinks I'm crazy, she thought, but she continued to cry out.

239

On the pavement in front of the Embassy, Julia saw the two men hurrying past, their eyes averted, their stride lengthy. Yes, she was safe. Oh dear God, she was safe.

They were safe. They must be. But only just. For, as the *Mercator* veered behind the berg, they could all see the wall of tormented water and ice was only a hundred yards behind them. The force hit the berg with a crashing, crunching, thudding sound, horribly muted, like a snarling, dying animal. But its volition was not enough to break up the berg, nor to surmount it. It rose and rose again, a demon composed of crushed ice and spray, fulminating at the great bulk of the tabular berg, lashing at the sheer hopelessness of its dying fall. The wave and its ice jungle gradually subsided into a turmoil of angry, spitting fury. Sea-birds wheeled above it, screaming in terror, and penguins fled, plunged, darted, staggered, escaped or were crushed by the gnashing, grinding ice.

A ragged, exhausted cheer came from every part of the *Mercator*, as men who had been too close to death too many times sat exhausted in the lee of their desperately sought, narrowly gained ice barrier. Some shouted, some wept – all were in ecstasy.

'We've got charmed lives,' yelled Forbes, pumping away at Maxwell's hand and then at the hands of every other officer on the bridge. 'Bloody charmed lives.'

'Don't you believe it,' said Maxwell. 'We've got nine lives – that's all. And this was our ninth.'

Amongst less restrained celebrations below, Taff Evans was heard to cry: 'Nothing can touch us. We're magic!'

But the celebrations in the *Mercator* did not last for long. As the tidal wave was dispersed behind the berg and the ice settled into dozens of strange, jagged, primeval formations, a great silence descended on both ship and sea. On the bridge, *Mercator*'s Captain and senior officers watched the colours on the ice diffuse in a myriad of different hues and the penguins resettle on their precarious ledge. In sentinel line they stared down at the *Mercator* and *Mercator*'s ship's company stared back at

240

them. It was the day after Armageddon.

11 February 1990
Drake's Passage

The mood of the *Mercator*'s company was subdued as she made her way across Drake's Passage in unusually moderate but misty weather, and it was not until they reached the vicinity of Beauchene Island that the westerly wind really started to freshen, bringing with it an uplifting of the men's spirits. Combinations of roll and pitch put the *Mercator* outside the limits for helicopter operations, and it was only when the ship found the ice of the Falklands that it became possible to launch one of the Lynxes from the heaving flight deck.

Mail bags were loaded into the helicopter and Maxwell joined the pilot and observer as the only passenger. As they flew steadily towards the football pitch next to Government House at Port Stanley, Maxwell felt extremely depressed. When they landed he was met by Gillett. They walked towards the building in merciful silence and it was only when they were inside that Gillett listened to Maxwell's account of the explosion and resultant tidal wave.

'A brilliant piece of seamanship,' he said and Maxwell smiled. How many more times would he be told this? he wondered. 'And there's a news black-out on the explosion. For the moment.'

'Why?' asked Maxwell with false innocence.

Gillett grinned sardonically. 'It's rather a delicate matter, isn't it?' Swiftly Gillett went on to another tack. 'It was tragic about Arrowsmith and Lucas. Like a miracle happening – and then finding it had never happened at all.'

'I'm still having difficulty in believing it – that and Petrowski.'

'Petrowski was a mercenary. He deserved all he got.'

'And Kenny?'

'He's under house arrest. I can tell you – it's caused the biggest stink since Anthony Blunt.' Gillett went over to his desk and picked up a pile of newspapers, dumping them down on a table near Maxwell. Black headlines screamed from *The Times*: CARNAGE IN THE SOUTH ATLANTIC. TERRORIST GROUP CARRY OUT THEIR OWN EXECUTION. HMS MERCATOR DISCOVERS AUTOMATIC MINING SYSTEM. HM AMBASSADOR UNDER ARREST. ALLEGATIONS OF SPYING. The *Sun* surpassed itself with ROYAL NAVY OPENS A CAN OF WORMS. BRITISH AMBASSADOR A TRAITOR.

'And that's nothing to what they're going to say about the latest event,' said Gillett.

Maxwell turned over the papers with growing amazement. The whole messy business seemed to have nothing to do with him at all, and when he tried to associate himself with it, a curious dream-like haze swept over his mind. 'One thing that puzzles me,' he said, trying to get a grip on reality. 'This business about Tennant. How did he get involved?'

'He was a homosexual – and you still can't be that in the diplomatic service and not expect to be blackmailed. Kenny found him very easy meat.'

'And Dunhill?'

Gillett laughed mirthlessly. 'There's nothing corrupt about Aubrey. He's a fussy little bureaucrat and enjoyed soft-pedalling anything that involved you.'

'He didn't exactly want me to get any glory,' said Maxwell acidly. 'I'd no idea he hated me that much.'

'Old habits die hard.'

'So did Rosemary. Very hard. I still can't see why they killed her.'

'God knows. That's one part of the puzzle that doesn't fit together at all. They risked a lot to do it.'

Maxwell drained his whisky. 'What the hell made Kenny a traitor?'

'I think you'll find he's been on their side for a good long time. That type always has.'

Gillett offered Maxwell another whisky but he refused. 'I need a clear head,' he said. 'One more and I'll be asleep on your carpet.'

'Be my guest.' He paused. 'James – there is one vital fact to emerge from all this, you know.'

'And what's that?'

'Your total vindication. You'll obviously be taken much more seriously in government circles now – not just seen as a bloody nuisance.'

'There's been a price to pay for that,' said Maxwell bitterly.

18 February 1990
2.00 p.m.
Montevideo

Directly the *Mercator* entered harbour Maxwell sent Browning and a detachment of marines to pick up Kenny. Browning replaced the existing Uruguayan armed guard with armed marines whilst he and his Sergeant Major went upstairs to the Ambassador's office.

'Are you the gentlemen Mr Kenny is expecting?' asked the receptionist in the outer office.

Browning, slightly flummoxed, replied: 'I am the Officer Commanding the Royal Marines, HMS *Mercator*.' His voice was officious but she gave him a pleasant social smile.

'He said some gentlemen would be calling. Will you come this way?' She opened two large baize-covered doors and ushered them into Kenny's office. He was sitting behind his desk, wearing a well-cut linen suit, working on some papers. He was very calm.

'These are the military gentlemen you were expecting, sir.'

'Thank you, Alice.' He smiled up at her.

'Thank you, sir.' An austere woman in her fifties, she walked out with the assurance born of long foreign service. Even if the Ambassador was under house arrest, she was not going to let civilized behaviour slip for one moment. Browning wondered if her confidence would be at all shaken by the knowledge that her boss really was a Communist agent.

'Mr Kenny, I am the OCRM from HMS *Mercator* and I have come to escort you to my ship under orders from Captain Maxwell.'

'You seem to have everything well organized.' He rose from behind his desk with a quiet dignity, making Browning feel slightly absurd. 'When we walk out,' continued Kenny, 'can it

243

be in a fairly casual manner? I wouldn't like to upset my secretary. She's been with me for a very long time.'

'That will be in order. But we shall have to search you before we go out.'

'Ah – the poisoned capsule syndrome. I'm afraid I'm not courageous enough for that. But please – do your stuff.' He raised his hands while the Sergeant Major searched him.

'OK, sir.'

'Thank you, Sergeant Major. We can now go.' Kenny looked round the office for a moment and then walked slowly to the door. Outside, Miss Appleby was typing.

'I'm just stepping out,' he said.

The *Mercator*'s launch was waiting at the steps of the Uruguayan naval base with three sailors, one of whom unfurled the Union Jack to show that the Ambassador was on board. A green Fiat drew up and out of it hurried two men, one of whom was Symons. Quickly they boarded the launch.

Once they reached the *Mercator* and the launch had been hoisted to deck level, Kenny was helped out and shown into Maxwell's cabin. He sat down heavily, the pose gone, suddenly hopeless. Browning and the Sergeant Major stood beside him, whilst Symons and his colleague hovered in the background.

'When we reach Ascension you will be charged with treason,' said Maxwell without a trace of emotion in his voice. 'I personally feel you should be charged with murder, but I suppose that's unlikely.' He turned to Browning. 'Will you take the Ambassador down to cabin 23. He's to be kept under close arrest until we arrive at Ascension and will be cross-examined by these two gentlemen.'

'Yes, sir.'

Kenny got up wearily. 'You haven't got any decent sea-sickness tablets?' he asked hesitantly. 'I'm a rotten sailor.'

21 February 1990
9.15 a.m.
Central Atlantic

Forbes and Maxwell stood on the bridge, looking into the murk. It was calm and the occasional flying fish could be seen over the fo'c'sle. Some members of the ship's company had been standing on the upper deck watching a school of dolphins swimming under the ship and round the bow, but the horizon was obscured by a blanket of tropical fog.

Maxwell spoke softly, in the damp greyness. 'I've had a signal about Julia Mendoza.'

'What now?' Forbes sounded desperate. He had been very quiet since they had left Montevideo and now Maxwell could see the true extent of the strain he was under.

'She gave herself up at the British Embassy in Paris.'

'Good God!' Forbes looked at Maxwell unbelievingly. 'What are they going to do to her?' he added sharply.

'I don't know – she's still under interrogation.'

That evening Maxwell saw Kenny again. He seemed very composed.

'I'm not here to cross-examine you. Mr Symons and his colleague are in charge of that department.'

'You wouldn't have to work very hard if you did. I'm quite prepared to tell you. It's not a very unusual story. I was recruited at Trinity, Cambridge. Where else?' He paused reflectively. 'But it was many years before they wanted me. Nevertheless, my convictions have always remained the same. I waited a long time. I was Third Secretary in Ankara, Second Secretary in Bonn, First Secretary in Ecuador and Stockholm. When I arrived in Madrid they made contact.'

'What on earth gave you the impression the Soviets had anything to offer?' asked Maxwell shortly.

'In my view, they have a very great deal and I've never been shaken in my beliefs. But there's not a lot of point in a discussion.'

'And you think that your beliefs justify all this carnage?'

Kenny shook his head. 'No – much of what has happened

could have been avoided. The organization was inexperienced.' He paused. 'But lessons have been learnt.'

'Yes,' said Maxwell. 'You've completely wiped out the poor sods who did the groundwork for you.'

'Not quite,' replied Kenny.

'Don't you even have any qualms over Rosemary Dunhill and the bloody hypocrisy you showed when you supported Aubrey?'

'I've told you – inexperience and unreliability have dogged this operation from beginning to end.' Then he suddenly seemed to remember Rosemary. 'We were having an affair. Unfortunately she became suspicious and might have done considerable damage if left alive.'

Maxwell hit Kenny across the face with the flat of his palm and he fell back on the bunk, the red weal glowing on his cheek.

'I'm sorry about that,' said Maxwell. 'I thought I had more control.'

Maxwell's angry return to the bridge was delayed by the communications office who had an urgent signal for him. Having read it, Maxwell walked on slowly, trying to work out what he was going to say to Forbes. The sea was flat calm except for the westerly swell running into Ascension. Tropical sea-birds plummeted into the waves near the shore, searching for fish, and Maxwell could make out the familiar volcanic mass of the island, with its trees and its grass, like an English meadow, high above the blackened beach.

'Nick.'

Forbes was staring out at the shore and at first didn't seem to hear him.

'Commander Forbes.'

'Sir.' He swung round.

'I've got news for you. They're flying Julia into Ascension.'

'What?' He was astonished, unbelieving. 'Is this some kind of joke?'

'I wouldn't have thought so. She's under arrest and doesn't have much choice.'

'But why are they bringing her all the way to Ascension?'

246

'To confront Kenny. Apparently, they reckon they'll get more out of him that way. She'll fly on to London with Kenny – as a principal witness.'

'And then?'

'She'll be tried in the UK.'

'What will she get?'

'Symons reckons that because she gave herself up it might not be too long.'

Forbes looked stunned. Then he said hastily: 'I don't suppose there's any chance of me seeing her, is there, sir?'

'I doubt it,' said Maxwell. 'But I'll try for you.'

Epilogue

'She's in the car,' said Maxwell. 'They won't give you more
than a few minutes.'

The Lynx landed and Forbes jumped down, running
towards the car and the nearest policeman. They spoke for a
few seconds and then the policeman opened the door and
Forbes stepped in quickly. As the door slammed Maxwell suddenly wished to God that Lucinda was walking along the
tarmac towards him.

Julia Mendoza looked much thinner in the face, and was
wearing a man's sweater and shapeless jeans. But the first thing
Forbes noticed was her sense of relief.

'I know he's dead,' she said, directly he got into the car.
'Please don't let's talk about him – it's too painful.'

'Let's talk about you then. James reckons you might get
away with a light sentence.'

'And then again I might not.' She smiled. 'I'm used to pris-
ons. I don't suppose yours are as bad as the ones I've been in.'
She looked at him closely and then added quickly: 'You still
know absolutely nothing about me.'

'You told me everything – or mostly everything – '

'That was all a lie.'

'It doesn't matter,' said Forbes quietly.

'I was born into a very rich Uruguayan family – a family that
believed in moderation. So did my brother at one time. My

248

childhood was not deprived – quite the contrary. The reason I did what I did was because of Gabriel. Did you know they murdered his sons? Did you know how much they tortured him?'

'I don't know anything about him,' said Forbes. 'I don't know much about you. But I'll still wait.'

She looked at him scornfully. 'What nonsense you talk.'

'I mean it.'

'You're just a romantic Englishman without any understanding of what we suffered – or what we were fighting for. You could never live with someone like me – someone with the memories I have. Before Gabriel and I went to prison, out of every thirty Uruguayans one had the job of watching the others. Students denounced each other. The person who kissed you one night would sell you in the morning. You could never forget that your neighbour was probably your enemy.'

'But that's over now.'

'In Uruguay – yes. But not in Chile or Colombia or Peru. And you know why Ola Roja survives? Because it's full of people like me who will go to any lengths, unquestioningly do unforgivable things, because their souls have been poisoned.'

'Gabriel maybe. Not you. The warning – and you gave yourself up.'

'I couldn't go on. That's all. I was very weak. And Nick – ' There was sudden desperation in her voice. 'There was something else.'

'What do you mean?'

'Something bigger. I knew Gabriel was keeping something to himself. I don't know what it was.'

'But how do you know?'

'No more than by the tone of his voice on the phone. But I know, all the same.'

Forbes thought of the ice island and the awesome explosion. Then he thought of the news black-out. 'I'm still going to wait for you,' he said.

'Then you're a fool.' Her face did not soften as he leant across and kissed her hard on the lips.

The military policeman began to knock on the window. 'I'll have to go now.'

249

'You must forget me, Nick.' Was there suddenly a trace of warmth in her voice or was it his imagination?

'I can't.' He began to climb out of the car. 'I just can't.' Forbes held out his hand to her and she took it gently, stroking his palm. Then she shrugged it away and settled back into the car.

They walked back to the Lynx and clambered on board. As they took off Forbes said: 'Thank you, sir.'

Maxwell grinned. 'I seem to have more influence than I thought.'

'I suppose you're their blue-eyed boy now, sir.'

'Not for long.'

'Why not?'

'I'm not made of the stuff of blue-eyed boys, Nick.'

'Thank God for that, sir.'

They looked down at the dwindling shape of the car and saw it start up, turning on the tarmac and heading towards the RAF VC 10.

'Kenny's on board already,' said Maxwell. 'Of course they'll keep them separate. But I was just thinking – when they're allowed to see each other, what an extraordinary meeting that will be.'

The explosion came as the car passed a Nissen hut. In numbed horror they watched the vehicle disintegrate, like a toy car smashed by an angry child. Then it settled, black smoke pouring from its dismembered parts, whilst the helicopter pilot kept swearing, using the same word over and over again. Forbes sat quite still as small specks of people began to run towards the smouldering wreckage.

'Julia,' he said quietly.

The helicopter veered towards the black smoke. Maxwell turned to Forbes but could think of nothing he could possibly say. Then they were back on the tarmac again and Forbes was out, ducking under the blades, running towards the acrid stench of the burning car.

Pray to God he's lucky, thought Maxwell.